To Bridget

GW01043785

Renegade

with warm wishes,

Jane Austin

LEAF BY LEAF

Published by Leaf by Leaf
an imprint of Cinnamon Press,
Office 49019, PO Box 15113, Birmingham, B2 2NJ
www.cinnamonpress.com

The right of Jane Austin to be identified as author of this work has been
asserted by her in accordance with the Copyright, Designs and Patent
Act, 1988. © 2022.
Print Edition ISBN 978-1-78864-934-6

British Library Cataloguing in Publication Data. A CIP record for this
book can be obtained from the British Library.

Designed and typeset in Adobe Jenson by Cinnamon Press.
Cover design by Adam Craig © Adam Craig.
Cinnamon Press is represented by Inpress.

Renegade is inspired in part by events surrounding the 'Angry
Brigade' described by Gordon Carr as Britain's first urban guerrilla
group. In fact there were a number of such groups across the
country, but this one attained notoriety in a lengthy court case in
1972. The characters in the novel are entirely fictional.

With warm thanks to York Novelists and to Farrell Burnett for
reading my early manuscript. Special thanks to my editor Rowan
Fortune for his care and patience.

Jane Austin was born in Liverpool, studied French, and lives with her husband in London. In the 1980s she was a political activist. She has since worked in a number of settings including schools, adult education and the University of York. Her debut novel, *News from Nowhere* (Cinnamon Press 2017), was showcased by New Writing North.

Renegade

For Sarah, Dave and Jim,
my dear sister and brothers.

Chapter 1

Justin lowered himself gently into a sofa at *Mellow Vélo Café*, trying not to spill a brimming mug. He looked at his son dismantling a bike with ease and Sanjay smiled back. The boy was in his element with likeminded twenty-somethings who'd put together a business plan and were making a go of it. It wasn't the career he'd imagined for his son, but the world had changed.

There was a scattering of newspapers, for old geezers like you, Sanjay had taken pains to say. He took a scalding sip of Colombian coffee and picked up *The Guardian*. He flicked through it out of habit, then did a double take...

'a little-known revolution in northern Syria... the Kurds have created a utopian area based on cooperation... an ecological society committed to women's liberation... Rojava...'

The background blare from the local radio station was interrupted by a newsflash in a bizarre moment of synchronicity: *A South Yorkshire man has died in Rojava, Syria, the first Briton killed while fighting against ISIS... joined a mobile guerrilla unit... hit by a missile launched by Islamic State militants...'*

Justin's heart pounded. His instinct was to get up and warn Sanjay, but he forced himself back into his seat. *Rojava* stuck like a barb under the skin. It was where Farida planned to volunteer in some women's group, and Sanjay had talked of a sponsored bike ride—it sounded innocent. Farida was her own woman and Sanjay would follow her to the ends of the earth, Justin knew that. He tried to relax and took a slug of the liquorice-black liquid, then studied the familiar décor with its posters of bikers in colourful flocks, flying up and down improbable gradients.

He could be overreacting given recent events, his own past under scrutiny. The risks he'd taken and decisions he'd made shouldn't overshadow Sanjay, though age and experience counted for something. Harpreet accused him of being controlling while he blamed her for mollycoddling. This old friction was petty in the greater scheme, particularly if Sanjay was caught up with a cause in a far-flung corner of Syria nobody knew much about—except that people got blown up there.

Sanjay was by his side. 'Hey Dad, you okay? You look a bit out of it.'

Justin looked through rather than at him and tried to block the inane babble on the radio. 'I don't like the idea of Farida going to Rojava—d'you know how dangerous it is?'

'It's a lot less dangerous than most parts of Syria. What's brought this on?'

Justin thrust the newspaper article under his nose. 'This, for starters. And the lad from South Yorkshire who got himself killed, but I suppose you knew about that. It's an unholy mess over there, Sanjay, with Turkey, Russia and the US fighting for control. Don't get mixed up in it—what if Farida wants you to follow her?'

Sanjay looked at his phone. 'Give over, Dad, I haven't got time for this. It's not what you think, believe me. We'll talk about it more once Mum comes back—where is she?'

'In a hotel on the Moors where they lock up lawyers for a week and retrain them. She'll be back next week.' He examined the floor, despising himself for this half-truth.

Sanjay touched his shoulder. 'I get why you're supersensitive about me being involved, but I know what I'm doing, Dad. Anyway, it's up in the air—Farida hasn't even been accepted.'

Accepted for what? he wanted to ask. 'Maybe we could go for a ride sometime?'

Sanjay was already on his feet. 'Sure thing, Dad. Must get back to work. Thanks for dropping by.'

He watched Sanjay's bouncing step, sporting leg muscles

like knotted rope. He levered himself as his grown-up son got on with his life. He shook his head as if to dislodge the email that kept replaying like an ear-worm and left him spinning.

Dear Professor Caffrey,

My name is Stephen Scott. You knew my father, Max, who died last year. My mum has since found his prison memoirs and he writes quite a lot about you. Could we meet sometime? I'd like to understand more about his life back then. Work sometimes brings me to Leeds…

Harpreet had always known about Max and how he'd been wrongly convicted in the 70s, because Justin had told her about the campaign. You're the patron saint of Lost Causes, she'd told him, and said she loved him for it. Decades later, the touching obituary by Max's wife had alerted him to a son and Harpreet had asked if he'd be sending the family condolences. He said he wouldn't. His evasions opened up a rift between them and this latest intrusion from the past had blown up in his face.

How come you never told me about this? She'd asked, after he'd told her about the email from Stephen and his involvement in the wave of protest and revolution of the day. She'd said, I don't know who you are any more, and he knew he had to come up with answers, if only for himself.

He dropped a gear on his carbon fibre steed and stood from the saddle in readiness for the hill and the last lap before home. The sight of their house always filled him with warmth, sturdily built in locally quarried stone, impervious to the elements. Autumn was late and the house was screened by a red-gold canopy of copper beech glinting in the early evening sun like fritillary butterflies. He pumped the pedals to the last moment up to the grey flagged drive. The adrenaline carried him through the front door and into the kitchen, then plummeted. He looked around and a prickling ran down his back, like snow stuffed down his shirt as a boy, before his brain could interpret it. Today he felt it as loss and shame.

The kitchen was a memory box, from the pencilled height-marks on the wall he wouldn't paint over, to the curling holiday photos of the three of them. Sanjay's fridge magnet from a distant geography trip to Orkney clung on. The dresser was filled with mismatched plates, it was their thing when they were newlyweds, to collect oddments of china. They'd never grown out of the habit.

Normally, he'd put a bottle of Chardonnay in the fridge and cook dinner for when she came home. He'd hear the front door clunk and her heels click on the tiled floor and she'd appear, wearing a navy suit and white shirt, her court uniform as she called it.

He conjured the silken day when he'd proposed, and she'd said yes, but would have to talk to her parents. It took a while. Nothing against you, they'd assured. When we fled Uganda, we knew that Harpreet might fall for an Englishman. They'd tied the knot two years later and Harpreet's parents had always treated him like a son.

What he hadn't told Sanjay was that Harpreet had finished her training course and decided to stay on for a few days, to think. Infuriatingly, there was no mobile coverage at the hotel and when he'd reached her on the hotel phone, she'd made it clear she wouldn't be sitting on a gate in the corner of a field to receive messages. She needed time alone before seeing him again and she couldn't say when. There was nothing more he could do and now there was this new worry about Farida going to Syria, which he was desperate to talk about.

The fridge leftovers turned his stomach and he resigned to cooking a frozen pizza, leavened by a large glass of red wine. This soon turned into a poisoned chalice as his head seethed with Harpreet's untethered rage.

'You were actually a member of *The People's Militia*? Is that what you're telling me? And all these years, I'd believed you were the nice guy fighting for justice and exposing police malpractice.'

'Corruption,' he'd corrected, and regretted it.

'Okay, let's get this straight. You identified with a group that planted bombs…'

'…but the bombs were symbolic, we only targeted property…'

'We!' Her complexion darkened. 'You were one of the bombers? Tell me this isn't true.'

It wasn't the moment to say that their aim was to show that workers could take power into their own hands, something he might have said to his students. He enjoyed his reputation as a renegade, while remaining opaque about his involvement, buried in the mists of time along with the Second World War, as far as millennials were concerned. Harpreet needed a different story. 'There was a Miss World Contest in 1970, you were too young to know…'

'Yes, yes, the one disrupted by feminists at the Albert Hall—what's that got to do with anything?'

'I was there, at least I was there the night before, helping to blow up a BBC recording van. I was the lookout. It was to make a political point about the exploitation of women.'

The sky was moonless, pricked with hard bright stars, the pavements gleaming with frost. The comrades' footsteps rang out in the frozen air and his spine tingled. His task was to raise the alarm as per the pre-op briefing. *If you spot anyone, whistle a tune. You can whistle? Good. Keep calm, even if you see the cops. Remember your cover? Calling on a girl you met, she said she lived round here. Nothing too specific.*

Harpreet pushed away the bowl of stir-fried vegetables he'd snipped and diced, cooked with juicy orange and cream scallops and cashews for extra crunch. She'd once said she'd married him for his cooking and he suspected she was only half joking. The meal had lost its magic. He met her smouldering eyes. 'I see,' she said. 'We've been married for thirty years and this is the first I hear of it? I feel betrayed.'

'By the time we met, I'd put it all behind me. There were things I preferred to forget.'

He'd interviewed her parents as part of a research project on refugees and there'd been a photo of their daughter in her graduation gown on the mantelpiece. It was Harpreet, and she'd agreed to be interviewed after work. It was love at first sight, at least for him.

'It's curious that you married a lawyer, isn't it? A form of subconscious self-defence, perhaps? You planted bombs and escaped justice, and now there's a memoir as evidence. What else do I need to know?' Her lips were curled thin.

There was so much more. Their arguments had always been hot, but today he'd stumbled into hostile territory and floundered. 'Look, darling, I know this must come as a ghastly shock... I never imagined I'd have to dredge it all up again... I've messed up and of course you feel betrayed, I get that. I should have told you long ago. Does that make me a bad person?' He'd yet to talk about his betrayal of Max, which he couldn't do without facing his own shame. How could he ever be forgiven?

The acrid smell of burning pizza brought him back to himself and he got up to inspect the damage. He chucked the incinerated object into the bin and ordered a takeaway curry on a mobile app, thanking the gods for modern technology.

Harpreet had impressed on him the importance of meeting Stephen ASAP and finding out what he wanted. A chance to connect with a hidden part of his father's life? To clear his father's name? Or revenge. He tried to step into Stephen's shoes—the email, after all, had been anodyne. *I'd like to understand more about his life back then.* It suggested a fondness between father and son and he imagined Max would have been good and kind as a father, just as he'd been as a comrade. He did reply, saying he'd be only too pleased to meet and talk about his old friend, Max. It begged the question of why they'd lost touch, which he hoped to avoid. As he pressed send, he realised he urgently needed to talk to someone who knew him back then and the only person left was Sofia, his old flame. His stomach knotted, but what did he have to lose?

Justin had made London his own, a place to reinvent himself. The way he'd met Sofia was something he loved about being in a big city, where a fleeting encounter could become intimate.

The Underground train swayed as he stood holding a leather strap in one hand and a book in the other, when he was thrown bodily against the person behind.

'Watch yourself,' a woman cried sharply.

'I'm so sorry,' he said, looking apologetically at the book, as if it were to blame. 'I got carried away.'

'I suppose one would, reading that,' she said, smirking.

'Ah, yes, gripping stuff!' He offered a lopsided smile and shoved the book into his duffel-coat pocket, not sure if she was mocking him.

'I've read it,' she said, serious. The train lurched and he grabbed tighter onto the strap for fear of colliding again. This was the moment he truly noticed her. If asked what she was like, he wouldn't have mentioned chestnut glints in her eyes or dark hair falling down her back. What captivated him was the vibrancy of her presence, which expanded to fill the space around her. He could have sworn other passengers had the same sensation as necks cricked in their direction.

The train jolted to a standstill and she edged towards the door. 'We can discuss Kropotkin over a cuppa if you like.'

He hurried after her feeling the shape of the book in his pocket.

They had several rendezvous in cheap cafés, over endless mugs of instant coffee. Justin found himself articulating his credo as Sofia teased it out of him.

'Why Kropotkin?'

'The whole anarchist thing—I'm fascinated by the notion of *propaganda of the deed* and doing something to shift the balance of forces.'

'Really? I can't make you out, Justin. Tell me more.'

'Let's say that on a spectrum from Gandhi to Che Guevara, I'm with Che. There's no such thing as a peaceful revolution.'

'So, you're not squeamish about violence?' she asked, provocatively.

'That's jumping the gun, isn't it? I believe a better society is possible and that conflict, however undesirable, is unavoidable. Dictatorships never cede power—take Spain, for example.'

Sofia's features sharpened as she told him how her parents met. 'Mum escaped Nazi Germany and went to Spain to fight the fascists after her parents were shot. That's where she met Dad, who was with the anarchists. They brought me up to understand how the world is divided into the powerful and dispossessed. How about you?'

'Whatever I say is going to make me sound spoilt and privileged, which I suppose I am…'

'Go on,' she encouraged, touching his sleeve. 'We don't choose our parents, but we can choose how we act in the world. Why have you rejected your advantages? That's the story I want to hear.'

He felt self-conscious and looked deep into the outsize mug on the table. 'My father owns an engineering business in Sheffield and expected me to take over. I was an over-sensitive child and he scared me. By eight I had an appalling stammer, made worse when he was anywhere near. Funnily enough he solved the problem by sending me away to school.

I realised that to survive, I had to fight back. Something clicked. I started rebelling against petty rules and cruelties and learned that if you stand up for something, things can change. Nothing earth-shattering, obviously,' he added, glancing from the coffee's filmy surface and allowing her to look him in the eye.

She acknowledged him with a steady gaze. He'd never spoken to anyone so openly and stripped of bravado; he found he trusted her. He wanted her to know it hadn't been all plain sailing.

'So, what happened next? You went to University, got involved in sit-ins and demos and stuff, I imagine.'

'I was kicked out of school and sent to live with an uncle who let me do my own thing. I went to night class in Scarborough and saw hardship. The lads I met swam against the tide, grappling for opportunities I'd been handed on a platter. That changed me. I realised I didn't have to work in shipbuilding or fishing to survive, but I *could* make a difference by exercising my freedom—the freedom to act in the world. We are what we do. So I came to London and studied at the LSE with every intention of getting involved in politics.'

'Very existential, I'm sure. But who decides whether our actions are good or bad? You could wreak havoc for the sake of having an adventure. Action for its own sake, so to speak.'

He took this as a challenge. 'I believe if I act in order to be free, it must be so that others can be free.'

She nodded conditionally. 'You're on the right road, comrade. Just remember, we don't act on behalf of the masses, but expose the contradictions of capitalism and its oppressive systems.'

He tried to melt her brittle exterior with a joke. *'Don't be daft lass, d'ya tek me forra wasak or summat?'*

'A *wasak?*' she giggled. 'Definitely not, unless that means a dark bearded man with eyelashes to die for.'

'Now you're taking the piss,' he said, catching her wrist, and knew they'd end up in bed sooner or later.

Sofia eventually invited him to visit the squat to meet the comrades. He felt this to be a sort of test. She'd been tantalisingly vague about their activities and said labels were a distraction. They were engaged in conscious communal living, challenging gender stereotypes and the nuclear family. For a horrible moment he'd imagined free love and partner swapping, but no, she reassured him, that's bourgeois hippy crap. It was then she'd outlined the *Miss World* gig at the Albert Hall, reeling him in. She spoke of the profits of the Mecca Corporation, sexually exploiting women in the name of entertainment for the gratification of men.

'Okay, I see where you're coming from,' he'd said, 'but *Miss World* is pretty popular with women too. My mother will be watching.'

'Sure, but that's how they trick us,' Sofia hit back. 'Women absorb idealised versions of the female body, which we see plastered on billboards, buses, everywhere, to persuade us to spend our pitiful wages on fashion and makeup. It's a con, don't you see?'

She said a lot more, but nothing about bombing the BBC van in the early hours, in an attempt to sabotage the event. He was well established at the squat before he knew about that.

Chapter 2

If he'd had to pinpoint the day he'd joined *The People's Militia*, Justin would have cited moving to the squat. He arrived at the stucco-fronted house with a pillared porch and a bright red front door. It was scorching and he was drenched in sweat from shouldering a rucksack and carrying a khaki holdall, relics of his father's wartime gear retrieved when he first came to London. Somewhere at the back of his head, Pa was telling him that squats are disgusting and squalid, fit only for druggies and dropouts. *What was he doing here?*

He pressed the buzzer nervously and Sofia opened the door almost immediately as though she'd been waiting. 'Welcome!' She flashed her devastating smile.

He followed her neat figure dressed in jeans and t-shirt, bracing himself at seeing the others again. Should he have brought something? A bottle of wine? He'd been tempted by a posy of violets from an old woman in the Portobello Road, *violets for your sweetheart, darling,* but thought better. Too obvious.

There'd been several meetings in cafés and pubs before he'd been accepted into what Rob called, 'the revolutionary direct-action movement.' This was a necessary stage before joining *The People's Militia,* he'd been told. They were part of a network, rather than an actual organisation. It was a dizzying leap of faith, harnessing himself to workers and the dispossessed to bring down the capitalist state and topple its leaders. What this would look like he couldn't imagine, only history would tell.

Rob, a slight and clean-shaven man, stood to shake his hand in a disarmingly old-fashioned gesture. 'Hi Comrade, good to have you on board.'

It was a homely scene with ragrugs that cheered up bare floorboards, which he'd reckoned must be hellish draughty in winter. There was a stained-glass pendant hanging at the window, glowing warmly that summer's day. Along one wall was a bookcase made up of planks of wood separated by stacks of bricks. He saw the wood was rough, the width and quality used in scaffolding, which he knew from working on a building site. The neat arrangement of books gave a pleasing order, offset by brilliantly coloured throws over sagging settees. Over the mantlepiece was a charcoal sketch of a reclining nude that captured the curve and heft of full breasts.

This place was unlike his student rooms, which he still hadn't got round to leaving since graduating. Bins had overflowed, and filthy dishes piled in the sink until somebody cracked and washed the lot—usually him.

Rob's partner, Vera, showed him a leaflet they were working on. 'It's for the dockers' march for a decent wage. We're calling miners and railway-workers to come out in support,' she said, in a Welsh valleys accent. 'We've got to hold our nerve, now there's a state of emergency…'

'…And now the army's been called out,' Justin chimed in.

'Too right,' she said, leaning in. 'The question is, *What is to be done*? Lenin tells us the past is a guide to action, we must factor in present day conditions. Today the time is ripe, comrade, time to smash the bastards who got away with leaving children to die under slagheaps, and take power.' He heard her passion and sensed it was personal.

Jess and Callum were absorbed in sorting boxes of dusty books and barely looked up, as if allowing him to find his place.

Sofia placed a huge teapot on the trestle table and Justin eased himself onto a bench. 'I hope you take milk and sugar,' she said, filling his mug with a caramel liquid. 'We took a vote and now we add condensed milk to the pot to save time.' The efficiency appealed, but he hoped the principle didn't extend to sharing bathwater.

Rob was the leader in a non-hierarchical way; a full-time revolutionary, scratching a living translating French articles for political journals. He wore a peaked Lenin cap and a wardrobe of black polo neck sweaters, as Justin soon discovered. A chain-smoker, he indulged a penchant for *Gaulloises* when he could afford them, but today was absorbed in crafting a thin rollup.

Callum and Jess joined them at the table and Justin learned how Rob and Callum met. 'We were at Oxford and right royal pains in the arse.' Callum grinned. 'We tore up our finals papers in protest at elitism. What a gas! I'd have been doing mathematical modelling in the City by now, but instead I've got a second-hand book stall on the Portobello Road—it's cool—keeps me in grass and Benefits cover the rest.' His t-shirt bore the slogan, *Smash the Patriarchy*, and his hair hung in thick coils like unravelling rope.

Jess, his girlfriend, was fast talking with an infectious energy. Bangles jangled at her wrists and she radiated a fragrance Justin couldn't pin down. Then it came, rosewater, his mother's favourite scent. 'We're involved in the community,' Jess told him, twirling her beaded braids. 'We campaign for housing and Social Security rights, as well as on women's issues.'

There was a great deal of talk about whether the levers of democracy could create change in a system where Parliament and the courts were instruments of the establishment, but he couldn't recall the detail at this distance in time.

His heart sank when Sofia announced she had to go to her life-drawing class. As she moved across the room and past the charcoal nude, he was thunderstruck to see that the portrait was of her. He was in too deep to not care and it pained him that she held him at arms' length. This was surely a political test, a ploy to test his commitment. He must live in hope. Jess showed him to his room and pointed out the bathroom. 'The bath takes an age to fill and uses up all the hot water. I hope you don't expect to have a bath every day after working on the building site.'

'I can always use the baths near work, otherwise you'll have to hose me down on the doorstep.'

'Callum and I share baths... you and Sofia...'

'No, we're not. Nice room, thanks.' Jess left and he dumped his bags on the floor and saw a stained mattress and sticks of furniture. For the first time he had a misgiving. It had all happened so fast and he'd been swept along by the excitement of building a movement and joining the vanguard, *The People's Militia*, a name they hadn't even used yet, not officially. He knew there'd be no going back if he joined them.

Justin shed his cycling gear in the corner of the office and dragged himself to the refreshment point. He hoped the morning routine would salvage the day after a disturbed night. He would rev the coffee machine, pop in to see Vanessa, and thereby delay emails as long as possible.

The *cc* habit drove him nuts. It cluttered up his inbox with everything from fun-runs to parking charge notices, which was before he got to students' emails. These were either pleas for time on assignments or complaints his lecture notes hadn't been uploaded onto the *Virtual Learning Platform*.

Vanessa's china-rose cup rattled in its saucer as he carried it across the corridor. They went back. She was a fellow sociologist and a veteran of Gender Studies.

'Justin, you're a sweetheart,' she said, eyes fixed to the screen as she pressed *send*. She got up and cleared a pile of papers from the armchair. 'Make yourself at home!'

'Thanks, petal.' He lowered himself, holding steadily to his *Today's The Day Everything Goes to Plan* mug and warmed at the prospect of leaving his computer to slumber. His gaze was drawn to Vanessa's screensaver, which glowed purple and green with images of the Yorkshire Moors, and this morning a painful reminder that Harpreet didn't want him to see him.

'So, how did it go with Kyle?' Vanessa peered over her leopard-print specs.

'Not great, to be honest,' he said, gulping coffee and burning his mouth. 'This management accounting bollocks doesn't allow flexibility. In the old days, you could put grant money into one pot and borrow from Peter to pay Paul. It all came out in the wash. The thing is, I've extended a couple of contracts, to get projects over the line.'

'Without funding?' Her eyes widened.

'It's in the pipeline.' He could see she knew this was a fib. 'I can't go laying people off for the sake of a few grand. Not when I see millions spent on the new Business School. It's obscene.'

'The spending or the building?' she asked, eyes glinting.

'Both.' He looked out of the window to see cranes already in motion. 'We're going to end up hot-desking the way things are going. The one advantage of these old prefabs is that the offices are too small to share.'

Sociology was about to be gobbled by the Business School and working in an open-plan office was Justin's idea of hell.

Vanessa changed the subject. 'And how's Sanjay? Still enjoying work at the bike-shop?'

'Yes, he's doing grand. I'm a bit worried about his political interest in Syria, it's such a hotspot. He's very keen on this girl who wants to volunteer out there....'

'...like father like son,' she said with a rippling laugh. 'You've only yourself to blame. Anyway, this thing about Kyle, you should let it go. Tactical retreat and all that. Fess up and get over it. And there's no point in kicking up about the merger, it's going to happen whether we like it or not.' She smiled encouragement.

'Okay, I get the message. Stop being such an arse and sort it. I wish I had your powers of persuasion.'

'Nonsense! Now, enough banter, or we'll both be out of a

job.'

He got up to leave. 'See you later, comrade.' It was their joke. He'd have suggested meeting for lunch, but these days Vanessa grazed on a box of rabbit food, so wolfing bacon-butties felt uncouth.

Back at his desk he scrolled emails. Did people work all night? Anything with an attachment he dumped into a folder for later and most others he deleted. Spotting Stephen's name, his heart missed a beat and he double-clicked. The message was cordial and professional, requesting a neutral venue. He'd suggested a Leeds hotel.

Justin was relieved at meeting somewhere anonymous, where there was no danger of bumping into anyone he knew. He would tell Stephen what a great bloke his dad was and discover what Max had said in his memoir. How bad could it be?

One of the few occasions he'd visited Max at Full Sutton in Yorkshire, he'd met Daisy in the prison waiting room, and she'd said, *he doesn't need friends like you.* They married soon after Max's release, he knew. She blamed Justin for Max being sent down and he could only suppose Stephen knew of her bitterness. He hadn't visited again. He got wrapped up in his PhD, work, marriage, whatever. Life got in the way, or so he'd told himself.

Sometime later, Max had written to him at Leeds University and had the crazy idea of them apologising to Peter Haddon for the distress caused to his family. The letter was seared onto his brain. It would have been suicide for his reputation to agree, so he'd ignored Max's request. When Harpreet had asked, *is there anything else I should know,* he knew he ought to have told her about the Peter Haddon affair, however incriminating. Panic bloomed in his chest and he did a few shoulder rolls in the hope that his rational brain would kick in. He got up and peered through the dust-laden blinds and took several deep breaths. Then he remembered forgetting to take his blood-pressure tablets that morning.

He felt his mobile vibrate and pulled it out of his trousers pocket, praying it was Harpreet. It was his sister Molly, and a call during work hours was bad news.

'Justin, sorry to do this. It's Pa. He's in A&E again after a fall. Could you get over? I'm away till tomorrow.' Molly took charge of Pa's care and he was emergency backup.

'He'll be in good hands, Molly, what more can I do?'

'Keep him company? He'll need pyjamas, toothbrush and pills. Could you drop by and pack an overnight bag?'

Talking to Molly was like listening to a satnav. If he went *off piste* she nudged him back on track and he knew he had to go. He belted back to Headingly, got out the car and headed to Sheffield.

The last time they'd had to rescue Pa, he'd been found by the carer on the bathroom floor, his emergency alarm hanging on the back of the door. There was no question of going into a home. Oh no. *Never say die*, was Pa's motto.

He's ninety, for Pete's sake, Justin thought, as the speedo inched up eating the miles along the A1. The descent into entropy was depressing: clothes flung onto chairs, socks and underpants on the floor, and heaps of half-read newspapers on every surface.

By now, he realised he'd missed the turn-off to his favourite transport café, but he wasn't too bothered. The old man was stuck in hospital after all and might even be pleased to see him. Football and family was neutral ground where they could communicate, though Justin didn't care about football. According to Pa, marrying Harpreet was the best thing he ever did and Pa doted on her. The next best was giving him a grandson. Years ago, there'd been a row over sending Sanjay to a Comprehensive school, culminating in Pa saying he'd pay for a private school. Harsh words were exchanged. Harpreet intervened by declining the offer gracefully, as only she knew how.

He turned off into the suburbs of his childhood and wound the car window. The November air caught the back of his throat with a taste of bonfires. As the old house came into view, he almost expected to see Pa as a younger man sweeping leaves from the drive. He hung to the image as he locked the car and rehearsed the code for the key-safe by the front door.

The glass-roofed porch smelled damp and was full of old coats and redundant walking sticks, now that Pa was confined to the house. Once inside, he made his way up past the stair-lift, hoping to find clean clothes in the airing cupboard. It was the arrangement Molly agreed with the Care Agency, whose badly paid employees were supposed to take washing to the laundry. There'd been the odd mix-up, and on one occasion Pa ended up wearing black and white striped satin pyjamas he'd refused to relinquish. *Makes me feel like the bees' knees and the laundry can go to hell,* was what he'd said.

Mercifully, Justin found an overnight bag and the purloined pyjamas were neatly folded in a chest of drawers. There was a whiff of camphor from Ma's mink stoles, from the days Pa's business thrived. He remembered the luxury of burying his face in the perfumed fur when she'd kissed him goodnight before going out to a dinner-dance.

He went downstairs to check the kitchen where Pa had fallen. There was an empty peach tin on its side and peaches spilt over the floor. He must have slipped and hit his head. Justin surveyed the mess and set to with a mop and bucket. The floor was filthy, and he cursed the Agency who should have been checking. Half an hour passed before he wrung out the mop and called it a day.

The wood-panelled hallway was embalmed with years of furniture polish. If Ma had lived, would they have moved? Molly thought Pa stayed on because he couldn't bear to let her go. Not morbidly. It was the garden he'd clung to. When they knew she was dying, they'd walked round together, and he'd taken notes on all the plants. Until then, he'd only been allowed to tend geraniums at the front. After she died, he'd developed a passion for horticulture and flowers bloomed all year round.

The geriatric ward was on the third floor and he mounted the stairs two at a time, Pa's holdall on his shoulder. The nurse in charge directed him to the bay. 'Mr Caffrey? He's at the end on the right and doing nicely. Should be home any day.'

Pa was sitting in a chair next to the bed, dressed in an indecently short hospital-gown. Justin felt his indignity and hurried over to cover his knees with a blanket. 'Hi Pa, what's all this then? Got a nasty bump on your face, I see.' He bent over and squeezed a gnarled fist.

'I've been worse. Where's your sister?' He looked up and Justin saw Pa hadn't been shaved.

'She's away a few days. You'll have to make do with second best. Shall we get you into these pyjamas?' He said, unzipping the bag. 'Can you make it over to the bathroom?'

Pa looked at the walker and the distance to be covered and his face fell.

'Never mind, I'll call for help.' He dug into his pocket. 'Here, I bought a box of your favourite mint chocs from the shop.'

Pa brightened. 'The shop? You could wheel me down there. I fancy a paper. And fish and chips at the café wouldn't go amiss.'

Justin's heart plummeted. This wasn't going to be a quick *hi and bye*. 'Sure, Pa, let's do it. We'll get you sorted out first.'

Easier said than done. The male care assistant pulled curtains round the bed and Justin waited on the outside. He heard, *like this, hold onto me, steady,* spoken with an easy patience he lacked. He heard his father speak in a dialect picked up in Burma, and the man caring for him laughed and answered in kind.

Pa emerged in his satin pyjamas and paisley dressing-gown. 'You look as if you've stepped out of a Noel Coward play,' said Justin, smiling at them.

'This is my son, the Professor,' said Pa, with a lizard smile on his lined face.

'Pleased to meet you, sir. Your father speaks good Hindustani. Learned under the British Raj.' There was a tinge of irony in his tone, which put them neatly in their place.

'Thank you for your assistance,' Justin said, extending a hand. 'My name's Justin.'

'I'm Murali,' said the middle-aged man returning his grip. 'It's a pleasure to care for your father.'

'We're going for a spin to the café, right Pa?'

'No need to shout, I can hear you. Make yourself useful and bring over that wheelchair. I'll go to the bathroom first.'

Murali smiled in complicity. 'Enjoy your lunch, gentlemen.'

The café thronged with health-workers, patients and visitors, and there was plenty of space between tables to accommodate wheelchairs. Justin parked his father at one by the window and joined the queue. Glancing back at the hunched figure with a bruised face, he wondered if Sanjay would have to do the same for him. He hoped not to stick around that long.

The words *senescence* and *obsolescence* circled in his mind and he mused on what would remain of him beyond academic footnotes. He caught sight of himself in the mirrored steel of the servery and saw an aging man with wiry grey hair and a rambling beard. He'd let himself go.

'Here we are,' he said, returning with a loaded tray, 'I even got you mushy peas.' He set down the plates and pulled the table nearer to Pa, to avoid spillage.

'You're a good lad. It's strange, seeing your own son grow old.'

'Steady on, I'm not that ancient. D'you want a napkin? Best tuck it in.' Pa had always been rather dapper and it was important to keep up appearances.

His father accepted his attentions. 'How old are you now?'

'I'm sixty-five, Pa. And with your genes, good for another thirty.' He watched his father attempt to open a plastic sachet of ketchup. 'Can I do that?

Pa handed him the sachet and peered through smudged glasses. 'Well, you're not looking too good. What's up? Trouble at mill?'

'No, no, work is fine, once you get past the paperwork.'

'You should have check-ups at your age. I hope you're looking after yourself.'

'Hey, what's this all about? Actually, I'm training for a cycle race in the spring. It's the *Tour de Yorkshire*. Sanjay and I have signed up.' He waited for a howl of derision.

'The tour de bloody Yorkshire? Give over. It's the Common Market gone mad.'

'It's just a bike ride, Pa.' The sounds of the café blurred and the snaking anxiety about Stephen crept back. Not just Stephen, but a past whose murky depths had been stirred. He felt an overwhelming desire to unburden and the words tumbled out before he knew it. 'I *was* feeling a bit off, actually. I got an email from the son of a mate who died last year. Intimations of mortality and all that.'

'D'you know, there's nobody left who calls me by my Christian name? It's what happens if you live long enough. People drop like flies.'

'I just wish I'd kept in touch; you know how it is? And now it's too late. It was Max Scott…'

'I remember, one of those bombers who claimed he was innocent. Sounded iffy to me. You helped him, didn't you? Always on the side of the loser, you were.'

'He *was* innocent, Pa, but mistakes were made. I'm going to see his son who wants to talk about his dad. It got me thinking, with Max passing, we've never really talked much, and we haven't always seen eye to eye.'

'Hang about, I haven't snuffed it yet!' Pa's eyes came alive.

'Hear me out, Pa. I know things didn't turn out as you'd hoped with the firm and all…'

Pa gave him a wary look. 'Well, I'm not sorry I sent you away to school, if that's your grudge.' He looked away. 'But I regret packing you off to live with Uncle Stan. Your Ma blamed me for that. I'll say this, Sanjay is a credit to you. You can hold your head high on that score.'

'You did me a favour sending me to Uncle Stan, that wasn't the problem. And any credit for Sanjay is down to Harpreet,' Justin said warmly.

'The lad's got real business sense, it must have skipped a generation. Sanjay's got a good heart and he's kind to his old granddad. You should be proud of him.'

'I *am* proud of him.' He couldn't remember when he'd last said so to Sanjay. 'The point I'm making, I've never been good enough, have I? I never measured up.' The instant he'd spoken, he imagined being free of Pa's lowering presence and had a fleeting sensation of lightness tinged with guilt.

'What've you ever had to worry about? You've never had to fight for owt.'

'So, choked with a silver spoon? Seems I can't win,' he said dryly.

Pa looked crestfallen. 'I'm too old to change and you need to grow up. Let sleeping dogs lie, eh?'

It was a hollow truce. Pa was happy enough to claim him as, *my son the Professor*. Taking credit where none was due. It didn't fill the void.

'How about Battenberg cake and a pot of *cha* for dessert?' Justin suggested, indulging their shared taste for the pink and yellow confection; his suggestion hit the spot.

Swilling a last mouthful of strong tea, Pa said, 'Now wheel me back to that piss-pot of a ward and see if I can get discharged for tomorrow. We can pick up a paper on the way.'

'Sure, we can do that,' said Justin before adding, 'I expect I'll be a truculent old sod, like you, Pa, if I live that long.'

He manoeuvred the wheelchair past chair legs and out of the canteen, and they trekked along corridors as Justin reined in a prancing panic at the prospect of meeting Stephen. Perhaps Pa was right; it was time to grow up.

Chapter 3

'What exactly *is* direct-action?' Justin asked, during his first session with Rob. The comrades would take turns to explain what they were about and it was clear they were in a different league to the student politics he'd dabbled in at the LSE.

'You have to understand the big picture,' Rob said, fingering a typed document held together with a treasury tag. 'Two years back, workers and students started a revolution in France and I was there. It was something nobody anticipated. It could happen again and we must be prepared to seize the moment.'

They were sitting upstairs in the office, furnished with battered desks and odd chairs, filing boxes stacked neatly on metal shelving.

'Yes, Sofia said you were in Paris in '68. What was that like?'

'Seminal,' said Rob. 'Totally seminal, completely blew my mind. Students and workers joined forces to oppose the establishment, oppression, capitalism, it was like a tidal wave of consciousness, a realisation we had the power to change things, change everything. Debord made sense to me, Guy Debord—heard of him?' He passed over the document he'd been playing with.

'*The Society of the Spectacle?*' Justin said, glancing at the title. 'You translated this?'

Rob made a dismissive gesture. 'Read it. It explains Situationism—it's part communist, part anarchist and with a vision that goes beyond either. Debord shows how working-class struggle is silenced and the traditional Left is part of the problem. The Trade Unions and Leftists want to keep things within the realm of politics and representation. Our task is to engage in *détournement*, to reappropriate language, images and culture and expose the alienation and separation people experience in everyday life. Capitalism makes us believe we want *and need* the commodities we knock ourselves out for day in day out. I'm talking about the poverty of everyday life, the sense that something is missing you can't quite put your finger on. Am I making sense?'

'Yes-yes, I get it...'

'As workers we're never considered in terms of our *leisure and humanity*, as Debord puts it. Once we're producing enough to survive, we're co-opted into consumption to keep the capitalist wheels turning.'

Justin opened the manuscript and saw it was divided into sections, each a sort of aphorism. He read aloud at random:

'*The spectacle cannot be understood as a mere visual excess produced by mass-media technologies. It is a worldview that has actually been materialized, that has become an objective reality.*' He looked up, puzzled.

'It just means we're all buying into a lifestyle with stuff that keeps capitalism going,' Rob elucidated.

Justin turned to another page.

'*The spectacle is characterised by the combined effect of five principal factors: incessant technological renewal, integration of state and economy, generalised secrecy and unanswerable lies, in an eternal present...*' He paused.

'D'you see? It's the big picture, Justin, and we have to challenge the con, expose the lies...'

'But how, exactly? What d'you actually do?'

'We're creative disrupters who reject the levers of democracy as instruments of change,' Rob said, reciting a credo. 'Our job is to upset the status quo.'

Justin registered a distant police siren and the smell of burning toast seeping through the floorboards. 'Go on,' he prompted.

'We're going to target the *Miss World* contest, linking up with women staging a happening at the Albert Hall. Jess and Sof will disrupt from inside the hall and we'll be on the outside.'

'Okay, I think I see where you're going with this,' he said, thinking Ma and Molly would be watching the spectacle as they did every year. Now he saw the world anew, enmeshed by capitalism in overlapping circles and ways that went deeper than he'd thought about before.

'If you're ready, you can join us on the op—think of it as an apprenticeship, but let's see how you feel after talking to the others.'

'Okay, that's cool. When is the contest?'

'Three weeks, back end of November. D'you ever go back to Yorkshire, Justin? Life's a bit different in the Smoke.' Rob's flat tones were from the other side of the Pennines.

'It's been a while—I don't have a lot to do with my folks. Family stuff.' He considered telling of a hard-bitten father who'd wanted a son in his own image, a man of towering rages who'd crushed him under his heel, but Rob looked away. He wasn't one for small talk.

It was clear that *The People's Militia* was small-scale and made up of those living in the squat. 'We're linked to similar organisations,' Rob asserted, without specifying. When Justin asked how they coordinated, 'We don't' came the reply. 'Each group responds to the political moment and our actions appear in the Underground Press. Some groups sell their own papers and newssheets.' He was with Rob and Callum in the basement print-room where the sound of occasional footsteps rang on the pavement above.

'Tell me about the *Miss World* op,' Justin pressed. 'What's the plan?'

'We target buildings using small explosive devices—just large enough to make a political point,' Callum told him. 'We take care not to injure people, not even the likes of those who beat up workers on the streets and in prisons.' He leant against the wall, hands in pockets and waited.

'So, you blow things up?' He'd half-guessed as much from the way Sofia had skirted round their methods, but the reality hadn't sunk in.

'What did you imagine, Justin? That we spray-painted slogans? We target oppressive institutions and other groups across the country are doing the same thing. The police have no idea where the attacks are coming from or what the next target will be. It's an uprising against the state that's impossible to pinpoint.' Callum was still propping up the wall and Rob pushed back his cap, exposing a receding hairline.

Joining was easier once he knew they targeted property not people. There was no way he was going to endanger life. Over the past couple of years there'd been a number of high-profile bombings on embassies, banks and tourist offices, attacking totalitarian regimes such as Spain and Greece. He'd heard something called the 1st of May group was involved. Nobody had been killed, which was remarkable considering the risks they took. He asked now what operations *The People's Militia* had carried out themselves.

'Okay,' said Callum, 'so we were kinda involved in blowing up Paddington Police Station a few months back. Our first proper job was firebombing the Conservative Association in Brixton, then we had a go in Wimbledon and Hampstead. Sofia does her own thing, international stuff…' A look from Rob cut him dead. 'We want you in on the *Miss World* job. You can act as lookout.'

'While you do what?' He felt foolish asking.

'Blow up the BBC van the night before. It won't stop the broadcast, but it should make the BBC think twice,' said Rob.

Justin had a tumble of questions about who made the bombs and where they found the materials, but knew it would take time to build trust. He had meetings with all four comrades, and they seemed to like him.

'Count me in,' he said, to wide smiles and raised fists.

He felt a sizzling excitement laced with fear, which took him back to school days. An old soak of a chemistry master who'd lost a leg in the war introduced boarders to homemade bombs. They'd set off the crude devices in the woods, then ran like crazy as these tended to go off without warning. The experiments stopped after a boy lost his fringe and eyebrows.

This was no game, and he would reserve judgment on the safety of the operation until after the event.

He watched Rob and Callum drop to their knees behind a square white BBC van parked up for the night. Rob nursed a carrier bag from which Callum took the bomb and placed it tenderly under the back axle. It was a simple enough device, using a blasting cartridge and a length of slow-burning fuse.

He stood rigid, nerves zinging as the seconds stretched. His ears tuned in as a police siren wailed in the distance. A pigeon flapped skyward and his heart lurched, as he shivered inside his donkey-jacket.

Justin did his best to appear casual, ambling along with hands plunged deep into pockets, counting the seconds under his breath. Setting a fuse wasn't an exact science. The bomb could go off any moment.

Rob and Callum were on their feet at last, putting distance between themselves and the van. Rob, shorter, pedalled the air next to Callum, who ran with long loping strides, cutting a striking figure in his shaggy afghan coat, hair streaming.

A plume of flame soared overhead followed by a roar that rent the air, and Justin took to his heels, leaving devastation behind.

The explosion followed by sirens brought an aged insomniac to the window of his flat in Kensington Gore, an unlikely witness to Justin's debut as an urban guerrilla. By then, the three were weaving through the streets to the safety of the squat. The burnt-out carcass of the BBC van, destined not to broadcast the *Miss World* contest, would soon be replaced.

Justin was trying to adjust the TV to stop the fizzing and the jagged lines that ran across the screen. It was an ancient set with an aerial fashioned from a wire coat-hanger. 'Stuff it, that telly's never going to work—let's watch down the Ladbroke,' said Callum.

The pub had an old-fashioned frowsty look despite the red and white paintwork and picket fence. In summer, there'd been green parasols and outdoor tables, where a young crowd hung out for the chat and beer. Justin led the way through the swing doors and felt an icy draught follow them. The air inside was thick with smoke and a coal fire blazed in the hearth.

'Could you stand me a half, mate? I'm a bit short of readies,' Callum asked, looking woebegone.

'Sure, drinks on me. We'll have to go to the saloon bar for the telly.'

They passed the door of the public bar, *Tap Room* painted onto frosted glass, code for *workingmen only*. Everyone knew their place. Justin preferred the public bar's rough and readiness; the beer was cheaper. They ventured into the carpeted saloon and ordered two pints of bitter.

Justin carried the drinks and Callum headed towards a couple of red plush stools at the back. The clientele was mostly couples having a night out. The men wore well-pressed shirts and the women had their hair up in beehives. Justin observed the fancy wall-lights and prints of racehorses, lending an air of gentility. He saw people as social types, he couldn't help it, and here was your classic aspirant working class.

The TV twittered from a high shelf and the show was

already underway. The camera panned the audience and the commentator was giving a round-up of the panel of judges. Justin recognised Joan Collins from the film, *Subterfuge*. She was sitting next to the Prime Minister of Grenada. 'They've got the big guns out tonight,' he remarked.

'Sure thing,' Callum said, with a grin. 'Have you ever seen anybody you knew on TV?'

'Sort of—my sister Molly had a friend who won a raffle to be in the audience of *Top of the Pops*. Molly went crazy when she saw her. It was weird, seeing the girl jigging about and smiling at the camera, as if she knew we were watching. D'you think we'll see Jess and Sofia?'

'Who knows? Jess said they'd got seats near the front to get a better view, if you see what I mean,' Callum said, lowering his voice.

Justin nodded. 'Nothing in the papers about last night.'

'Well, tonight won't go unnoticed, that's for sure,' Callum said, looking round the room. 'Look, there's Bob Hope.'

The guest presenter strode onto the stage. 'Good evening, one and all! Good to see you on this beautiful occasion! You'll have seen the spoilsports demonstrating outside—well, I for one am happy to be here at this cattle market… mooo… I've been backstage checking the calves and it's quite a sight! The fight to save our wildlife has many rewards. I don't want you to think I'm a dirty old man. I adore these girls, and here they come, aren't they beauties?'

Justin felt anger at this arsehole clapping the air like a ringmaster, as a drum-roll brought in a shimmering procession of scantily clad women. Each was draped with her national banner. The camera zoomed in on Hope, getting a close-up while he commented in lecherous tones, introducing the contestants who curtsied before leaving the stage.

Then something changed. There was an alteration in pitch among the audience, so distinct, you could almost put your hand out and touch it.

'Hey, what the hell was that?' Bob Hope looked horrified as he ducked objects hurled from above, and the sound of a football rattle whirred like an approaching missile, gathering momentum until the din was thunderous. The camera showed the audience in uproar, then whipped back to the hapless presenter hit by a flour bomb, frantically dusting his suit.

Justin let out a low whistle as the cameras swung back to the crowd. Smoke was rising from the auditorium and women were clambering over seats and heading towards the front.

The spectators in the pub gasped.

'Bloody hell, it's a bear pit,' said a man sitting nearby.

'It's them blasted women's libbers ruining a good night out—I'd show em a thing or two, if I got my hands on one,' said another.

'I wouldn't rate your chances,' said the woman next to him, 'they'd ave you for breakfast,' followed by an outbreak of good-humoured laughter.

'It's happening,' Callum said, shielding his mouth. 'We're exposing the *Society of the Spectacle*…'

Glued to the set, they watched as women launched themselves at Bob Hope. 'It's Sofia—and Jess!' Justin gasped, barely able to contain himself.

The orchestra played valiantly while chaos reigned and it was some minutes before a sonorous voice said, 'Ladies and gentlemen, we apologise for this unfortunate interruption, but rest assured the show will go on!'

Justin watched, wide-eyed, as uniformed guards swarmed and manhandled protesters to the floor. The camera shot blanked and a card filled the screen, promising that normal service would be resumed. The screen came alive after a long minute and Bob Hope emerged from the wings, arms aloft as he brought the house down. The reaction in the pub was mixed and Justin heard nervous laughter, as though people had glimpsed a brief rip in the membrane of normality and had a narrow escape.

Bob Hope was back in the saddle. 'Ladies and gentlemen, this is useful training for Vietnam! I'll be over there with the troops before long. I want to tell you, anybody who would try to break up an affair as wonderful as this, with these wonderful girls from the entire world, has got to be on some kind of dope, ladies and gentlemen, believe me…'

Callum eyed his half-finished pint. 'Should we go? Jess and Sof are bound to be at the cop-shop after that performance.'

'Sure, let's get out of here,' Justin said, draining his glass.

The air outside bit their cheeks and Callum pulled his shaggy coat tight. 'That was cool, what the girls did—I'm proud of them.'

'Me too,' Justin said, 'even better than our bombing efforts.'

'Just different, mate.'

'A year ago, I'd have said that women cheapened themselves by entering beauty contests. I'd have blamed them for it.'

'I know where you're coming from, like stopping yourself looking up mini-skirts on the tube. We're socialised into seeing women as sex objects and that's what tonight was about. To show women as people, not fodder for capitalism. It took me a while to get it, but we still fancy the pants of them, don't we?' he said with a beguiling grin, 'Jess and Sofia, I mean!'

4 December 1970 to International Times

PRESS RELEASE 1

We expect the news of the machine-gunning of the Spanish Embassy in London on Thursday night to be supressed by the bourgeois Press.

It's the third time over the last month that the system has dropped the mask of the so called 'freedom of information' using a D Notice to hide its vulnerability.

'They' know the truth behind the BBC van bomb the day before the Miss World farce; 'they' know the truth behind the four Barclays Banks were either burned or badly destroyed.

'They' also know that active opposition to their system is spreading.

The People's Militia doesn't claim responsibility for everything. We can make ourselves heard in one way or another. We machine-gunned the Spanish Embassy in solidarity with our Basque brothers and sisters. We were careful not to hit the pigs guarding the building, which represents British capital in fascist Spain.

Solidarity & Revolution and Love

The People's Militia

Chapter 4

Justin watched helpless as Harpreet scoured the inside of the oven, her back firmly turned.

'Listen love, we need to talk about Sanjay,' he appealed, 'could you leave off cleaning a bit and I'll put on the kettle?' He should have known better.

'Not unless you're offering to clean the oven, which would be a first.' She flashed him a look over the mask she wore against the noxious fumes.

He felt he pulled his weight doing most of the cooking and shopping, which let him off housework in his book. Left to himself he'd have a cleaner, but Harpreet wouldn't hear of it. There was an uneasy truce over the division of labour, which broke down with the occasional spat. Since her return home, everything had taken on a raw edge. He bided his time, poring over what Sanjay had said at the kitchen table, jigging his knee.

'So, Farida is volunteering for what exactly?' he'd asked, trying to sound non-judgmental.

'The Women's Protection Units, called the YPJ who are fighting ISIS…'

Justin grabbed him by the shoulder. 'Stop! Farida is joining a *military* unit? Is she crazy? You said she was working for a grassroots women's organisation…'

'I know, and she is, but obviously there's more to it…'

'Hang on,' he said, trying to take this in, 'she'd already left the country when I saw you at the café?'

'She flew to Istanbul that night and then to Irbil, the Kurdish capital in the north of Iraq. From there, she was getting a car across the border—I haven't heard from her yet—she warned me, reception isn't good.'

'Christ!' Justin said, head in hands, 'this is even worse than I thought.' He looked into the middle distance, with the dawning thought that Sanjay was taking the first missteps that could end in disaster. It wasn't too late to get him back on track.

'Have you any idea of the risks, to *you* as well as Farida? What if men in dark suits turn up looking for a suspected terrorist...'

'...because that's what all Muslims are like, right?' Sanjay's fist clenched as a telltale vein throbbed in his forehead.

'It's what the security services suspect when someone goes to Syria—they don't read the small print.' Justin made his tone reasonable. 'I know that Rojava is a progressive cause and that your hearts are in the right place...'

'Chuffing hell, Dad, listen to yourself. D'you think being a member of the Labour Party and the Ramblers gives you the right to judge me? You did your own thing back in the day, but you've no idea about what's happening now, under your nose. Like when there's a terrorist attack, anyone who looks like they might be Muslim, meaning brown, gets abuse. And if you wear a headscarf or carry a backpack, you're fair game. Farida saw a way to make a difference and I support her totally.' Sanjay's fist was shaking; he was near tears.

'Look, we got off on the wrong foot, but you *do* realise Farida will be classed as a foreign fighter? Getting back into the country could be tricky, and before you say it, yes, I *know* she's a UK citizen, but with her father's background...'

'...a political refugee after being tortured in an Algerian jail—how can that be held against her?'

'Isn't it obvious?' his voice trailed as he contemplated the vagaries of his predicament and tamped down mounting anxiety. 'What I'm saying is that taking direct action in the heat of the moment can be dangerous, and I speak from some experience. Fighting ISIS is suicidal—sorry to be so blunt, but that's how I see it.'

Sanjay stood and filled a glass from the tap, back turned. He drained the glass and turned slowly to meet his father's eye. A young man who was hardly recognisable as the little chap who answered in English to his mother's Urdu and spent seaside holidays with his grandparents, counting the steps up to Whitby Abbey, *aik, dow, teen, char*. How they adored him! What had his boy become?

'Okay Dad, let me explain.' He stood four square, facing him, exuding a quiet confidence. 'Farida wasn't groomed online or anything sinister, she's going into this with eyes wide open.'

'How did she get involved?' Justin asked, wishing he'd taken a closer interest.

'It started with raising funds for a charity after she heard an inspirational talk about the YPJ. You've got to understand the context—the US is backing the Kurdish defence forces against ISIS, and as the Brits support the Americans, fighting ISIS isn't against the law. At least not yet. It's like the civil war in Spain, where foreign fighters supported the revolution—George Orwell and all that.'

'And look how that ended,' Justin added, which Sanjay ignored.

'Revolutionary forces led by the Kurds are carving a space in northern Syria to build a form of direct democracy where women play a leading role; that's what Farida wants to be part of. It's what she believes in and it's why she's headed for Rojava.'

'We don't want to lose you, son,' Justin said, summoning Harpreet in her absence, 'we don't want you following her out there.'

'Don't worry on that score. She needs me here to raise the profile of the YPJ and she's going to write a blog on what's going on.'

Justin got to his feet and closed the space between them to give Sanjay a hug, something he hadn't done in a long time.

'Wow Dad, I wasn't expecting that. It's cool, okay? We'll fix a date to get out on the bikes, cos you need to get in shape for the *Tour*. How about we ride over to Grandad's? I'd like to see the old man.'

Justin's heart clenched at the fondness between Sanjay and Pa, lovely in its simplicity.

Justin looked up to see Harpreet stripping off blue rubber gloves and tying her hair back into its tortoiseshell clip. She wore an old tracksuit and looked hot and bothered after her labours. He poured jasmine tea from a glass teapot and her face softened. She'd withdrawn her warmth since he'd spoken of his insurrectionary years; he knew he was on probation. Her spring-cleaning offensive did nothing to dispel the distrust between them.

As Harpreet gathered herself, he hoped their love for Sanjay would heal the rift. 'So, you've spoken to him?' he ventured.

'Yes, and I told him he must step back from this stuff and I imagine you said the same. I gave him the gist of the memo we got at work and I hope he'll take it on board.'

'What memo?' It was the first he'd heard of it.

'A briefing for the Crown Prosecution Service about the Kurdish People's Protection Units, or YPG as it's called. It's not a banned organisation, so far so legal. However, there's a grey area round links between the YPG and the Kurdistan Workers' Party, which *is* proscribed. The YPG is like the military wing of the political entity, just as the IRA was to Sinn Fein. Farida has joined the YPJ, the women's section of the YPG, and in theory she can't be investigated. However, anybody who makes it to Syria will be watched, that's for sure. If the Americans pulled out of Syria the UK policy could change overnight. Which means Farida would be considered a security risk when she came back. She'd be taken to a detention centre for interrogation.'

Justin thought of Farida's family who'd already suffered so much, and the young Yorkshireman who would never come home. 'That's a horrendous thought, but how can we protect Sanjay? It was so much easier when he was little and fell over, we could make it better.'

He saw dark rings like tea-stains under her eyes and a sadness he hadn't noticed. She looked up from the amber liquid in her cup and said something he wasn't expecting. 'Sanjay once told me he felt he didn't properly belong, and I can sympathise. You can never be British enough in this country, however hard you try. I guess he's decided not to try any longer and Farida has given him something to fight for. *And* he's fallen in love, which can't be helped. This time out we can't protect him, only warn. Obviously, the business you're mixed up in complicates matters.'

He felt the clamour of his existence pumping through his veins, where adrenaline and self-righteousness had once numbed him to danger. The bombing of the minister's house came unbidden with an image of the cat superimposed. A tiny black and white bundle, she'd emerged from an outbuilding into the yard, as he'd searched for the back door. She wound herself insistently round his legs and wouldn't be shooed. Time split between the reality of the cat under his arm and the enormity of the blast when his mind almost departed his body. The cat leapt into the bushes and burglar alarms pulsated as loudly as the factory hooter he'd known as a child, and equally terrifying.

'There's something I need to tell you, darling. It's about Max. He went down for the Peter Haddon bomb, but he wasn't at the scene. I was. I'm appalled when I think back on it—his wife and daughter were at home at the time.'

Harpreet recoiled. 'You bombed a government minister's home? *Why*, in God's name?'

'The attack on the minister of employment was symbolic—we were protesting anti-union laws.'

'So, you and whoever else got away with it? Max took the rap? It's beyond belief, Justin, what planet were you on?'

Justin shook his head, grappling with fractured shards of the past. 'We exercised group discipline and solidarity… we considered the state the enemy and the likes of us, the enemy within. They picked off Max because he was easy to frame as he had a previous conviction. The rest of us were clean and we believed his best chance was a defence campaign—hopelessly naïve, of course. There was no question of giving ourselves up, which would have been to capitulate to bourgeois morality. It was a pact of honour nobody broke.'

Harpreet studied him intently. 'You made a collective vow of silence and lived with wilful amnesia in order to reinvent yourself? I'm trying to understand you Justin, I really am.'

Was this true? He'd *chosen* to forget and created an identity of the good guy sniping from a safe distance, is that how Harpreet and the world would see him?

When he didn't reply, she said, 'D'you know what I think? You're having a late-life crisis. Things are going badly at work and now Stephen has walked into your life threatening your reputation and you're filled with self-pity.'

His heart pounded. 'Okay, I get it. I'm white, middle-class and male, tilting at windmills from the bastions of academic privilege. Is that what you think? You've been happy enough to pander to that version of me all these years.'

'It was the version of yourself that you chose to show me, until now.' She looked over at the improbably bright painting they'd chosen because it reminded them of their walks at Bolton Abbey, picking their way across the stepping stones. 'I can't help thinking of my parents and their choices. Survival for us meant playing by the rules. It's what they drummed into me. *Study hard, adapt, don't draw attention to yourself.*

'When we first arrived in Leeds, we shared a house with distant relatives who resented us occupying a room in their cramped space, and their daughter was embarrassed to walk to school with me. I soon learned to scuff my shoes and *speak Yorkshire*, much to my parents' annoyance. Your kind of rebellion wasn't an option for a refugee, and a girl. I became a lawyer to tackle injustice from within the system you derided.'

Her look was steely. 'I think this is the first time the difference in our backgrounds has mattered.'

He'd been transformed from loving husband to self-regarding imposter. Was there a way back? He retreated to that first shimmering summer when they'd courted. For courting it was. It had been a slow getting to know one another, 'walking out' as Harpreet's mum put it, which at its most intimate meant holding hands in the park. Back then, Harpreet looked up to him for his brains and experience. The balance had shifted.

The decision to allow Max to move in split the group down gender lines. The women were wary. 'Unknown quantity' and 'loose cannon,' were phrases bandied about; Max didn't fit the mould. Justin had first met him at the Benefits drop-in session where Max was labouring over a form. He needed a place to crash and Justin's instinct was to take him to the squat. It didn't go down well.

At a group meeting, Justin said, 'I propose we recruit Max to the group as we've agreed we need to expand. We need comrades like him or we'll end up reproducing ourselves. He has more experience of life than all of us put together.'

Rob backed him up. 'That's right, Max is unemployed and homeless, thanks to the bloody Social Security system. And he's skilled, he'll make himself useful.'

Jess screwed up her freckled nose. 'There isn't exactly a job-description, is there? *Full-time revolutionary required, willing to bomb banks or similar.* I know it's about politics but chemistry comes into it too. Max gives me the creeps.'

'Me too,' Vera added, with a nod to Jess.

'Well, how *do* we recruit? On politics or gut feeling?'

Callum said crossly.

'Don't look at me like that,' said Jess. 'Living here is a meal-ticket for someone like Max, he *has* been in prison after all...'

'...for God's sake, Jess, the man lived in a night hostel and did time for petty theft. Does that mean he isn't one of us? Legality is a fetish, remember? The law isn't there to protect us and it's certainly done nothing for Max.'

'Cool it, Callum,' Sofia cut in. 'We're all entitled to an opinion.'

'Not if it's a wrong opinion, unless you hold the petit-bourgeois notion that opposing views are of equal worth.' Callum sneered.

'Don't tell me what to think, you patronising prick,' Sofia swiped back. 'I can name half a dozen women who would be far more eligible.'

Callum was incandescent. 'So that's it, women are more entitled? This is class war, sister, the sex war is a sideshow...'

'No!' Justin jumped in before Sofia lost it completely, 'it's both! We can't defeat capitalism while women and minorities are oppressed. As for Max, he's been tried and tested by life, and I say we recruit him not out of charity but because we *need* him.'

'We're going round in circles,' said Rob, moving from the table. Rob hated conflict.

They simmered in silence under a haze of cigarette smoke, then Justin played *My Generation* on the record player, hoping they'd dance out their differences. It worked. Everyone took to the floor and bopped, even Rob let his hair down, so to speak.

They would eventually reach an uneasy compromise and Max was invited to join. He went pink under his unruly red hair and said he needed his freedom and could never be a full-time politico. Anyway, he expected to leave in the summer to pick strawberries in Kent and until then just wanted to help out. True to his word, within days he'd made himself indispensable in the kitchen as well as in the print room. The shelf in his bedroom was soon piled with library books he borrowed and returned regularly without the inconvenience of a library ticket, a quirk that endeared him to Justin.

Chapter 5

His mind went down a rabbit-hole, piecing the components that had exploded so spectacularly on that fateful night. Callum had laid them out meticulously on a bench in the abandoned lock-up they used as a bomb-making factory. It was his induction into making an acid-delay explosive device.

'First, no smoking, or we'll be toast.' Callum fixed him with sharp blue eyes. 'You okay with this, mate?'

'Yeah, sure, just show me how we put this lot together.' He couldn't imagine how a bomb was to be made from these items, rather like when Pa had declared they would make a steam-engine out of a heap of *Meccano*.

'No sweat. We place the cartridge into the paper bag, like so...' He'd watched as Callum lowered the cylindrical contraption into the bag.

'Now grab that jar, it's a potassium chlorate and sugar mixture. You can pour it in, that's it, gently, about a third full, so we've got room for the bottle of sulphuric acid.'

Justin's hands shook as he replaced the jar on the bench. This was a lot more precise than bomb-making at school, where they'd made concoctions of sulphur, charcoal and saltpetre.

'Next is tricky,' Callum said, pulling on brown rubber gloves. 'I'm going to fill this Milk of Magnesia bottle with sulphuric acid. Gloves are a must.' He poured the liquid gingerly into the blue Milk of Magnesia bottle and screwed on a metal cap. Pointing at this, he said, 'The top has the centre cut out, replaced with an erodible paper membrane.'

'So, keep the bag and the bottle separate, right?' Justin said, to check he'd understood.

'You've got it. Once you're on site, you upend the bottle and wedge it into the sugar-mixture. And get the hell out. The acid will drip through and set off the mixture, which in turn will explode the blasting cartridge. It's an acid delay technique—not as fine-tuned as I'd like.'

He felt a vice clench his chest and breathed hard. 'What's the worst that can happen?'

'Apart from getting nicked? Getting your face blown off, I guess. If you follow instructions it's not a huge risk. You'll find the adrenalin slows down time and you feel in control. It's afterwards you get the heebie-jeebies.'

He remembered carrying the bomb in a shopping bag, nestled in the crumpled pages of a *Rolling Stones* magazine. In his pocket was the Milk of Magnesia bottle, ready to plunge head-first into the lethal mixture. Once in the yard, the bottle slipped his grasp as he pulled it from his pocket and hit the backstep with a crack; he risked an uncontrolled explosion—this much he had time to process before registering a tremendous blast from the front of the house, courtesy of Rob. He rammed the bottle-head into the mixture, grabbed the cat, and fled. Seconds later the ground reverberated under his feet and the bomb let rip a thunderous roar and lit the sky a purplish yellow.

He was shaking head to foot when Rob grabbed his arm and dragged him along a wooded snicket that dropped down to the railway line. They'd timed it catch the 20.13 and had taken the precaution of buying tickets in advance.

They stumbled onto the platform and Justin stood hands on hips, gulping the crisp night air. His cautious side informed him he could have been killed, or maimed for life, missing a hand or arm. The horror took over and his body heaved as he wretched helplessly onto the track, deaf to the approaching train.

They'd known the minister's family would be home, having reconnoitred the target a day earlier. On that occasion, a Mercedes Benz had driven up the drive and lights had flooded the side of the house. A girl of about thirteen ran out to greet the car and closed the gates as the car crunched across the gravel.

When Justin worried that someone would get hurt, Rob said, 'Cool it man, we're not blowing up Parliament, but it'll be enough to make the neighbours think it's bonfire night.'

The bomb was meant to be personal, to frighten Peter Haddon, the minister who led the attack by the Conservative government on the right to strike. The months spent labouring on a building site where men were 'let go of' at a moment's notice, left him angry at the precarity of men's lives. The strike was sacrosanct, he had no doubts. That was then. The reckoning was to come.

Max was juggling a panful of eggs and tomatoes when Justin walked into the kitchen.

'You okay, mate?' Max asked, tacitly acknowledging last night's job.

He nodded, reluctant to talk before lining his stomach. 'Rob's gone for the paper,' he filled in, dishing the meal onto an antique willow-pattern platter salvaged by Jess. 'Grab the plates and we're set.'

He'd woken to the waft of fried breakfast and reached out, to find Sofia's side of the bed cold. Now, she looked up at him from folding leaflets. 'Hey, flower, you've had a good kip. You were dead to the world this morning, so I didn't disturb you. Rob said it went well last night.'

'Not too bad.' He blanked out the bungled acid bottle, but couldn't ignore his throbbing wrist clawed raw by the kitten in her frenzy. He'd felt nothing at the time.

The front door clattered open and Rob walked in with the paper, handing it straight to Justin. 'Inside page. I guess the blast was bigger than we thought.'

There it was, the wrecked kitchen with a gaping hole where the door should have been. He scanned the contents and passed the paper to Sofia. 'You read it,' he said, and made an effort to eat.

She flattened the page and read: *'Two bombs have exploded at the home of Employment Secretary, Peter Haddon, causing serious damage. The first device went off soon after 19:45 at the front door. The second device went off a few seconds later near the kitchen of the house in North London, where moments earlier, Mr Haddon's wife Fiona, had been preparing the evening meal. The explosions blew out windows and extensively damaged the ground floor.*

'Mr Haddon, his wife and their daughter Philippa, 13, left the house after the explosions and took cover in a neighbour's home. No-one was hurt.

'The blasts came after a day of protests against the new Industrial Relations Bill, which passed its second reading in the Commons. The Government hopes to reduce industrial disruption by introducing the idea of strike ballots and a cooling-off period before any action is taken. Labour and the Unions claim the proposals are too restrictive and infringe workers' freedoms.

'The police hope investigations will lead to the arrest of those responsible for the bombing. Mr Haddon will not be drawn on whether he believes the attack is politically motivated.'

Justin scrutinised the faces of Sofia, Rob and Max to see if they shared his horror.

His throat tightened and the contents of his stomach turned to cement. 'I could have killed the girl, I mean, if she'd been in the kitchen, she'd be dead.'

Sofia frowned. 'You're letting this get to you, Jus. There'll always be risks, and nobody was hurt. Guerrilla action is like sending flares up into the sky to warn that working people won't be treated like shit any longer. That's what we do.'

Justin looked Rob full in the face. 'Were you scared? Or was it just me?'

'It's only human to feel fear, comrade. Last night was a test and you came through. Fear feeds on itself if you allow it. You'll get used to it.'

Justin reached for a cigarette and smoked while the others ate in silence, save the children playing in the street. Max's pale grey eyes met his as he washed down breakfast with a mug of tea. He was brawny with a lived-in face and wiry outcrops of golden hair, which sprang from his forearms. To Justin he was a man hewn from the calcified layers of life and he trusted his craggy presence.

'The Haddons and the like don't have to live hand to mouth, like the rest of us,' Max said, addressing Justin's unease. 'It's no joke being on strike, I've been there, and strike pay don't keep a sparrow alive. If men walk out it's because they've got no choice…'

'And *women*,' Sofia cut in, 'remember the Ford's sewing machinists strike? All they wanted was fair pay…'

'Okay, keep your hair on.' Max made no allowances when talking to Sofia. 'We've all got our shit to deal with. Popping off a few bombs will get the wind up the bastards but it won't get rid of them. I'm not against it, mind, don't get me wrong. What I want is a better world for my wife and kids if I have any.'

'You want a family? That's not for me, comrade,' Sofia said, avoiding Justin's eye. 'The revolution needs people with nothing to lose, willing to go the whole way.'

Max gave her an indecipherable look. 'I'd like to meet you in ten years, lady, and we'll see where you're at. I know you're capable of anything.' This earned him a snort of derision.

Beyond the brief spell spent in prison, they knew little of Max's past. He'd worked on the railways and lost his job after a breakdown, which he wouldn't talk about, except that he'd spent years in children's homes. When Justin asked if this was the cause of his grief, he'd said no, the homes weren't too bad.

'I'm up on charges for the *Miss World* demo,' Sofia said, directed at Max. 'I'm pretty sure I can talk my way out of it and get off with a fine at most.'

'You're not one of them beauty contest chicks?' Max asked, with a wily grin.

'That's me,' she said, punching his arm, and he let out a low gleeful rumble.

13 January 1971

PRESS RELEASE 2

The Minister for Employment got it last night. We're getting closer.
*   We are no mercenaries.*
*   British democracy is based on an empire of blood, terror and exploitation.*
*   Its government has declared vicious class war.*
*   The Industrial Relations Bill aims to make it a one-sided war.*
*   We are fighting back, and the war will be won by the organised working class, with bombs.*
*   POWER TO THE PEOPLE!*
*   The People's Militia*

If he had the power to wind back time and change a single event, Max wouldn't have addressed any envelopes.

Rob came into the print room. 'Hey guys, could you address these for me? Here's the list.' It was the press release to the media.

'Sure thing,' Justin replied, looking over the typewriter, while Max was engrossed with a spanner inside the cranky printer.

He'd been over and over what followed as if capturing the detail might change the course of events. He could easily have typed the addresses, but said, 'Want a go with the typewriter? I can show you if you like.'

Max took one look at the keyboard. 'Nah, I'll write them by hand.' Once he'd wiped the grease from his hands, Justin had zipped six through the machine. Max sat and addressed the remaining two. Now guilt gnawed at him, whichever way he replayed the scene.

Another fantasy he indulged was a trick of fate where he never met Sofia on the train. He still wondered whether he was more a recruit than a lover. When he'd moved into the squat, they weren't yet a couple. At work he'd boasted about living with his girlfriend and the blokes wanted to know if he was *getting any*.

He wasn't. The sexy buzz had fizzled out and he stopped attempts to kiss her or even hold hands. It was driving him crazy, he wanted her so much.

'Can we chat?' he asked one morning, when the others were out.

'Sure,' she said, letting her hair fall over her face and not looking up.

'About us…' he half-stammered, 'I know there is no *us*, but d'you think there could be?' He felt weak with longing.

She looked at him with caramel eyes. 'It wasn't the deal when you moved in, Jus, you knew that?'

His heart raced as he prepared to go into emotional lockdown. 'I'm here for the group and the politics, which is separate from any relationship with you, I'm clear about that. I never took it for granted that we'd get together… but I dared to hope. I need you to know how I feel,' he said, sotto voce.

She slid a hand across the table. 'I know, Jus, I've been holding out on you. I couldn't leap into bed before knowing you'd moved in for the right reasons.' She came round and stood close, caressing his cheek and beard. Her lips brushed his, slow and unhurried, and he pulled her in until she melted against him. He burned up with desire and kissed her deeply, falling in love as if for the first time.

When he'd returned from the BBC van job in the early hours, she was curled asleep like a dormouse. His body was humming with adrenalin and he struggled to slow his breathing, afraid to disturb her. He felt her reach out and wind herself wordlessly round him—they were always ready for one another, but this was different. They made love with the urgency of a breaking storm until both lay back, breathless. 'Wow, it's like I'm re-entering earth's orbit,' he said reaching out to touch her.

She fumbled at the bedside for a cigarette and he kissed the spot between her shoulder blades.

'Sorry I didn't wait up,' she said propped against the pillows and lighting up for them both. 'It'll be easier next time.' She didn't ask how it went.

'You've done this before? You kept that quiet. Was it Paris?'

'If I told you, I'd have to kill you, sweetie,' she said, exhaling a steady stream of smoke. 'Now let's get some beauty sleep, lover-boy. You're very good, you know. You'll make someone a good husband one day.'

Another reminder that this wasn't to be *happily ever after*.

Chapter 6

'Love you in a skirt—you've got gorgeous legs,' he said to Sofia's reflection, as she stood scrunching her hair in front of the mirror. She had on a soft wool powder-blue suit she'd found in a charity shop. 'Why don't you leave your hair loose? I prefer it.'

'Too hippy,' she pouted, 'I don't want them gawping.' Slowly and deliberately, she applied a pale pink lipstick that left her lips glossy. The woman had film-star good looks.

'You're beautiful,' he breathed, catching her by the hips and kissed the nape of her neck.

'*Not beautiful, not ugly, but angry!*' she quipped from the Women's Lib chant and turned to kiss him despite the lipstick. He wanted her desperately, but didn't dare make her late for court.

Justin chose a spot on the public benches several rows behind the gathering streams of women, some carrying banners and placards. The formal surroundings took him back to the hallowed halls of the L.S.E. subverted for sit-ins and hot debates about Lenin, Trotsky, Mao and Ho Chi Minh. Occupying the space had felt like a rehearsal for the revolution.

The magistrates' court was almost intimate, designed to keep people in their place. He took in the elevated seats for the magistrates and the gated dock like a sheep pen. It resembled a theatrical set where everyone played their allotted role and accepted the game's rules. The judges and the judged.

There was no sign of the magistrates, just the Clerk of the court sorting documents and glancing up now and again as if distracted by the mounting tension.

He'd insisted they take a taxi to court and had bathed in

the luxury. It was another London from this perspective, shielded from the stench of overflowing dustbins, shitty pavements, smashed windows and broken off railings. Walls and hoardings were daubed with graffiti, sometimes poetic. On one occasion Sofia read, '*The Tigers of Wrath are Wiser than the Horses of Instruction.* What the fuck?' For once, he knew more than she did.

'Something about reason and energy, attraction and repulsion, good and evil. We need both or there's no progression,' he'd said.

She'd looked at him askance. 'Says who?'

'William Blake, a visionary poet and revolutionary ahead of his time.' This knowledge he considered cultural baggage, little knowing he'd lecture his students on cultural capital in years to come.

'Court rise,' the Clerk instructed, and the hubbub subsided. Three dumpy middle-aged women lowered themselves into their seats. Sofia was escorted from a side door and his heart missed a beat at her entrance, head held defiantly high.

The Clerk read the charges, '*Being in possession of offensive weapons at the Royal Albert Hall, including stink bombs, smoke bombs, a bottle of ink, paper bags containing flour, and wantonly throwing missiles causing danger to Miss World contestants.* How do you plead?'

'Not guilty,' Sofia answered, clear as a bell.

Like a fool he imagined her saying, *I do*, in a quite different scenario, but what was he thinking? Sofia would never be tied down.

'Where's the defendant's lawyer?' the chairman asked, curtly.

'There is no lawyer, ma'am, the defendant is conducting her own defence,' the Clerk replied.

The magistrates conferred, interrupted by shouts of, '*On trial against Miss World*, and *Women are people too*,' from the women supporters.

'Any more interruptions and I'll clear the court,' the Clerk barked, as Sofia stood serenely, holding her notes.

Justin watched as she drew herself up. 'I'm here because we dared protest against a so-called beauty pageant where women are paraded like cattle for public entertainment. We have no quarrel with the contestants, in fact some have since spoken out in our favour. We protested against being judged by our looks and bodies. Bob Hope made the point when he said, *I don't want you to think I never give women a second thought—my first thought covers everything.*'

'Get on with it!' the Clerk snapped, ignoring a titter.

'We stood up for our rights as women to be taken seriously, and as for causing danger, that's ridiculous, flour and stink bombs harmed no one, except Bob Hope's pride.'

The women whooped and clapped, drowning the Clerk's calls to order, then started a piercing ululation, and Justin knew it was going horribly wrong. As Sofia was ushered out of the dock, she managed to blow him a kiss.

'Clear the court!' the Clerk ordered and as the trilling reached an ear-splitting pitch, the sound emptied the court faster than any fire alarm. Justin followed the women outside as they sang, *We shall overcome.* He stood alone, the comrades had stayed away *to put the Pigs off the scent,* worried frantic about what was happening to Sofia. A police siren screamed from a distance and the women's singing flared to a crescendo, traffic came to a standstill and a police van with blue flashing lights mounted the pavement.

Justin stood slack-mouthed in horror, as police plunged into the melee. '*Get off our bodies!*' the women cried, as police hauled out two women, dragged kicking and screaming into the van. Wham! The doors slammed and the vehicle took off with a screech of tyres.

Panic gripped him. He had to find Sofia. Inside, he saw people standing, sitting on benches, waiting, and he approached as a black-gowned clerk brushed him aside. He *had* to get back into the courtroom, but a policeman barred his way. 'Court's in session, sir, it's closed to the public. Please step aside.'

Close to tears, he sat like a stuffed shirt in his borrowed tweed jacket.

'You all right, mate?' an older man asked, and it was all he could do not to blub.

'Not really. It's my girlfriend. I'm not sure what's going to happen to her.'

'She been shoplifting or something?' The man's face creased with kindness.

'No, she, er… she threw things at the *Miss World Beauty Contest*…'

'One of them women's libbers,' he chortled, 'I shouldn't worry yourself. The worst she'll get is *bound over to keep the peace*.'

'Really, not even a fine?'

'I doubt it. My lad's in a lot more trouble.' Justin waited for him to go on. 'Working while claiming Benefits. I'd like to see these magistrates keep a family on tuppence ha'penny a week.'

At that moment Justin looked up to see Sofia walking straight towards him.

'Will that be her? The pretty one?'

And she was in his arms, crying, as he pulled her close.

The old man got up, tipped his cap and said, 'Take good care of her, son.'

'I got off with a caution,' she said, sniffing into his shoulder.

'Well done, babe. Your speech was stunning—blew my mind.'

Holding hands as they stepped outside, Sofia hobbled along in her tight skirt and kitten heels, and he felt a deep tenderness.

Their bus was signalling to pull out from the kerb and without warning, Sofia grabbed his arm and they both jumped onto the moving platform.

'I could ave you put off for that,' the conductor shouted, but he didn't, and they legged it to the top deck. The front seats were empty, and they collapsed in a heap, hysterical with relief.

He told her about the women being arrested and she gripped his arm. 'What? That's really bad news! Let's hope they don't name names because if they do, and the cops will link the *Miss World* demo with the BBC van bomb.'

'Christ, that puts me in the frame.' He swallowed hard.

'I doubt they've even got a file on you... except...' she tailed off.

'Meaning?'

'In connection with me. I'm on their radar—the Women's Movement is just a cover...'

'What?' he spluttered. 'Sooner or later, you're going to have to tell me...'

'I've told you, the less you know...'

'Don't treat me like an idiot,' he said, elation curdling to anger.

'You don't own me, Justin, and as for your little pet, Max, he's leaky as hell.'

'Don't start, that guy hasn't got a disloyal bone in his body...'

'Until he's had a few and shoots his mouth off; having a record makes him vulnerable. The thing about you, Justin, is you've got a clean slate. That's a valuable asset. As we've said before, if one of us goes down the rest of us close ranks. You'll never have to feign ignorance on my account if you don't know what I've done.'

'I don't think I'd do well under interrogation.' A shiver fluttered down his spine.

'None of us knows, petal. That's why we work in cells.

We compartmentalise.'

It was twilight when they walked down a street where Edwardian streetlamps made purple shadows of everything. The first sign of trouble was a flashing blue light outside the house. When his pace quickened Sofia held him back. 'Relax, Jus, and remember they'll make out they know stuff they don't. It's going to be okay.'

They walked up the steps and through the wide open front-door.

'Mr Caffrey, I presume? Detective Inspector Havering.' A man in a beige mac stood in the living room and flashed police I.D.

Justin nodded offhandedly. Keep cool, was the rule.

'And you must be Miss Vergara or is it *Ms?*' he smirked.

'What are *you* doing here? Bugger off unless you've got a warrant,' she snapped.

Justin heard the sound of scraping and knocking upstairs, as if furniture was being shifted. A man in overalls walked out of the kitchen carrying a clear plastic bag.

'The warrant under the Explosive Substances Act,' D.I. Havering said smugly, flapping a document pulled from his pocket. 'We're onto you lot and we'll keep looking until we find what we need.'

'Or plant it,' Sofia flipped back.

'That's enough, young lady,' Havering said, more conciliatory now.

But Sofia was on a roll. 'You've already turned over half the squats in town and found nothing, so it's the next logical step. We'll get home one day, and there'll be a small arsenal stashed under somebody's bed. It won't have our fingerprints on it, that's for sure,' she fumed.

Havering's face twitched. 'We've picked up your friends at Bow Street and they've been remarkably helpful. Another outburst from you, Miss Muffet, and you'll be joining them.'

Sofia plonked herself at the table, glaring, as if ready to pounce. Justin found her irresistible, demure and dangerous in her pale-blue outfit.

Havering crossed the room with the rolling gait of a man with a gammy leg. He stepped over books, pamphlets and leaflets strewn across the floor. They'd been knocked off the bookcase, leaving melted candle stubs on the makeshift shelving. The old guy bent awkwardly and scooped a handful of leaflets and waved them at Justin.

'Been printing a bit of propaganda on the side?'

'Dangerous things, ideas,' Justin retorted.

Havering looked at him steadily. 'Anarchists, aren't you? Like the students in Paris. *The story of terrorism is written by the state and it is therefore highly instructive,*' he read from the leaflet.

'I'm not an anarchist, I'm a libertarian socialist, for the record,' Justin quibbled, playing for time.

The detective raised his eyebrows to the ceiling as the banging continued, and Justin followed the progress of a fingerprint cop working with powder and brush on every available surface. Another knelt in dusty corners taking photographs with a flash-camera.

Havering looked over at the posters of Che Guevara in combat gear, and one of a woman in striking silhouette holding a Kalashnikov. The settees looked sad despite vivid Indian covers and jostled for space with saggy beanbags.

Havering motioned Justin to sit at the table and lowered himself into the chair opposite. Above them hung a saffron shade, emitting a dim glow. Justin surveyed the debris of mugs, bowls and cereal packets and saw them through Havering's eyes.

'Anything you say is off the record,' said Havering, tapping the blunt end of his pencil on the table.

Sofia snorted and rolled her eyes.

'As I'm sure you know, the home of a Minister of State was bombed recently. If you have any intelligence, now is the moment to share it.'

'We know nothing, and even if we did, you'd be the last to hear about it,' Sofia said, overly defensive, for Justin's liking.

Havering nodded, unperturbed. He looked at Justin. 'We've picked up a friend of yours. He walked into us after drinking at the Ladbroke.' He paused, waiting for a reaction.

'Who would that be?' Justin asked, knowing full well it was Max.

'Mr Scott. He's helping us with our enquiries. We've reason to believe he may know something about the bombing, even if he wasn't directly involved. And we've yet to nail someone for the BBC van stunt at last year's *Miss World* contest. We think they're connected.' He looked pointedly at Sofia.

'I don't know what you're talking about,' Justin said, his throat dry as sandpaper.

Havering pulled a crumpled Photostat from his pocket and placed it on the table between them. It read; *The Minister for Employment got it last night. We're getting closer.* It was a copy of their Press Release.

'Recognise this? We'll be borrowing your typewriters to check for a match.'

Justin tried to look bored as Havering took out a chequered handkerchief and wiped something sticky off his hand.

'You're wasting your time,' Justin said, and regretted rising to the bait.

'So, you're part of *The People's Militia?*' Havering's tone was conversational.

'No, we're not, we don't believe in organisations.'

'Ah, so there is a *we?* And you admit it exists.'

'I don't know if it exists. You're the detective.' He could feel Sofia radiating white heat and expected her to blow any second. She surprised him.

'If it's all the same to you, Detective, I'm going upstairs to slip into something more comfortable. It's been a heavy day, what with one thing and another.' She gave a seraphic smile and sashayed off without a backward glance.

Havering put the pencil behind his ear and leaned forward. Adopting a fatherly tone, he said, 'I detect a middle-class lad with a chip on his shoulder. Otherwise, why live like this?' He surveyed the room. 'I happen to know you're fairly new to it, on the periphery, so to speak. Unlike certain others, you didn't drop out of university, and you're not really cut out to be a brickie. Not too late to change your mind. Think about it. Help us, and we'll help you.'

'I've got nothing to say to you, neither here nor at the station,' said Justin, pulling away.

Havering got up as if to go. 'And another thing,' he looked up the stairs, 'the little Spanish piece—drop her, if you know what's good for you.'

Justin leapt up, incandescent, as the detective's lackeys clattered downstairs.

'We're done here,' Havering barked at them, and to Justin, 'we'll let ourselves out.'

They'd left once Sofia came down, ponytail swinging.

'What's the matter, Jus? You look like you've seen a ghost.'

'That Havering guy really psyched me out. The thing is, Max addressed some of the Press Release envelopes.'

'In that case, let's hope I'm wrong about him being leaky,' she said, biting her lip.

Chapter 7

Max
HMP Brixton

I lie on the mattress and feel the energy drain from me after Justin's visit. He's full steam ahead with the defence campaign, says the masses are on my side. It helps to know folk believe in me but I've got no faith in judges and juries.

There's a high patch of sky at the window of my cell and I lose myself in it. In a moment I'll psyche myself for my exercise routine before taking the air in the prison yard. Keeping fit is how I survive. What counts is how you carry yourself—body language is everything. And eye contact, of course. You learn whose eye to meet and whose to avoid. I cope by skating on the surface of prison life, a discipline learned in children's homes that serves me well.

When I'm in the dumps I revisit happier times, like when I was a rail guard. In a flash I'm in the brake-van and feel the rhythm of the wheels on the track and the train rocking beneath me. I would read discarded newspapers and take along books from the lending library. For weeks *The Ragged Trousered Philanthropist* was wedged into my guard's bag, alongside the Bardic lamp, a carriage key and emergency detonators. It's funny how these were the closest I got to using explosives. Lying here, I can smell the diesel and hear the clicking of points and the hooter's wail as the train approaches a crossing.

Time to get off my arse. I strip to underpants, prop the bedframe under the window and tie one end to the bars knotted with a pillowcase. I've got about thirty minutes before we're let out into the yard. Pull-ups first. I press my back against the bedframe and heave myself up, one, two, three, up to twenty on a good day. My arms feel leaden and I pace myself, stopping after fifteen. I've got forty press-ups to go. Five minutes to spare and I sluice myself down with this morning's shaving water and dry off with a towel the size of a fig-leaf. Humming with adrenaline now, I wear an invisible shield so no one can touch me.

I pull on my tracksuit as the door clatters open. 'You coming?' asks the screw. The question is rhetorical. An hour outside come rain or shine keeps me sane. I walk out, rolling my shoulders, eyes forward and clocking anyone in my peripheral vision. They've got me down as a bomber, which is up there with bank robber in the pecking order and gives a degree of protection. Attacks in the showers are rife, particularly after a visit. *Getting stuff in* is normal and if you don't, you're a liar or a freak. They've come to accept I never have coke or jelly babies to trade.

I'm looking through the wire mesh to the landing below, when I hear, 'Got any snout?' It's Edwards, a waif of a man with a drug habit. 'Here mate,' and I hand over a wad of tobacco wrapped in bog roll. We both know this is an exchange. 'What's going down?' I ask. 'A bloke topped himself last night. Middle landing. Bedsheets job. There was a hell of a racket, you must sleep like the dead.'

'Poor bastard,' I say, and my mood crashes. We're in a slow-moving line shuffling down the steep metal steps and I cling to the handrail, nerves in shreds. I could do without this snuffing out of life. It's somebody else's story. Except it isn't. I know what it is to be that desperate, but I'm a different person now.

'Step it up,' barks a young screw with a bottle-brush moustache. The new ones are all short back and sides and strut about like little Hitlers. The men are eking out their time outside the cells and catching up on who'd been *ghosted*, lingo for suddenly transferred to another jail.

Four gates later, the biting air slaps me full in the face; most men hang around the perimeter smoking and I break into a jog alongside a dozen others. There are big bruisers as well as smaller compact men like me, running and shaking out their limbs. Today there are a couple of dogs out, each pulling on a short leash and barking in snatches. I once saw two men beating several shades of shit out of each other and a dog leapt between them and sank fangs into flesh. Not pretty.

Parsons joins me and I slow because he's old. 'Who was your visitor? The good-looking lad with long hair.'

'Justin, one of the comrades. They're running a defence campaign to get me off.' We've talked politics before and we're on the same wavelength.

'Did you do it? Bomb the MP's house?' Parsons asks, puffing out each question as his lungs labour in the cold and damp.

'No, but I knew about it.' Parsons is solid, there's something about him I trust.

'So, you'll be down for conspiracy?' Parsons wheezes.

'It's possible, but Justin says the magistrate should throw out the case at committal stage because of lack of evidence. Let's stand over here and talk,' I say, to save his heart.

Parsons is serving a long stretch for bank fraud. 'Believe in it do you? Smashing the state?' He fumbles for smoking tackle and we stand under the shadow of the walls.

'Sure, I believe in people-power and sticking it to the rich. No point in asking nicely. The comrades aren't just a bunch of hippies like the papers say, they're for real.'

Parsons chuckles, half-hugging himself against the cold and puffing out smoke. 'My son's a hippy and lives in a commune. Never done a day's work in his life. I don't get it, me.'

I look up at the walls, like ramparts studded with barred windows. 'I was living rough when I met them and they took me in. They talked about fighting for a better, fairer world, and I wanted to help.' I start running on the spot to keep warm.

Parsons nods. 'So, what's all this about getting you out? Over the wall is it?'

'I bloody hope not.'

'Why are you covering for them? If they were charged too, your lawyer could get you a lighter sentence.'

I look across to see if he's joking and see his nose is dripping and turning blue. He's deadly serious.

'I'm not a grass, Pearson. And anyway, the more of us on the outside the easier it is to fight back.' It crosses my mind that Callum, for one, wouldn't take the hit for the rest of us. Justin would, I'm pretty sure of it.

Parsons salutes me. 'You're a one-off, mate. Respect. I hope it works out for you; I really do.'

A screw is walking towards us and almost throttles an Alsatian at the end of its leash.

'Scott! Parsons! Break it up!' The snarling hound is ready to take a bite and a current of fear runs up my legs. Violence and extortion are one thing but fraternising is off limits. We raise fists in a gesture of low-level defiance and jog our separate ways.

Back in the cell, the last meal of the day is congealing on a metal tray. The slop of carrots and greens and lumpy mash is dished alongside banana-custard with no trace of banana. I joined the 'vegetarian society' for a small subscription, to get a more balanced diet. I'd expected eggs and cheese and occasionally fruit on the menu, luxuries rare as hens' teeth.

I eat mechanically and open the notebook filled with quotes from *The Society of the Spectacle*.

Revolution is not 'showing' life to people but making them live. A revolutionary organisation must always remember that its objective is not getting adherents to listen to convincing talks by expert leaders, but getting them to speak for themselves, in order to achieve, or at least strive toward, an equal degree of participation. (Guy Debord)

My first taste of socialism in action was when we voted on the food kitty. We knew how much food money we needed each week, but hadn't agreed how much each should cough up. Callum said it should be less when you're skint, which is most weeks in his case.

We discussed whether those earning should pay more. Justin squirmed and I said it wouldn't be fair, we can all afford food, even on Benefits, and we saved money by cooking as a collective. After we'd all had our say we voted to contribute equally, though Callum abstained. If it's that complicated amongst mates, how the hell do you run a whole society? It's something I think about a lot.

It's a long stretch till morning, so I occupy the time writing for the Free Max Scott news-sheet.

The Free Max Scott campaign is a constant reminder that I'm not alone. They can lock me up for 23 hours a day, but they can't cut me off from your support.

My story is simple. My mum brought me up and we were happy enough. She met a man who beat her up and in the end he killed her. I tell you this, not because it happened to me, but because it happens every day. We live in a society where we turn against each other. This I know. My friends helped me understand why. Our economic system and the technology that reproduces it, are based on isolation. From cars to TVs, so much of what is produced creates lonely crowds. People aren't only isolated in prison, but also in everyday life.

I've been called many things from misfit to weirdo, oddball and worse. It will take an army of misfits to change the world, so let's band together now!

Thank you for your letters, cards and gifts.
Max Scott

The cell door clatters open and a screw bends stiffly to pick up the tray. I get up to help.

'Thanks, fella. Truth is, I'm getting too old for this game. If they were all as quiet as you, there'd be no bother. I don't know why they've got you in solitary.'

'A corrupting influence, apparently. Bit of a joke, in this place.'

The old guy shrugs. 'Well, another bomb's gone off. It was on the wireless earlier. Ford showrooms this time. At least they can't have you down for that one.'

The door closes quietly and I lean back in the chair. Someone believes in me who shouldn't do, or at least shouldn't say so and it makes me feel fully human.

It's become a weekly ritual, the trip to court for committal proceedings. I'm in the back of a van, sirens blaring blue murder. People must wonder what kind of a dangerous criminal is in there, as we scream across the city and bring commuter traffic to a halt. An axman or train robber most likely.

I'm hand-cuffed to a screw and thrown against his weighty mass as the van rattles round corners. His breath stinks of stale beer. It's an early shift. The cuffs are rubbing my skin and the air is sour in the windowless space. I steady, going over Daisy's letter in my mind.

Dear Max,

How are you? I can't imagine you caged in a cell, you were always one for the outdoors. It's strange thinking back to them days. We had our moments, didn't we? Remember when we climbed out the window and played cards on 'the flat roof? We smoked ourselves silly and played poker for matchsticks. And that time we wagged off school and biked out to Bellflower Wood, and you said it was like the world turned green, the place thick with leaves. We lay on the ground and looked through the branches and it was magic.

They had us in the office and wanted to know what were we doing together, which is ironic, because we were quite innocent in that way, while the house-parents were at it like rabbits. Leastways they didn't touch us, a blessing.

Did you do it, Max? Or are you protecting someone? Like that time some lads pinched a tenner and we all denied it, except you went beetroot with your pale freckled skin. They had you grounded for a week, but you never grassed. Because if you're protecting people now, think on. You don't deserve to take the rap, even if you are mixed up in it.

I'm writing now the twins are in bed and I've got a bit of peace. They're good girls. I'd like you to meet them. I'd visit if you were nearer, but I can't afford the fare to London. Let's hope you're out soon, if those lawyers are any good.

Don't let the bastards keep you down, little fella.

Your friend forever,

Daisy

She loved me well when we were youngsters and now she's reaching out across the years. The kids at the home taunted me about ma's murderous death but Daisy was different. We had a pact not to talk about parents and between us created an adult-free world of our own. Daisy bled into her jeans once and I was shocked to see her as a woman. It was a catapult moment, made me grow up, just turned fifteen. Not long after, the children's home fixed me up with a railway job and I had to leave.

A screech of brakes announces our arrival at the magistrates' court. Getting out of the van is an awkward business. Like reluctant conjoined twins, we have to coordinate to avoid falling over each other. Once inside, it's straight to the cells, another tricky sideways manoeuvre down a narrow spiral staircase. The screw is now sweating an acrid stench I can't escape.

Unclamped, I sink onto the bench to wait. It could be five minutes or five hours before I'm produced in court. Being held in suspense is the prisoner's lot.

I'm reprieved after half an hour and stand in the dock.

The magistrate glances up over spectacles in the merest acknowledgement of my presence, before returning to the files in front of him. His job is to consider whether there's sufficient evidence to proceed to trial.

There's a handful of supporters in the public gallery, which lifts my spirits. When they're warned by the Clerk not to *disrupt proceedings* they settle down.

After more paper shuffling, the magistrate confers with the Clerk. 'Remove the prisoner,' the Clerk says abruptly, and I feel the chafing of manacles at my wrist before being dragged back down the steep stairwell.

We return to the van and the whole process is reversed except the sirens are silent. Week on week, I watch the magistrate examine the accumulating papers to decide my fate. The longer it takes, the more likely I'll end up at the Old Bailey, or so say the jail-house lawyers, all too willing to advise.

And each week I have to recover my equilibrium, first shattered on the night of my arrest. I honestly believed it was a mistake, they'd picked up the wrong guy, even as the cop beat me up. He had on a short-sleeved shirt and bulging biceps, with *Rosie Forever* inscribed over a livid rose tattoo. The image seared on my retina before a punch to the cheekbone sealed up my eye. I've had blinding headaches verging on migraine ever since. No permanent damage the quack reassures me, it's all in the mind.

The van sways, my vision swims and I'm eyeing the bucket in the corner, praying I won't need it. I focus every fibre of my being to keep control. It's a skill I deploy to bland my face to calm at the first sniff of aggression and I can steady my heartbeat when alarms ring at night, because some poor bugger has finally lost it.

I submit to the routine body search, drop my kecks and squat bollock naked for a visual inspection. I remove myself by pretending it's happening to somebody else. Job done, trousers hoisted, it's time to go back to my cell. But no.

'The Deputy Governor wants to see you,' the screw says. 'Now.'

I fill my lungs slowly. 'Why?'

'Not a clue, mate.'

The next five minutes are spent crashing through gates, walking along corridors and finally, taking a lift. I've never been summoned to this exalted level.

The Deputy's office is austere and so is the man. He stands with arms behind his back and inclines his head telling me to sit.

'I'll send for you when I need you,' he tells the screw.

I note the bare walls save a cluster of framed certificates. The desk is furnished with a blotter, a letter-rack and a telephone. There's also a glass paperweight, which if shaken would create a shower of snow. It's the only concession to frivolity in a room that reeks of despair.

'Appearing here is usually a cause for concern,' says the Deputy, sat behind his desk. 'Not on this occasion. I like to take an interest in special cases.'

'I see, sir,' I say, though I've no idea what he could mean.

'I hear you're keeping fit and making the most of the vegetarian menu,' he says in semi-jocular tones. 'And you're pally with Parsons. I hope you're not thinking of leaving us.'

So this is what it's all about. We've been observed in the yard and Parsons is well capable of staging a break-out. There'd be a warning not to fraternise and that would be that.

'No, sir. No plans of that sort. I'm hoping the magistrate will throw out my case before it gets to trial. I'm in limbo until then.'

'I hope it works out for your sake, but we're not here to discuss your case. I just want to know what makes you tick, Scott. Coming from your background. The appalling loss of your mother. I'm sorry.'

'Her murder, sir. Yes. It shaped my outlook, you could say.' The Deputy looks like an old-school military type, not given to sentiment. What is he hoping for? A display of emotion?

'And you gave years of service on the railways, before falling on hard times?'

'Yes, sir. Though I brought it on myself, to be fair. The demon drink, sir.' I've never used the term in my life; it's as if I've been abducted into a bad melodrama.

The Deputy leans in. 'And you like reading? Political philosophy and Kafka, the librarian tells me. I'm impressed.'

So, spies everywhere. 'Catching up on my education, sir.'

'Not the usual diet of Denis Wheatley's occult novels. A pernicious influence, in my view.'

'I wouldn't know, sir. I've never read him.' Another part of my brain is working overtime. Does the magistrate have a hotline to the prison, or are both men members of the same Masonic Lodge? Perhaps the magistrate has mentioned a puzzling case and asked the Deputy, does he know the man? He's clearly linked to the crimes, including bombing a minister's house, I hear the magistrate saying. Rather Wild West, isn't it? And the Deputy would offer to dig around, see if he could shed any light. Off the record, of course. You scratch my back and all that. The comrades often talked about how the establishment worked.

'And your *comrades* are keeping your spirits up?' he asks with deliberate emphasis.

'My friends, sir, yes. They're looking out for me.'

'But you call them comrades, don't you?' he persists.

'Why do you ask, sir?' I'm on dangerous ground.

'As I said, I'm curious to understand you. Your apparent commitment to a cause, to the point of refusing to name those who may have been involved. That level of loyalty is rare, especially in here. Maybe you're being threatened?' He pulls a packet of cigarettes from a drawer, flicks it open and offers me one over the desk.

I hesitate, then take the cigarette and accept a light tendered to the tip. After months smoking roll-ups, I bathe in the sweet-smelling cloud of blue smoke puffed from a straight cigarette. The Deputy sits back in his chair and lights up himself.

'No, sir, I'm not being threatened. And my friends are mounting a campaign to defend me. Even if I knew who planted the bombs, I don't believe that would make any difference to my case. My background, as you put it, puts me in the frame.'

'I see,' says the Deputy, nodding. 'You're wrong, of course, but I'm sorry you feel that way. You sound like a communist. Proletarians have nothing to lose but their chains, and all that.' His tone is almost chummy.

I decide to skirt round this, but admit that yes, I am angry about what had happened to my mother, but I can't bring her back. Now I'm rambling on about the squat and transforming the square into a place where people could escape for a while. 'There are families living in one room, paying rent to landlords who own whole streets. That's what makes me angry; the rich exploiting the poor. It doesn't have to be that way; it isn't a law of nature.' A surge of energy runs through me and I watched the Deputy for a reaction.

'You obviously have a very high IQ, which needs to be schooled, and I'm minded to attend to it. I'm recommending you for an English course. You'll join a class.'

This is unexpected. I inhale deeply, playing for time. I release a lungful of smoke. 'Why me, sir?' There must be a catch.

'It's an order, Scott. I'm sending you to classes. Is that clear?'

'Yes, sir. Thank you.'

'One last thing. I'm told there are rumblings of an escape and I expect you to keep me informed if you hear anything.'

Without waiting for a reply, he must have pressed a buzzer under the desk, because the screw appears from nowhere.

I've missed the exercise hour, but for once don't care. I'm back in the cell in time for the dinner tray, if you could call it that in the middle of the afternoon. I shovel down food as I ponder the chance of an education, which could speed me into another life. And the price is to act as the Deputy's stoolpigeon, which isn't going to happen.

I open a grey exercise book stamped *Property HMP Brixton*. Despite this it belongs to me and makes me part of a community of adult education students, says Elisabeth.

She acts older than her looks. She's a hard taskmaster who expects great things of us. There's no messing about in her class. We all call her 'Miss' out of respect and you could hear a pin drop when she speaks. She brings in newspaper articles and encourages us to write short pieces of our own. There's an old-fashioned blackboard and easel she fills with beautifully curved script, showering herself with chalk in the process.

She encourages us to write for 'Posterity with a capital P' in the form of a diary or memoir. I talked a bit about work on the railways and how the signals were lit by lamp-men who shimmy up signal-posts, just as they did a hundred years ago. 'That's fascinating Max, it's the kind of social history you don't find in textbooks.' It had never occurred to me that workingmen's lives could be of interest.

I keep a diary at the back of the exercise book and read yesterday's entry.

Daisy's letters keep coming, yet we haven't seen each other since we were kids. She's seen horrible mugshots of me in the papers and still writes.

She says her twins are a handful, but she wouldn't be without them for the world. Their dad buggered off and I tell her she must be a great mam, like she was to me at the orphanage.

I'd like to be their uncle or something, so I can spoil them rotten when I get out. Then it dawns that if I'm sent down, they'll likely be grownups by then. It's like a door has slammed shut on my life.

H.M.P. Full Sutton

The trial went ahead and I was lumbered with Briggs as my lawyer, about as useful as a chocolate teapot. I swear he isn't the full shilling. I'm recording what happened for Posterity, as Elisabeth would say.

The charges against me: Conspiring with Robert Rigby, Callum O'Leary and Jessica Bissett, unlawfully and maliciously to cause explosions likely to endanger life or cause serious injury to property.

They tried to link me to the BBC van bomb, which happened before I even knew the comrades. Briggs asked the Jury to consult their folders, to ascertain that I hadn't known my alleged confederates at the time of the bombing. 'In any event, the co-accused haven't yet been to trial. The cart before the horse, so to speak.' Briggs came over as apologetic, leaving me at the mercy of the prosecution.

'Mr Scott, is it right to say you moved into your accommodation within days of the BBC van explosion, invited by your co-accused?'

'I moved in after we met at a Claimants' Union meeting. I knew nothing about the explosion.'

'Nonetheless, you moved in within a week of the bombing, which occurred on November 19th last year. The meeting you speak of took place on 24th November, five days afterwards. You moved into The Grove almost immediately, did you not?'

'Yes. I was homeless and they offered me a room.'

'It seems a very hasty decision on the part of the household, to invite in a complete stranger at such short notice. Are you sure this was the first time you'd met? Perhaps you'd run into each other at the local public house, the Ladbroke, which I believe you frequent?'

'I'd never met them before. I can't prove something that didn't happen.'

'That's all my Lord.' The prosecuting lawyer sat down, having sown the seeds of doubt.

The handwriting expert failed to discredit the envelope evidence and my hopes fell through the floor. She swore that my signature and the writing in my address book was penned by the same person who'd had addressed the incriminating envelopes.

The prosecution had me by the balls. 'Mr Scott, can you tell the Jury whether or not you addressed these envelopes?'

'I don't know, it's possible. I often helped out with leaflets and the like. If I did, I certainly didn't know what was to go inside them.'

'So, you unwittingly addressed envelopes in a household that held regular meetings of a revolutionary nature, and you didn't stop to wonder what they might contain?' He didn't wait for an answer. 'But you do now, don't you, Mr Scott? A press release. I draw the Jury's attention to item number 29b in your folders.' He paused for the Jury to find the page. 'Let me refresh your memory, Mr Scott.'

I knew it all too well and shuddered when he got to the part about fighting back with bombs.

'Do you agree with the sentiments expressed in the missive, Mr Scott?'

Briggs got to his feet and appealed to the Judge to disallow the question as it was prejudicial to my case. I wasn't on trial for my political views, he said. The Judge made a dismissive gesture and Briggs sat down. The cross-examination continued.

'Let me put it another way, Mr Scott. Are you a member of The People's Militia?'

'No, I am not.'

'So, you agree such an organisation exists?'

'That's a trick question. I don't know if it exists.'

'Do you support the notion of attacking democracy with bombs, as the press release suggests?'

I turned to the judge. 'Can I answer in my own way?'

The judge agreed with a nod. He must have decided it would

make him appear more impartial if I had my say, especially as Briggs wasn't doing me any favours.

I fixed on the Jury. 'I've done things I'm not proud of in my life, but I'm not a violent man. I've held down a job, had the respect of fellow workers. I fell on hard times after a mental breakdown. The comrades befriended me and I began to believe in myself for the first time in years. Those of us at the bottom of the pile have to fight for our rights. Otherwise, when things go wrong, we have no control over our lives and decisions are made over our heads.

'I don't know anything about bombs, except that there's been a great number of them in the past few years. A lot of people are angry and I can understand why. So no, I'm not a member of any People's Militia. And my best chance of justice is being heard by a jury that understands that surviving in today's world can be tough. Very tough. My future lies in your hands.'

When I sat a cheer went up from the packed gallery. My heart soared, until I looked across at the prosecutor and saw an angry vein stand out on his temple. He proceeded to argue that the press releases I'd been willing to address showed it was highly probable I was part of the bomb plot in question.

The thing is, I wasn't. And if I'd known what went into the envelopes, I'd have thought twice before addressing them, though I may have gone along with it. That's how it was, we were all in it together.

In the end, the Jury found me not guilty of the Miss World bomb, but they did find me guilty of conspiracy for the bombing of Peter Haddon's home, the Minister for Employment.

The judge called it, 'The most evil conspiracy I have ever had to deal with.' He turned to me and said, 'I do not doubt that you were chosen as a tool in conspiracy by people more sinister than you are, and I suspect more intelligent. I must equally face the fact that you knowingly embraced that conspiracy.'

When he read out the sentence two women on the Jury cried out, and I couldn't understand why. It was too much for me to take in straight away. Fifteen years. There's no way to quantify that stretch *of time. I'll be an old man by the time I get out.*

We get newspapers in the library here and The Guardian *said the sentence was exceedingly severe. 'Scott's opinions, as distinct from his actions, are the understandable products of a wretched life.' Almost as insulting as the judge, who thought I was too stupid to know what I was getting into. The gutter press worked itself into a frenzy: 'These guerrillas are the violent activists of a revolution comprising workers, students, teachers, trade unionists, homosexuals, unemployed and women striving for liberation. The Red Badge of Revolution creeps across Britain.' Sadly wide of the mark, but still... one day maybe.*

I never returned to Brixton. The van drove straight out of the Old Bailey all guns blazing, for hours. Now I'm in Full Sutton, a high security prison in the wilds of Yorkshire. The only light in the darkness is that Daisy can visit. It's an hour and a half away by bus and she brings her girls.

If the comrades stand trial, there's hope I can appeal my sentence, depending on what happens to them. I've tried not to succumb to anger and bitterness, but right now I feel I was the victim of a social experiment that went badly wrong. It's not that they didn't care, they did, especially Justin. On sleepless nights I torture myself with what would happen if I told the truth about the bomb that put me away. I can't afford to think like that, it's not who I am... and yet...

Chapter 8

Harpreet's words rang in his ears as he set off on his bike. *Tell Stephen how you feel about Max, remember you're the key to his father's past. Don't hold back. Imagine Sanjay asking about you and the details he'd want to hear.* She was right, he thought, this was about Max and not assuaging his own guilt.

He'd tell Stephen about the time Max smashed open the gates of the garden square, incensed about a little lad who broke his arm trying to scale the railings. He made short work of snapping off the chains with bolt cutters and put up a banner declaring the square a *liberated zone*. Kids meant everything to him and he wanted them to have somewhere decent to play. Storming the square released a tornado of communal energy. People stepped off their porches to claim a patch of nature and fill their collective lungs. Max built a swing from offcuts brought from the building site and someone found a rope to attach to the seat; middle-aged women rocked up with wheelbarrows and garden forks to clear the undergrowth and mothers organised a rota to watch over toddlers. A posse of teenagers unscrewed a bench from a nearby park and staggered along the streets dragging it to the square. The women with wheelbarrows unbent their creaking backs and hailed them as angels, not vandals.

Justin flipped back to the day he'd passed a couple of girls playing hopscotch and one said, 'Hey mister, where's the mister who put up the swing?' She looked over at the garden square, its gate hanging open.

'Max? Ah, he's gone. He won't be back for a while. I'll tell him you asked.'

'In prison, is he? My da's in prison. Mam says she's not having him back.'

He'd looked at the little kid with her hand-me-down clothes and dusty plimsoles. 'Tell your mam to come by if she needs anything.'

The girl looked down at the squares chalked in white on the cracked pavement and threw a pebble into one of them. 'I'll tell her,' she said and carried on hopping. Her friend narrowed her dark eyes with suspicion, and he walked on, imagining her mother had warned against speaking to strange men.

He arrived at the hotel with time to spare as the wind was behind him. He padlocked his bike to a municipal rack and walked to the brutalist building of concrete and glass. It was softened by a curtain of moss and cascading tropical foliage down one wall, as if in remorse for its other hideous sides.

In Justin's mind's eye, Stephen was short and stocky with a rash of red hair like his father's. A tall, fair-haired man in his thirties crossed the empty hotel lobby and held out his hand. 'I'm Stephen, you must be Professor Caffrey. Pleased to meet you at last.'

'Stephen, good to meet you too.' He was the spit of Daisy, with her cornflower blue eyes.

'We've got an office to ourselves and they'll bring refreshments,' he said, leading the way to a business suite and a room with glass partitions. They settled into low armchairs and Stephen pulled a folder from his satchel in a relaxed, off-hand way.

'Before we start, Stephen, may I say how sorry I am for your loss. I would have attended your father's funeral if I'd known. I hope there are no hard feelings about the past.'

Stephen inclined his head. 'This isn't about recrimination, Professor.'

'Please, it's Justin.'

'Thank you, Justin. I'm on a journey to get to know my dad better. I know you were close at one time.'

Justin looked him up and down, dressed in a smart-casual suit, tieless, and fashionably tapered brogues. At a guess he worked in arts and media. Definitely not a public sector type.

'How is your mother?' Justin asked, hoping to glean how Daisy felt towards him.

'Well, thank you. They'd hoped to travel when she retired, but she was still working when Dad died. It was his heart. All very sudden. He and I were particularly close because he was a stay-at-home father. Later, he got a job with a children's charity, which meant a lot to him. I'm sure you'll understand why.'

He began to feel hot in the small space and wiped his brow. Heavy molecules of musky aftershave saturated the air. It was a relief when the door opened and a young woman brought in a tray of tea.

Justin watched as Stephen poured with practised ease, which was pure Max. He wanted to say how touching this was. 'When Max moved in, he took us in hand. If we didn't wash the pots, he'd call us a bunch of slouchy layabouts, in the nicest possible way. I was very fond of him.'

'That's good to know,' Stephen said, stirring in quantities of sugar. He evidently had his father's sweet tooth. 'Dad would talk about you all. It made a huge impression on him, living with educated people, as he saw it. I never understood why he seemed so grateful after what happened. That's part of what I'd like to unpack.' He gave a strangled cough.

Justin felt his pulse quicken. 'You said he left a memoir; did he mean to publish it?'

'I don't think so. It was more a journal of personal reminiscence.'

An eloquent silence fell between them.

'What more can I add, I wonder?' He couldn't take his eyes off the dayglow folder on the arm of Stephen's chair.

'That's a good place to start. First, I'd like you to read an extract, to give you a feel for what I'm about to propose.' He handed over a typed sheet and Justin's heart stuttered in anticipation.

Notes from a survivor:

This was going to be 'big-bird,' I knew that as soon at the cell door clanged shut. Fifteen years was more than I could contemplate. I'd be in my forties if I served the full term.

It was The People's Militia that started me on this road. After Rob went down for seven years, my sentence was reduced on appeal. I served seven years to his five.

Justin led my defence campaign and did what he could on the outside as well as visiting faithfully while I was in Brixton. He even came to Full Sutton a couple of times after I was sent north. Things petered out after that. I know he felt guilty about me taking the rap for the conspiracy charge. I was angry, but that came later through counselling, when I finally realised I should have told the police who was responsible.

I used to be in awe of those youngsters, literati who quoted Marx and spoke French. I trusted their judgment. I've long since realised they were in a fantasy world and I was dazzled by it.

What would I say to Justin if we met today? It would go something like this: We were from different worlds, you and me. I had to go to prison to get a degree. And if you'd gone to prison, you wouldn't be a university professor now. I've learned to be angry that you betrayed me, but I'm angrier at the class system that divides us. It's because of the system that we met in the first place, and now we're on opposite sides of the barricades. When you ignored my request to meet Peter Haddon, I knew you'd gone over to the other side.

Justin looked up. 'I didn't know how he felt but I'm not surprised. He's right, we should have turned ourselves in. None of us would have accepted that at the time.' He sidestepped the Peter Haddon question.

Stephen spoke in a voice husky with emotion. 'I'm a filmmaker and I want to tell my father's story. The memoir offers ample material, but your testimony would make all the difference, a chance to shine a light on events. It will be a short film to show how my father was let down by the system and by his so-called comrades.'

Christ, this wasn't what he'd expected. He felt he was drowning. 'Are you approaching any of the others?' he asked, desperately treading water.

'Sofia turned me down. Vera, the Welsh MP, won't touch it for political reasons. The two who were acquitted are off the radar, and as I'm sure you know, Robert Rigby died some years ago. So that leaves you. I imagine you'd like to think about it.'

'To state the obvious, you must feel angry about what happened to your father. And therefore with me,' he said, clattering his cup into the saucer.

'Look, the storyboard will follow the differing fortunes of *The People's Militia* in a social context. And yes, I want to set the record straight and express what my father wrote in his journal.' He tapped the yellow folder. 'Maybe you can tell me about life back then, and talk about Max.'

It was clear that whatever the film's slant, he wouldn't come out well. A scenario flashed through his mind: homage to a dead father, a vulnerable man befriended by the loony-left, jailed for a crime he didn't commit. Panic coursed his veins at the thought of Harpreet, her parents, heaven forbid, and Sanjay seeing the film. He would try and fill in some gaps and talk about Max in all his humanity.

'Well, as I said, Max was the grownup in the household and poured common sense over petty squabbles. We invited him to live with us because he was working-class. And because we liked him, of course.' He cringed at how patronising this sounded.

'Gave you a veneer of authenticity, so to speak,' Stephen said flatly.

'Maybe so, but it wasn't why we wanted him to join *The People's Militia*. Which he never did, by the way. He kept away from politics other than reading and studying and got stuck into local issues.'

Stephen gestured a refill and Justin accepted. 'What kind of issues?'

'He loved kids and helped turn the garden square into a playground. He broke into it because the Local Authority kept it locked—they tried to browbeat us with trespass notices but caved under public pressure. Max organised a brilliant kids' party to celebrate—he said children were precious cargo and deserved respect.'

Stephen's features softened. 'That sounds like Dad.'

'He wasn't comfortable around women. Vera was the exception. I found them together once.'

'Meaning?' Stephen said, colouring.

'Nothing like that. She was weeping and he was listening. She'd been telling him about her brother, buried under tons of liquified slurry…'

'Ah, Aberfan, beyond shocking…'

'It was her brother's tenth birthday, Max told me later; the little lad was six when it happened. Vera never talked about it with the rest of us, not even Rob, I suspect. Max was different, he had a particular way with people. I didn't have a clue, looking back, I was too raw and full of myself. Emotional intelligence wasn't a thing back then.'

Stephen uncrossed his legs and opened the folder, jotting something down. 'What was the vibe between you? I mean, you weren't exactly The Red Army Faction or the Brigate Rosse, were you? More Citizen Smith?'

Justin winced at the mention of the hapless would-be revolutionary then remembered his workmates had dubbed him *Che*. 'Who were we? Good question. We were part of a wave of revolutionaries who opposed fascist Spain, the Vietnam war and we were radicalised by the uprisings in France in May '68. I bumped into Sofia, literally, while I was reading *Kropotkin* on the tube. She was a member of the 1st May group, though I didn't know it at the time. They bombed banks and embassies linked to Franco's Spain and

I'm pretty sure they supplied our explosives. When I joined, *The People's Militia* had already bombed one or two police and army targets but were still under the radar. Sending out Press Releases changed all that. The authorities couldn't make head nor tail of the attacks.'

Stephen placed his mobile phone on the table between them. 'D'you mind if I record this?'

'Go ahead. It's all on public record, though you'd have to dig around the archives a bit.' It felt good to say out loud what had been stuck in his head for so long.

'You were saying, about the attacks…'

'Yeah, the operations were anarchistic without an obvious connecting thread, which threw Special Branch into a spin. The targets listed in one of the press releases, were *High Pigs, Judges, Embassies, Spectacles, Property.*'

'*Spectacles* as in Guy Debord's thesis on Situationism, I presume. A bizarre proposition for the police in the '70s…'

'They didn't get it; it was playful and performative without the hectoring tone of The Far Left…'

'Apart from the actual bombs…'

'We only targeted property…'

'Peter Haddon was a near miss…'

'It was a botched job…'

'Did it give you pause?'

'You have to understand how it was back then—seismic cracks were opening up with war and resistance everywhere: Cuba, Vietnam, U.S. Civil Rights, then Paris in '68 when workers took over the factories. The Spanish Civil War was like yesterday, where anarchists had taken over swathes of the country and established libertarian communes, just as Kropotkin had envisaged. Food and products were sold or exchanged on behalf of the community—can you imagine that in today's world?' The old passion flooded back and flashed up an unexpected answer to his own question. *Rojava.* Why hadn't he seen it before?

'Were there arguments between you?' Stephen prodded, running a hand through his hair until it stood on end.

'We fell out over setting off a bomb at Ford's for the centenary of the Paris Commune. It was Rob's idea. He wanted to link it to Max's defence campaign, and I argued against it. He said, Max's frameup and the car workers' strike were part of the same struggle and a bomb at Ford's would send a message. I said I didn't think Max or the Ford workers would thank us for it, and to count me out. In the end, another group did the job and Max was cited in the Press Release, so Rob got his way.'

Stephen turned to a section in his folder and pulled out a sheet. 'I think I've got it. Is it this one?'

Justin took it, shaking his head. 'I haven't set eyes on this for well over forty years.'

PRESS RELEASE 3

It's FORD TONIGHT and we are celebrating the hundred years of the Paris Commune, and the revolution that won't be controlled. We reject the senile hierarchies, the poverty pimps, the Peter Haddons, the Bob Hopes, and the channels provided via MPs, social workers, the sell-out brigade.

You call us anarchists, commies, the bomb-mob, but you are wrong. We are the woman or man sitting next to you. Violence isn't us, it's the police, the army, the prisons. Be warned, every day our comrade stays behind bars will be avenged. MAX SCOTT IS INNOCENT. The future is ours.

POWER TO THE PEOPLE
The People's Militia

'Christ, did we really write that? It would be enough to get you locked up on the spot today.'

Stephen threw him a wry smile. 'What I want to explore in the film, is the group's moral compass and why you and Rob didn't give yourselves up. The memoir makes your responsibility clear. Did you write Max off, on the assumption he was going down for conspiracy anyway? I'm not saying that you did. Simple facts never tell the whole story. I want to give an honest account of my father's life and your testimony will be an important part of this, Justin.'

They said their farewells in the hotel lobby, Justin smiling as bands of steel tightened round his chest. Stephen ran out into the street holding his satchel over his head and flung himself into a taxi. It was raining stair-rods. Justin pulled on his wet-weather gear and headed into the deluge.

Chapter 9

Sitting in his office, the chuntering of a cement mixer was an unwelcome reminder of the encroaching Business School, an eyesore that would tower over the campus. And to add insult to injury, it was funded by a football club magnate who'd pitched in his ill-gotten millions. Gone are the days, he thought, when buildings recalled the names of men and women of learning.

He blotted out the noise by clamping on headphones and selected *Bach Preludes and Fugues*. The perfectly crafted pieces for harpsichord guaranteed composure before his meeting with Kyle.

'Justin!' Kyle came from behind his desk with a genial smile, gesturing to one of the democratically arranged armchairs. In another sat Maureen, Head of Human Resources, tablet in hand.

'Coffee all round?' Kyle asked. His personal assistant materialised through a side-door.

'Maureen will take notes, if that's alright with you, Justin? Keep us all on track.'

Justin nodded and placed his file on the coffee table. 'I've brought the accounts you asked for.'

'Don't bother with that. I just wanted to explore a couple of ideas with you. As you know, we're bringing Sociology into the Business School. All under the same tent, so to speak.'

Me pissing out instead of pissing in, he thought, and waited for Kyle to continue.

'There are important synergies between our two programmes and we think a pick-and-mix degree would improve student recruitment. Win-win, don't you think?'

Justin was saved by the entrance of the PA deftly wielding a tray. The reed-like young man poured coffee, enquired discreetly about milk and sugar, then vanished.

'It's like this, Justin,' said Maureen, patting her chignon. 'Student numbers in Sociology are in freefall. Our proposal will boost numbers and we can wipe the slate clean on your budget deficit.' She glanced down at his folder.

'Two birds with one stone, so to speak,' Justin threw in. He hadn't anticipated this manoeuvre. It was a ploy to dissolve his department. The payoff was to clean up his mess.

Kyle steepled his fingers and frowned. 'It's rather more than that. We'd be offering students more choice and there'd be economies of scale. You'd be relieved of your head of department role and the hassle of managing money.'

Justin reconfigured his tactics. 'I see where you're going, Kyle, and I'm with you in principle. I've decided that the rough-sleepers project, which has overrun, is untenable after all. I'm prepared to close it. Yes, that means losing short-term staff, but we have to cut our losses. I'll inform the funders and square up the budget.'

If Kyle was surprised, he didn't show it. 'Excellent, I see we're talking the same language. And you'll come into the Business School for the next semester.'

Justin had no desire to be shoehorned into Kyle's empire, nor the steel and glass high-rise it would inhabit. He had one last card. 'I'm sure my colleagues would welcome closer collaboration across disciplines. To smooth the transition, I propose we keep the identity of Sociology intact and create a Centre within the Business School.'

Maureen made as if to speak, but Kyle held up a silencing hand. 'That's a constructive suggestion, thank you, we'll give it due consideration.'

So, clearly a *no*. Kyle leaned in with a lizard smile. 'Have you plans for your future, Justin? When you do retire, you'd be welcome as *Emeritus Professor*, you have my word.'

'Thanks, Kyle, I'll bear that in mind.' He wouldn't be found dead hot-desking with some junior researcher, which is what had been graciously offered.

'I'm delighted we're agreed,' said Kyle, already on his feet, extending a hand, as Justin levered himself from the low chair.

'Indeed,' Justin said, unable to return the enthusiasm. He nodded at Maureen and left the folder of awkward figures on the table; the problem was no longer his.

He was glad to be back in his cramped office, it contained him and allowed him to think. The past was now an advancing tsunami and Kyle had lost his sting. He sat with legs stretched and propped on a pile of journals, the must read at some point pile that had the virtue of being chronological, the pages pristine between their covers.

Had he lived a lie for the past forty years? Or compartmentalised, as Sofia had taught him, split himself off from the truth. What of guilt? He'd felt terrible about Max at the time; at some level he'd been the sacrificial lamb, the first convicted, and for something he didn't do, unless you counted conspiracy, which was debatable. If asked whether he'd considered turning himself in, the answer was *no*. How to explain the group mindset? They considered Max a hostage, to lure out the rest of them in the war against the state. Surrender was out of the question. In hindsight, they'd got it right about police tactics, the dirty tricks brigade was out in force. The Old Bailey trial of the *Notting Hill Three*, as Rob, Callum and Jess would be known, was the longest in history and sucked a year out of his life. All this, plus the breakup with Sofia and the way she'd left him. And Ma dying a week before the verdict would be forever linked to the calamity. He'd lost all sense of who he was and made his escape up north.

Justin looked at the photo of Harpreet in a silver frame above his desk, away from the clutter. It was a spur of the moment thing, a long weekend break in Lisbon, one of those offers in a Sunday magazine. He'd folded over the page with its postcard perfect vistas and swivelled it towards her over the breakfast table. She'd taken one look and said, 'Yes!' It rained for three days, but no matter. They'd held hands, haunted the alleyways and deserted shops and dined like princes on seafood and wine. Afterwards they found their way back to each other in bed, they were pitch perfect—he'd forgotten how good they were together. Her skin glowed and her smile was radiant, leaving no doubt about her feelings for the him as she faced the camera. And that was only last year.

Since he'd told her about his past, their love had gone slack, deprived of the invisible tautness lent by everyday intimacy. Harpreet had made it clear she was reserving judgment, needed time. She approved of his decision to cooperate with Stephen and had made him talk it through, to articulate his feelings. The film clearly wasn't revenge on Stephen's part, more like restitution on his, he'd concluded. He had no illusions that Stephen would give him an easy ride, nor did he deserve it.

Worst case? He'd be put out to grass, which Kyle was already seeing to. The law's long arm was unlikely to reach him now, but he'd lose his good name. Sanjay would be hurt, which would be painful. Harpreet's judgment brought the worst shame, more than he could bear.

He nursed his soul with youthful memories of working alongside men with the weight and heft of authenticity, something he'd lacked his whole life.

Filthy, noisy, unpredictable, this was his London, he observed, stepping off the bus into the early morning light. The Mile End Road had thrown off its used and dusty look and sun burnished the windows of cars and shopfronts. He fell into the rhythm of easy strides as his canvass workbag swung on his shoulder. It was no penance to go to work on a day like this, even though there'd be a lorry of bricks waiting to be unloaded.

They were building a Council block, still at the foundations stage. It was said to be ten storeys high, but nobody knew. He arrived at the shed early and set about the important task of brewing tea, filling the kettle from a tank and lighting the gas ring. Jim, the foreman, came in holding a blue and white enamel mug. He had a permanent limp, which Jim told him was down to a scaffolding accident, not the war.

'Tea's up in five,' Justin said, dropping a handful of teabags into the pot.

'I'm one brickie down,' Jim announced without preamble. 'Today you can work for John and Carlson.' They had an informal agreement he'd assist two bricklayers when required, and in return, Jim let him slope off early for what he called, *your political shenanigans.*

He busied himself with the kettle and asked, 'Should I start with John first?' as he was the senior of the two brickies.

'Yes, and when you've finished with Carlson, the two of you can unload the lorry.'

Others trickled in and lined up for their mugs or cans to be filled. He didn't mind being tea boy; it made him feel part of the gang, a ritual that got the day off to a good start. Jim overlooked the time lost, which meant the men were ready to pull the stops when required.

'What's all this then, Che?' asked Mervyn, peering into his half-filled mug. 'Has the bleeding tide gone out, or what?' They called him *Che* because of his dark hair held back with a bandana.

'Sorry, mate, pot must've run dry. Hang on.' He refilled the teapot from the giant kettle.

'Did you blow anything up at the weekend?' Mervyn went on, with a sly grin.

He was used to the joshing. Everyone got it. You were pigeon-holed and expected to live up to your reputation. He disliked Mervyn, who made lewd jokes about women and pinned nude centrespreads on the shed walls.

'It was my turn to cook, so I spent most of it in the kitchen. Sorry to disappoint you.'

'Cooking? Un-bloody-believable. Them women's libbers ave got you by the short and curlies, son.' He turned to rally support and got a chorus of non-committal grunts.

Sean piped up. 'You should try it, Merv, it could spice up your sex life.'

That did it. The shed rocked with laughter at the idea of Mervyn doing a kindness to the woman he called, *the fridge*.

'Right fellas,' Jim said, barely raising his voice, and proceeded to allot the day's tasks, with a warning that work had to be done by knock-off time.

'Yes, guv,' they replied, and meant it.

John was the master when it came to bricklaying and normally paired with a more experienced labourer. He was Polish and had a laconic humour.

'You want to be a brickie, Che?' he asked, looking over wire-rimmed specs. 'Or maybe you follow the example of the great Mr Churchill.' He chuckled. 'You like to build walls for a hobby, like he did?'

Justin turned over a pile of wet cement with a spade; he had no idea what John was on about, but knew he was being got at. 'Need more in your bucket?' he asked, ignoring the jibe.

'Yes, but not too much or it hardens. Half-full is enough, Che.'

'Sure thing. My name's Justin, by the way.'

'I know that Che, and my name isn't John.'

Justin stood, spade mid-air. 'What *is* your name?'

'Stanislaw. Here, they call you John if you're foreign.'

He shovelled cement into the bucket. It was obvious, when you thought about it; all the foreign blokes were called

John. 'D'you prefer, Stanislaw?'

'No, John is easier.'

He felt indignant that someone's identity could be rubbed out, and *John* wasn't even a nickname. He wanted to ask how it felt, but couldn't, seeing John's face shuttered in concentration.

'Why you get mixed up in politics?' John asked, wedging a brick into a bed of cement.

'To change things, to make the world better,' he said, hearing the inadequacy of his reply.

'Politics means war and changes nothing for ordinary people. Germans invaded my country, then came the Russians. I am happy England is my country now.'

'Were you a pilot?' Justin asked, knowing there were Polish airmen during the war.

John peered in puzzlement and shook his head.

Justin watched him raise his trowel and split a brick in one deft movement; he placed the smaller portion in a gap in the wall. It fitted perfectly.

'I was a soldier. I escaped to France, and when Germany invaded, I came to England. Always a refugee.'

Justin looked at this man in awe, standing small and slight in a washed-out singlet, the experience of ten men etched into the furrows of his brow. Pa never spoke about his war in Burma and when he'd foolishly asked if he'd been a POW, he'd reached for the whiskey decanter and clammed up.

'Politics is for power, Che, not fairness. Believe me.'

'If workers took power, the profits of labour would be shared,' he ventured.

'What are you, boy, a commie?' He spat out a glob of phlegm in disgust. 'I hate communists,' he said in lowered tones, as if afraid to be overheard. 'They've done nothing for my country, and now they're taking over the Unions. I tell you, Che, the commies take power for themselves, not us.'

Justin saw Jim approach and made as if to move. 'I'm not

a commie, by the way. I don't like Stalin any more than you do.'

A bitter smile crept across John's face. 'At least in England, you are free to say that.'

'You've not done nothing but gab, this morning,' Jim berated from a few yards off. 'Get your arse over to Carlson, he's running out of cement.'

'Sorry, Guv,' Justin said, stung.

Carlson looked up from his trowel and pushed his cap to the back of his head. He was a bricklayer who worked slowly and methodically, with none of John's panache when it came to slicing bricks. 'The boss boot you over here?' he asked with a toothy grin.

'I got talking to John. Big mistake. I'll make up fresh cement.' He brought over buckets of sand, dry cement and water, and mixed them evenly. It reminded him of stirring flour and sugar, butter and eggs, to bake cakes with Ma and Molly.

Justin knew two things about Carlson: he lived in Notting Hill and they were both twenty-two years old. Born in Grenada, he combined his cockney accent with a Caribbean burr.

'How much money d'you send home?' Carlson asked, picking up from a previous conversation about handing wages over to his mother.

'I don't send any,' Justin admitted. 'They don't need it.' It was so partial a truth it felt like a lie. 'I live with my girlfriend and she isn't working, at least not in the usual sense. She writes articles for a magazine.' Another half-truth. There was no way he was going to mention the nude modelling.

'And you do the cooking?' Carlson said, trowel in hand, waiting for the cement.

'Yup, we take it in turns. There's a rota for cooking and cleaning. There are six of us. We all make a mess, so we all clear up. That's the theory, anyway. We want to change society starting with ourselves.

'Here's a fresh batch. Tell me if it's too sloppy,' he said, handing over half-a-bucketful.

Carlson tested it by dripping a trowelful back into the bucket. 'That's perfect, thanks, mate.'

He was warmed by the easy generosity and returned Carlson's smile.

'The women at our house don't let us men near the kitchen. It's where they go for a chinwag, so we go out. You can't hang out on the streets with the police looking for trouble, so we go to the Mangrove Restaurant. D'you know it?'

'Sure, I've heard of it. The cops keep raiding the place.'

'That's right, man, trying to close the place down and they never found no drugs, not even a spliff. It's where folks hang out and there's no law against it. I was on the march against police harassment.'

Justin shook his head. 'I don't know how they get away with it. A mate of mine is in prison for something he didn't do.' He leant on his spade and felt the sun burning his back.

'What's he in for, this friend of yours?' Carlson scooped cement onto his trowel and laid it smooth as butter onto the next brick.

'Planting a bomb. There was a bomb, but it wasn't him who did it.'

'That's heavy, man. The Panthers are over here organising for Black Liberation.' Carlson placed brick on brick with precision and looked up with a diffident smile. 'There'll be no revolution here, Che. Nothing like that ever going to happen in England.'

The assertion, so simply expressed, was like a punch to the gut. Was *The People's Militia* acting inside a bubble of its own creation? Was he a fraud, living a life he could never inhabit? A rising doubt crept up, threatening to overwhelm him.

On the top deck of the bus home, he was sucked into the sun-slapped dream of cars and travel, writ large on giant billboards, which spawned thoughts of French slogans, *Métro, boulot, dodo*—Metro, work, sleep, and *Sous les pavés la plage*, Under the cobblestones the beach, opening up space to dream.

Glancing at his phone, he saw a string of flashing messages.
#bataclan #Parisattacks
Charlie Hebdo and now this
Farida arrived safely in Syria
We need to talk

He switched to his newsfeed and saw the destruction: mobile phone footage of mayhem, a woman clinging to a windowsill, a man wading through blood, disfigured bodies, and the scream of sirens as the police charged behind a metal shield, hit by twenty-seven bullets as it later transpired. The toll of death and wounding was yet to be counted.

It was as if Sanjay was shaking his shoulder and saying, *look Dad, this is what's happening now! Farida's mission is to stop the madness.*

We're responsible for this mess, Justin concluded, especially those on the so-called Left, whose sense of outrage was blunted. Sanjay would surely be sickened to hear him wallowing in his own past. A knife twisted in his gut.

Chapter 10

Justin scraped mud off his bike, Sanjay's text and its urgency ran like a banner headline in his brain. The horror of the Paris attacks flooded social media—bombings and shootings targeting people enjoying an innocent Friday night. Hundreds dead or injured.

It had the hallmarks of the London attacks ten years back, except that was *Al Qaeda* inspired and today it was *Islamic State*. The London bombings were closer to home. He and Harpreet had stolen a weekday to walk the woods round Bolton Abbey and stopped in awe at the ruins standing crisply under a crystal sky. They'd picked their way across the stepping stones spanning the river Wharfe and ordered a bottle of *Yorkshire Heart* with their meal at the local pub. *To us*, he'd said, as they clinked, *and to more days like this*, she'd replied. Waiters swept in either side to serve halibut in a fragrant sauce (he refused it call it *jus*) and they shared a portion of polenta chips. They'd communicated their joy and pride in Sanjay, who'd announced he'd signed up for GCSE Urdu with a class of girls despite the lads calling him a wuss. *He was a long time coming, that boy*, she'd said tenderly, and they'd held hands over the table, remembering getting pregnant after years of trying.

Harpreet had taken an early train to London for a conference the following morning. He knew she'd be crossing the city as the bombings began. He'd left message after message on her mobile, *Darling are you alright? Call me! I'm out of my mind with worry. I love you.* They'd spoken when she was on the train and she'd promised to text—it was how they touched base. The silence told him she'd switched off her phone or worse; he couldn't begin to imagine as reports came through of unnumbered dead and wounded, like a war zone. He made a pact with a God he didn't believe in: if she was safe, he'd reach out to Max after all these years and apologise. She'd arrived at her meeting early and knew nothing of events until an announcement was made. She called home immediately. He'd wept with relief.

Three of the four bombers were local and one left a videotape for the world's edification. *Your democratically elected governments continuously perpetuate atrocities against my people all over the world... you will be our targets until you stop the bombing, gassing and imprisonment and torture...* from a young man born and bred in Leeds, a husband and father, and a learning mentor at a local primary school.

It felt it was his job to know current trends. He was shocked that they'd escaped his notice. Had he taught young men or women for that matter, carrying this burden of anger and hatred? The *War On Terror* brigade had got back into the saddle and there was a sharp rise in racist attacks. It was a watershed for Justin and now the Paris attacks demanded he tune in, or rather Sanjay did. His left-leaning fence was becoming crowded and he was in danger of falling off over airstrikes in Syria. To bomb or not to bomb was the question. Condemning the invasion of Iraq had been easy by comparison. It brought him back to Farida who'd made her way to Syria. And to Sanjay, who expected him to pay attention.

He attached the foot pump to the front tyre and took satisfaction in watching the dial creep up to 80lbs and he hadn't even broken sweat. It was a beautiful invention. Repeating the process on the back tyre, he tried taking a retrospective view of his own political engagement. He'd laid out the bare bones for Sanjay, that he'd done things that should have landed him in jail. *Gees, Dad, I didn't have you down for an urban guerrilla,* was his initial reaction.

If his account of himself wasn't all good at least he'd tried to be honest. How he'd taken to heart the cry, *Be realistic, demand the impossible* and bought into the drama of direct action, the leap of faith that bombs would reveal what lay beneath the surface, conduits for revolutionary energy. He admitted that his workmates had rubbed the corners off him on that score. After his flight north, had he lost his political soul? His ambitions changed as he poured himself into research and teaching, earning respect even as a thorn in the side of the bureaucracy. The heady hopes of youth had faded. Did this make him a cynic? He'd come round to suspecting the unfettered consumption of resources demanded by global capitalism would destroy humanity, but this was too dark a prospect to share with his son.

The bike was shining, gears adjusted and wheels ready. The plan was to ride over to Sheffield and spend the night at Pa's, getting the train back in the morning. It was a long haul but good training if he was to attempt *Le Tour* next spring. When Sanjay's footsteps rang across the drive he walked out of the garage and gave his son a bearhug embrace.

Once they'd notched up a good few kilometres, they stopped at a bikers' caff just outside Wakefield. It was a windowless shed with harsh lights and bland wipeable surfaces that spoke of utility not comfort. The air was humid and the windows and walls ran with condensation in contrast to the November chill outside. Justin pulled off his helmet, sat and felt a ferocious thirst. He took a long pull on his water bottle, hardly touched till now.

'Did you use the hydration tablets I gave you, Dad?' Sanjay asked, in the tone of someone who already knew the answer.

'Drat, I forgot,' he said, not having taken on board the lecture about electrolytes.

'It's basic, Dad, why make it harder for yourself? You need to drink a lot more or you'll get dehydrated.' He gave a long-suffering sigh.

Justin tolerated this berating by his son, the self-appointed health tsar, and handed over a ten-pound note. 'Toasties and chocolate cake? My shout.' He watched as Sanjay joined the queue of Lycra-clad bodies, some top to toe in black, others in fluorescent yellows and greens and one woman in pink and blue swirls.

Bikers balanced plates of food and giant mugs on tin trays, picking their way through the narrowly spaced tables. The mugs took him back to being teaboy, and Bert's unusual drinking habits. He was a quiet man, a casual labourer who lived in digs with no mod cons, only a sink and a gas ring. He'd crack eggs into a can of milk for breakfast, swilling it before gulping it down. It was his staple diet save for the beer. He was paid a daily rate, *on the lump*, no sick pay, zero security. It would be good to know what had become of him, though given the social patterning of mortality, Bert would almost certainly be dead.

Sanjay returned with thick toasted sandwiches oozing cheese and mugs of dark tea. 'Here, get this down you,' Sanjay said, passing him a steaming mug.

Justin took it gratefully. 'Tell me more about Farida— where is she, exactly? How's she being trained?' It was no throwaway question; it was driven by his need for detail to keep anxiety at bay.

Sanjay was already deeply involved with his toastie and spoke in snatches. 'Don't know, she's not allowed to say.'

'And the training?'

'Early days. She's settling in, meeting people. Going to Kurdish classes. She's good. Says it's cold at night.' Sanjay could be frustratingly vague.

'I'll text you the link to her blog,' Sanjay offered, perhaps sensing his impatience.

Justin squared himself to discuss the meaning of the jihadist attacks, the meat of things for Sanjay. When tense, he suffered an acutely heightened sense of hearing and the clatter of trays and cutlery reverberated like a hailstorm on a tin roof.

Sanjay's eyes levelled with his. 'I remember when I was a kid wars were distant, like in Afghanistan, or inevitable, like in the Middle East. Then the attacks got closer to home and I became part of the story without wanting to, because of the way I looked. Most of it was under the radar stuff, hostile glances, people backing away and then it got really bad after the London bombings with those Leeds lads. I started cycling to school, remember?'

'Because of that?'

'Yeah, because of the hassle on the bus. A few of us did.'

'You never said.'

'It's obvious, isn't it? When people saw us coming, they saw mad bombers, simple as that. It's taken me a few years to get my head round it, to be honest. After meeting Farida, I read on the various groups, never realising there were different kinds of Muslim, like the Sunnis and Shias, quite apart from the extremists of Al Qaeda, and the so called Islamic State. Throw into the mix a population of 30 million Kurds spread across four countries and you'd think, those guys don't stand a chance. That's where things get interesting.'

Justin looked at his son and tears pricked his eyes. He bit his lip, not wanting to make a fool of himself. Sanjay was grappling to find his place in the world on a journey that had taken him far from home. 'Why the Kurds?' he couldn't help asking. 'The world is full of displaced and marginalised peoples. The People's Protection Units have been extraordinarily successful against Islamic State, but they're reliant on US aircover, arms and logistical support. The Americans aren't fans of self-determination and my guess is they'll pull out of Rojava when realpolitik dictates. Once ISIS is driven out, they'll want to appease Erdogan, who hates the Kurds.' The nerve-jangling background noise was muted as he warmed to his theme.

Sanjay threw up his hands, incredulous. 'What are you saying, Dad? You think they should tell the Americans to piss off? I don't buy this peacenik Stop the War stuff, it's purist bullshit. The Kurds *do* want US support to stop the rape and murder—that's real politics. They're canny enough to make strategic alliances while fighting on several fronts. *"The Loser Left"'* he made speech marks in the air, 'doesn't get there's an actual revolution going on, or if they do, they wring their hands expecting defeat. They claim intervention won't make Britain safer, but what about Syria and the Kurds? They'd rather polish their anti-imperialist credentials than demand help to drive back genocidal fascists. It was Kurdish fighters who liberated the Yazidis trapped in Mount Sinjar in northern Iraq, remember? Massacred in their thousands and abandoned by the rest of the world.' He jutted his jaw.

Justin nodded and resumed eating his toastie, holding back on a lecture about the carving up of the Ottoman Empire in 1916 by the Brits and the French, which laid the basis for over a century of regional conflict. The revolution in Rojava couldn't undo the legacy of imperialism and going in all gun's blazing wasn't the answer. Indeed, he had no answer, life wasn't that simple. Rather than say so he stepped onto common ground.

'I knew a woman once who was passionate about liberating Spain from fascism. Her parents both served in the International Brigades in the 30s when whole cities were democratically organised and industries controlled by workers. It was a radical vision of the future very similar to the one you describe in Syria. I don't dismiss what's being achieved there, Sanjay, I'm just cautious.'

'The People's Protection Units took back Kobani earlier this year and that's where Farida's gone—I don't know where exactly. She's staying in a women's house where they train volunteers. It's huge what they've done, but they do need more help,' he said, less emphatically than before.

'It's a winding road to revolution and it's easy to take a wrong turn. There's something else I didn't tell you about my rebellious youth.'

Sanjay's face flickered with interest. 'The bombing? You said nobody was hurt?'

Justin cleared his throat. 'Not physically. I'm not proud of what I did and it's come back to haunt me. There was a comrade, Max, who went to prison even though he didn't actually plant any bombs. He died last year and his son Stephen has been in touch. He wants to make a film about what happened to his father.'

'Christ, Dad, it gets worse.' His eyes widened.

'The explosions aren't on my conscience, but Max is. He was put away for something the group did—me included.'

'I'm beyond stunned, I mean, how could you keep silent all this time?'

'You're right, why didn't we speak out? It was a collective conspiracy of silence, resisting the forces of law and order and with our twisted logic we betrayed Max. The police had evidence he'd addressed envelopes for press releases that claimed responsibility for one of the bombings. It was enough for Max to go down on charges of conspiracy.'

'Sounds like this Stephen guy wants to know what happened to his father and to be honest, I'd be the same.' He waded into a wodge of chocolate cake. 'What's at stake?' he managed.

'My reputation, for what it's worth.' He thought of the campaigns he'd waged for social justice over the years, now wiped off the slate. He'd been an expert witness to parliamentary select committees on building standards, giving evidence on short-cuts and substandard materials. He'd demonstrated that at least half a dozen tower-blocks were accidents waiting to happen, but inertia had prevailed. Impossible to convey the freight of a lifetime's work to one so young.

Sanjay bent the plastic chair backwards, hands clasped behind his head. 'This isn't actually about politics, is it Dad? Who was Max, exactly?'

Justin rubbed his right calf to prevent creeping cramp and reached for his water-bottle. 'It was never a level playing field between Max and the rest of us. He already had a record, so it was easy for the police to target him. When the police searched the house and found nothing, the detective goaded me, knowing I'd feel guilty if Max was charged with the bombings. He was a wily old guy. He hinted that if I cooperated, he'd go easy on Max. It was a line I refused to cross, none of us would have done.'

'You've got survivor's guilt,' Sanjay said matter-of-factly.

'My biggest regret is I never acknowledged in so many words that he paid for my freedom. The film could be a chance to put that right.'

'What does Mum think?'

'She's pretty mad at me and I wouldn't blame you for feeling the same. She says if it went to court, it could go either way depending on the forensics. In practice, she doubts the CPS will follow it up. Not in the public interest.'

'I get it. So you feel like a skunk for what happened to your mate because you didn't end up in jail. Obviously you owe it to Stephen to put the record straight. I'm not judging you, well I suppose I am, but I guess you did what you thought best at the time.'

A beat passed as Justin basked in this partial absolution. Sanjay shifted in his seat as if there was more to say.

'What is it?' Justin asked.

'Mum's not leaving you, is she?'

'I hope not,' he said with forced joviality.

'Because with Farida gone, I don't know, that would really cut me up.'

'Yes, it would be unbearable, but Farida will surely come back.' It was more question than statement.

Fleeting uncertainty crossed Sanjay's brow. 'Yes, she'll come back, but I don't know if we'll still be together. It depends on how deep in she gets, which is how we left it. YPJ women don't have partners though volunteers aren't under the same discipline. I have to respect her decision whatever it is. There's zero chance of me popping over, if that's what you're worried about; it's the last thing she'd want.'

Justin leaned over and gripped his son's arm in a silent gesture of solidarity.

They snapped on helmets, pulled on fluorescent jackets and stepped teetering on cycle-shoe cleats into the freezing air. Justin was a recent convert to Lycra and today was glad of the insulation. He caught a glimpse of himself in the window, a slightly rotund deep-sea diver.

The next couple of hours were gruelling, as they pushed on until they reached the cycle path parallel to the M1 motorway. The end in sight, they slowed to a conversational pace and discussed *Le Tour* in May. Sanjay was all for doing the 78k route while Justin thought the 50k route more realistic, as his knees and hips creaked under the strain of today's workout.

They caught sight of the pea-green roofs of the giant Meadowhall shopping centre, the immense cathedral to consumerism Justin had vowed never to set foot in. Once they'd passed the monstrosity, it wouldn't be far to the leafy suburb of Sheffield where Pa lived.

They let themselves in using the key-safe box, because Pa never heard the doorbell. Once inside, the sound of the TV led them to the snug where the old man spent most of his days.

'Hey Pa, we made it,' said Justin moving into his eye-line.

He heaved himself up. 'You're here!' His face creased with smiles at seeing Sanjay.

'Hello, Grandad, good to see you old fellow,' Sanjay said, bringing him into a hug.

'Don't stand about, make yourselves at home,' he urged. Eyeing Justin, he added, 'I don't like the look of you, your nose is blue. Sanjay, go and run your father a bath before he catches his death. I'll fetch a mug of tea with a dash of Scotch.'

Justin sank into the easy chair and shivered. Maybe he'd overdone it in this icy weather. His fingers were numb and cheeks aflame as the blood rushed back. His heart was going like the clappers. After closing his eyes a few seconds, he woke covered in a green tartan blanket. He must have drifted off.

'Bath's ready,' said Sanjay, beside him. 'Drink your tea before it gets cold.'

It was an effort to lean forward, every joint stiff and sore. Maybe this was how it felt to be ninety. The tea tasted peculiar until he remembered the Scotch. He touched the pulse on his wrist. 'Heart's settling down. I'm not popping my clogs yet.'

'You had me worried there, Dad. I've put your clothes in the bathroom.'

Sanjay offered his arm for support and Justin hauled himself upright.

'Let's get you upstairs and you can have a good soak.'

It took him back to the squat when he would wallow in the bath and catch the cooking smells of garlic and spices wafting up the stairs. He imagined he must have been happy back then, as he'd never had occasion to ask himself the question.

'Steak and kidney pie,' said Pa, placing a tin with a magnificent crust on the table, alongside peas and mash.

Sanjay had changed into a tracksuit and looked clean and shiny. He was moving deftly round the kitchen finding plates and cutlery. 'Sit down, Dad. Feeling better?'

Justin was aware of their sideways glances. 'Good as new, thanks.'

'Dicky heart?' Pa asked.

'Nothing wrong, Pa. I'll be right as rain tomorrow.' Thank God they'd planned to take the train back to Leeds.

'Grandad was telling me about the old days,' said Sanjay, as they tucked in. 'About how he became an engineer.'

Pa took up the story. 'I was good at mending things and bluffed my way into the Royal Engineers when I joined the Army. After the war I went to night school. My father said I'd be better off as an apprentice mine engineer, but I didn't want to follow him down the pit.'

Justin had heard variants, but never this version. There'd been a mixture of pride and shame and he'd never sought to dig deeper.

'I started at a small engineering shop and worked my way up. By the time I was your age,' he said, looking at Sanjay, 'I was more or less running the place. Then I bought it out. I'd married your grandmother by then. When your father was born, I hoped he'd take over the firm, but it wasn't for him.' He looked over his glasses at Justin. 'When he told me he was studying Sociology, I said, how d'you make a living from that? Then he got a job on a building site and said that was Sociology!'

Sanjay looked up to smile. 'Dad was a bit of a tearaway, a 60s wild child. I never wanted to go to Uni. Does that bother you, Dad?'

Justin wasn't prepared for this. 'Not really. Well, slightly. You'd have done really well in engineering and you missed out on student life.'

Sanjay nudged his grandfather. 'And I work in a bike-shop and love it. What d'you make of that, Grandad? Is today's generation better or worse off?'

'It depends what you mean by better off. Neither you nor your father had to go to war, which is a good thing. Making things with your hands and using your brains are both good things. Regular work for regular pay is also good, but seems less and less possible nowadays.

'This meal, for instance. Magda spent several hours shopping and cooking and left it ready to heat up. I pay her a decent wage, because I can.' As an aside to Justin, 'I've started paying her privately, by the way, instead of wasting money on the Agency.

'The rest of the week she dashes from house to house in fifteen-minute slots and gets paid a pittance. She pays for her car and petrol and is classed as self-employed. People who work like that are definitely worse off than we were.'

Justin was startled by this insight, and at the way his son had teased it out of him.

'I agree with you, Grandad, there's a lot needs changing. The way we're destroying the planet, for starters,' said Sanjay.

'Ah well, that's another story. It's too late for me to worry about.'

RojovaSyria Blogspot 1

If you follow me don't expect an account of gun-toting women in colourful headscarves, which is the hyped-up reality presented by the media. Expect a world where women are led by women, who may lead men into the battle but not the reverse. What would that look like?

Let's back up a bit.

Rojava is an autonomous region in northern Syria in a country embattled against itself and Islamist jihadists, variously called ISIS, IS (Islamic State) and Daesh (the term used by its opponents).

Rojava embraces the principle of Democratic Confederalism which replaces the demand for a separate Kurdish state and embraces all religious and ethnic groups in a system of self-administration. There is no need for the state when citizens are elected from face-to-face assemblies in villages, towns, neighbourhoods and cities in an organic network of governance.

The most startling feature of the revolution is the central role of women. They are at the heart of the project. According to thinker, Abdullah Ocalan, The Revolution is Female. 'No social group has ever been exploited physically and psychologically to the same extent as women.' Gender oppression is the cornerstone of capitalism and to defeat it, we must get rid of established gender structures, he states.

There is a system of male/female dual leadership in place and a minimum of 40% of decision makers at all levels have to be women.

So far, so historical and political.

What gives me the right to talk about the revolution?

I'm British-Algerian and my father is a refugee after suffering torture in Algerian jails. My beliefs? feminist and secular, though I identify as Muslim. I also speak Arabic. Oh, and I'm a science teacher, which may be of use in defusing explosives.

Before I sign off, let me introduce you to Yezda, one of our tutors who's been in the movement for twenty years and a seasoned soldier. I asked her about love. 'We fight for a new kind of love, just as we are becoming new kinds of women. If male and female fighters have sexual relations it may cause misunderstandings. It's your job to exercise restraint while we work through the early stages of the revolution.'

Farida
November 2015

Chapter 11

The chill from the cycling spree had left him achy, made worse by his draughty attic study. He looked up from his desk at trees laid bare by blustery winds and at the rooftops, a pleasing patchwork of purple slate and more recent red tiles. The horse-chestnut beneath his window creaked and twisted its gnarled branches against a mottled blue sky.

Justin needed a distraction from reliving the past, an experience he found disorientating. Today he was jotting notes on *how politics was lived at the squat* for the benefit of Stephen's film. There was to be a scene shot to camera where Stephen would ask him about the politics of the group before homing in on Max's story.

His mind drifted as he surveyed the archaeological layers of books and papers surrounding him, and thought, not for the first time, that a fire would make short work of it all. He kept an old vacuum cleaner under the eaves, which he rarely used. He never had visitors. Harpreet called it his den before the man-cave was invented.

Leaning back, eyes closed, he was transported to the night of the party. The group had just split up to be less of a target for the police. Callum and Jess were living in a feminist squat that included men and two babies. The household had voted for a rota of shared care by both sexes, from nappy changing to four-hourly bottle feeds. How Callum coped, Justin couldn't imagine, let alone the poor babies. He'd helped Rob and Vera move that afternoon, to an attic flat in a house that overlooked a projectile of flying concrete in the shape of the new A40, a monument to speed and efficiency that sliced through a swathe of West London. He'd been glad to escape the oppressive atmosphere and get back home.

As he walked into the kitchen, Sofia was saying, 'I wonder who'll turn up?' as she helped Jess stack sausage rolls onto a platter, the air heady with wine, cinnamon and cloves from a steaming vat of punch.

'The usual headbangers from *Workers' Struggle*,' he'd filled in, mentally adding the apostrophe they omitted because it looked phoney.

'I hope Rob and Vera can make it—how did the move go?' Sofia asked.

Justin let his tool-bag drop to the floor. 'Not great, to be honest. It's hot as Hades up there and the flyover traffic is like, practically in the flat. We couldn't open the windows because of the noise of lorries hammering past and I imagine it's no better at night. I left them having a bit of a tiff.'

'What about?' Sofia flashed back.

'Vera wants a baby. Apparently the Women's Collective said it's her right and Rob accused her of spending too much time with people who think men are the problem, not capitalism and the ruling class.'

'It's about time she told him,' Jess said, arranging parsley in decorative clumps.

'So you knew?' he said, looking from one to the other. 'Why don't you women share stuff?'

'We do,' said Sofia, 'with each other. What business is it of yours? If Vera really does want a kid she should get on with it. I don't see why she needs Rob's permission.'

'Who's talking about permission? Okay, maybe Rob came over a bit strong, but they should discuss it.' He'd felt sorry for Rob, however useless he'd been when confronted by Vera's tide of emotion.

'What else did Rob say?' Sofia asked, with a look that told him he was on a losing wicket.

'Rob said the rules for life as a revolutionary were different and it just wouldn't work. Vera argued that if we're leading the masses to shape human history, whole families must be involved. Rob talked about cadre discipline, but he'd lost her by then. She tried dragging me in, asked if women had to be proto-men to be revolutionaries. I left at that point, it was too heavy.' Vera had added that she knew Sofia went on missions to bomb banks and embassies, it was an open secret, but that she wasn't like other women. This, he kept to himself.

'What d'you think, Jus? Are you with Rob on this?' Sofia asked, more gently.

'About having kids? I'm definitely not up for that, I'd be crap at it.'

Both women burst out laughing, and the fumes from the punch combined with being let off the hook left him giddy.

His job was to tidy for the party. 'Just clear a space, move things against the walls, use your common sense,' Sofia said.

'Shall I take the dining chairs upstairs?' he called from the living room.

'Leave a few, but make sure people can't trip over stuff,' she called back.

'And the standard lamps, aren't they in the way? Don't you think they should go too?'

'No, we'll need them when it gets dark. Leave them. Candles are dangerous when the place is crowded,' she said, voice rising.

'Are you sure? They create a nice atmosphere.' He was gripped by indecision.

She strode in, wearing her wine-stained apron and marigold gloves. 'For Christ's sake, Justin, it's clearing a space, not an exercise in dialectical reasoning. Why can't you do as I ask?' She stood open-palmed. 'God, see what you've done to me? I sound like my mother!'

In a moment she was next to him. He felt the brush of her lips and a shower of butterfly kisses on his face. It was what he loved about her, how she could turn on a sixpence, laugh at herself, and throw a handful of stardust into the air. The resentment of a moment ago dissolved and she was his again.

The house filled up in dribs and drabs, first with families who drifted off at dusk to put the kids to bed, then with teeny-boppers intent on smoking a free spliff. Even they wandered off, once the music became too demanding for their tastes.

Justin found himself standing on the side lines of a group in tetchy debate; loudest among them was Ross, from *Workers' Struggle*.

'We have to build fractions in industry,' Ross was saying. He wore a brown suit borrowed from the 50s, and a dozen lapel badges, from *Ban the Bomb* to *Stop the Vietnam War*.

'Fractions of what, darling?' asked a slip of a woman with Yoko Ono shades, sidling up.

'I mean political cells in factories and mines and so forth,' he said, barely acknowledging her, even though she'd fed him the line.

'The problem with you lot,' she persisted, 'is that you're more interested in tearing each other apart than openly joining the Labour Party and kicking out the Tories.'

Ross shook his head in mock despair. 'The Labour Party isn't a party of revolution, sweetie. *We* are building a party of the working class.'

'Why don't you join them, these workers of yours?' asked the woman in shades, angling her head to show a finely wrought profile, as she blew a plume of smoke outside the circle.

'Thanks Tina, I love you too,' Ross replied, and moved to block her view.

A neighbour and fellow jogger Justin recognised, said, 'As for the crazies who blow things up, I mean struth, what's that all about?'

Justin stepped forward. 'I don't think we've actually met. Name's Justin.'

'Pleased to meet you, Justin. It's Clive, from across the square.' He extended a hand and displayed an even set of white teeth. 'Our place is a wreck too, but we bought it for peanuts and we're doing it up ourselves.'

'Okay; well this is a squat, so no overheads. Sounds like you're a budding property developer.' He noticed the designer shoes.

'Wine dealer, actually. I specialise in Burgundy. Goes down well in the City bars. I'm agnostic about politics, but I'm all for getting into Europe. Wine flowing freely without tedious red tape! Tell that to the Labour Party. They're on the wrong side of history on that one.'

Ross shouldered himself back into the conversation. 'Workers of the world have nothing to gain from a capitalist Economic Community, my friend, but if you've got any plonk going cheap…'

They all laughed and Ross joined in to show he got the joke. 'Going back to the bombers, Clive, I'm with you on that. I'd have them shot.'

Tina was back in the game. 'I didn't know capital punishment was a *Workers' Struggle* party line.'

'That's rich coming from an ex-Stalinist, Tina,' said Ross. 'I'm amazed the Labour Party allowed you in.'

Tina shot him a venomous look. 'Piss off, Ross! Who d'you think you're kidding with your undercover tactics? Joining the Labour Party to destroy it from within, that's the aim, isn't it? As for fractions in the workplace, the Unions wouldn't give you the time of day.'

Clive looked bemused. 'So you lot aren't even on the same side?'

'Not exactly,' said Justin, and with two pints of punch on board, he embarked on some points of political clarification. 'We probably all agree that Russia is a failed socialist experiment thanks to Stalin. Capitalism is trickier, because the Labour Party is okay with it…'

'Wrong!' Tina interrupted, 'What about *the common ownership of the means of production, distribution and exchange?* It's in Clause IV of the constitution.'

'Come off it, Tina, Clause IV is a relic from 1918, and even then it wasn't revolutionary. It's aim was to make the party a non-revolutionary vehicle for socialism, in contrast to the radical movements in Russia. Don't you get it?'

Clive grinned. 'This is fascinating, to hear you arguing about the Russian revolution as if it were yesterday! Where do *you* stand on this, Justin? Are you with today's bombing brigades?' He chuckled at his own wit.

'I see change emerging from the politics of everyday life, springing from networks of activists outside sterile political banners... squatters, claimants, feminists, Black people, the marginalised of society. It's their actions that will awaken revolutionary consciousness, not sitting in meetings imbibing a political line that changes with the weather. Guerrilla action is the spark, though it isn't the revolution. It shows that the State is flimsy as a house of cards and once we lean together against it, the whole pack will come tumbling down.'

'You mean bombs as theatre? As metaphor?' There was a dawning of light in Clive's eyes, if only from intellectual curiosity.

Ross chewed nervously on his bearded lower lip. 'That went completely over my head, Comrade, not to mention your average car worker. As for bombing an army recruitment centre, what does that achieve? When it's working class lads who are facing bombs in Belfast?'

'That's really the point. To warn youngsters against signing up to an army of occupation and getting blown up defending imperialism. The message is crystal clear.'

Tina raised a pencilled eyebrow. 'A *billet-doux*, how thoughtful,' she said with searing sarcasm. 'Also rather patronising towards lads in need of a well-paid job. Once the Labour Party is back in power, we can seriously rock the boat. Blowing things up is counter-productive.'

Justin was on a roll. 'Direct action is legitimate when the

state denies workers their rights and makes outlaws of whole layers of society. In fact, rebellions are spread by popular response to repression, particularly in wartime. By the end of 1918, even the Metropolitan Police were on strike and the Labour Party's Clause IV was an attempt to divert the growing mood of anger and disillusionment.' He'd thrown this in with the fleeting thought that she was recruitable.

'You imagine car workers planted the bomb at Ford's? I hardly think so,' Tina said, agitating a cloud of blue smoke in front of her.

Clive played the patriarch. 'Look, whatever you may think of capitalism, Justin, you're not going to bomb your way out of it. That's assuming this is all theoretical and you're just an armchair anarchist.'

'The revolution is the man or woman sitting next to you on the tube, Clive. It's just a matter of time.' He was on a roll, enjoying the surprise on the faces of a growing audience, when Sofia arrived at his side and took his elbow, pulling him away.

'You don't know who these people are, Jus, we're probably being watched. I've got a job. Vera's turned up with her Women's Collective posse and they're baying for blood. Could you pour drinks mixed with a shot of animal magnetism? Tell them you're a bricky's labourer—bourgeois women love a bit of rough.'

Recovering the memory he felt a greater shock than he had at the time. Sofia could be utterly cynical in the interests of the greater good, as she saw it. He'd wondered if she was acting as double agent when she knew things she shouldn't and was never picked up by the police. DI Havering had tried to warn him off her and must have known more than he let on. He'd never doubted her commitment, but suspected she could be totally amoral about means and ends.

She came back to him now, with her dramatic features

and a studied carelessness. That night she'd looked stunning, yes, he'd tell Stephen so, in a black shimmering trouser-suit and her abundant dark hair held in check by a silver headband. No trace of makeup or jewellery, she wore ballet flats and was easily the most arresting woman in the room. Could she tell him anything he didn't know after all these years? He was tempted to find out.

His phone bleeped a reminder of a call from Molly. She'd taken to scheduling him in every couple of weeks, and he'd wondered why, but still enjoyed chats about films, family, food and the *aged one*. Molly had a circle of walking and concert-going mates and regaled him with lively anecdotes. An unexpected addition to the family, she was younger by five years. It wasn't until after Ma died that they'd come to know each other. Molly and Harpreet had never hit it off, though they shared a fierce social conscience and worked with similar *client groups*. He broke off to consider the expression that reduced human transactions to the market place, an example he used with students to show capitalism's appropriation of language.

Molly called on the dot and he was surprised at the lift he felt on hearing her voice.

'Hi Jus, how's tricks? Pa said you had a funny turn after the ride.'

'I'm fine thanks, just got a bit cold. How was your hike in the Dales?'

She laughed. 'Challenging in a word. We took in the Peaks over three days; Pen-y-ghent, Whernside and Ingleborough. The peaks are so elemental, I find putting one foot in front of the other clears my mind. I'm planning a trek in the Himalayas next year. I'm going to retire Jus, turning sixty has been a watershed.'

'Goodness, that's out of the blue, retiring I mean, you're still a spring chicken.' He saw her younger face framed with dark bouncy curls, now silver grey like his own thick mop.

'I'm tired of crisis management, you know what it's like. Crazy caseloads and young social workers burnt out after a few years. And I want to get in big walks while I'm fit and able. You'd keep an eye on Pa?'

'Sure,' he said, with less enthusiasm than intended. 'I may be retiring too before long.'

'Sanjay said you were in some sort of trouble.' He heard concern in her voice. 'Work getting you down?'

She'd be relentless in drawing it out of him, so he'd give her the headlines. 'Remember the guys involved in *The People's Militia*? You met them when you visited that summer. Max, who was in prison by then, died last year, and his son has been in touch. It's dragged up the bombings business.'

Molly knew the whole story. 'What does his son want? How much does he know? Why are you even talking to him? What happened to that witch, Sofia?'

Was that witch or bitch? He wasn't sure. This was pure Molly, gushing forth a torrent of questions to find out everything at once.

'Steady on, sis, hear me out. Max's son, Stephen, wants to interview me for a short film he's making about his dad. He already knows I was one of the bombers and that Max wasn't. Max left a memoir. I owe it to Stephen to give my version of events, however partial. It's for others to judge the rights and wrongs.'

Her tone adjusted to reasonable. 'Think carefully about this, Justin. In today's climate what you did would be judged as terrorism, not some radical piece of street theatre. You'll be a one-day wonder and classed with ISIS or the IRA. I wish you'd told me about this sooner.'

'It's a matter of conscience, Moll, however belated.'

'I think it's suicidal, Justin, you should go back to Stephen and say you've changed your mind. Let him make his film, he can't prove anything.'

'Thanks, sis, it's good to have you on side, I mean that.'

Molly would always be his champion. There was a pause before she came back.

'It's weird, isn't it, to think Sanjay is supporting a revolution in Syria while your renegade past is coming back to haunt you. D'you think he's trying to outdo you somehow?'

'I don't think so, he's far more together than I ever was.'

She let that go. 'And the others? I know Rob was killed in that ghastly car accident, in Nicaragua, wasn't it?'

'A bus, actually, on a mountain pass; the road disappeared in a landslide and the bus fell into a ravine. He'd only been there a few weeks, supporting the revolution.'

'Poor Rob, so earnest and *so* polite. Vera pops up occasionally as a Welsh MP. What about Jess and Callum?'

'They went to ground, maybe changed their names, I don't know.'

'And Sofia, did she drop out of the picture?'

'She joined an organisation in Paris that fought the fascists in Spain. Harpreet spotted her name once, in a magazine at the hairdresser's. Turns out she came back decades later and set up a pottery in Lincolnshire. She'd be over seventy if she's still around.' He followed her on social media occasionally and knew she was alive and probably kicking.

'I wasn't keen on her because she had her claws into you. She gave me a crash-course in women's lib, I'll give her that. I thought of her this week when some prick at work said he didn't think childlessness was a *valid lifestyle choice*. I tore him to shreds, said that reproduction didn't define us, and I for one, was perfectly happy. Poor lamb, he didn't know what hit him.

'I should be going, pet. Same time in two weeks? Text me if anything comes up. About Stephen, that is.'

The phone clicked to silence and he felt elated by Molly's love and straight talking common sense.

Chapter 12

When Franz Kafka crashed into his dreams, Justin wasn't overly surprised; though he didn't welcome the intrusion. The source was easily traced, a one-man show at the Edinburgh Fringe where he'd booked a blizzard of tickets and he and Harpreet had zigzagged across the city between shows, remembering little of any of them. Except now, years later, Kafka's *Letter to His Father* surfaced to torment him. Played by an angst-ridden actor in a makeshift venue, scraps of the monologue reassembled by arrangement with a part of his brain over which he had no control.

'*I'll rip you apart like a fish,*' Herr Kafka threatened his son, who wrote in reply, '*I knew that nothing bad would happen (yet as a child I didn't know this), but your words served as a sign of your power and you always seemed capable of doing something.*' So what? Pa had never laid a finger on him. '*It was dreadful when you shouted left and right at the table,*' this was nearer the mark, '*until mother seemingly came to the rescue.*' And there it was, perfectly distilled. *Seemingly.* Ma had never been able to protect him from Pa's mood swings and as Molly pointed out, suffered from undiagnosed depression.

His ninth birthday was marked by the appearance of a black and white cat found cowering in the coal shed, and she was the best present he'd had. Ma made a bed from a cardboard box lined with a square of old blanket and Justin placed the bed on a low shelf in the scullery.

'There'll be kittens before long,' Ma said, one evening. 'She'll need to be left in peace.'

They called her Perdita and Justin fed her food scraps. She wound round his legs and purred.

'How many kittens will there be?' Justin asked.

'Up to five or six. She's still very young and quite small.'

'They'll have to go,' Pa said from behind his newspaper.

'She can keep one, then we'll have her spayed,' Ma

intercepted.

Pa lowered the paper and Justin knew something bad was about to happen.

'We'll drown the rest, and Justin can help me do it,' Pa said.

It was the year he'd learned that kissing Pa goodnight was for girls and he must shake hands at bedtime. Drowning kittens as a rite of passage, hadn't been mentioned till now.

'He'll do nothing of the kind,' Ma said firmly, 'we'll give the other kittens away.'

Pa beat a hasty retreat with, 'You spoil the boy, Kathleen,' and they all knew he'd overstepped the mark.

The kittens were a grey and white seething mass, feeding blindly for a week. Justin crept in to give choice morsels to Perdita and completely forgot his father's threat.

It was Sunday and Ma was at Mass, when Pa said, 'We'll see to the kittens this morning, son. You can choose which one to keep. Pick the liveliest, mind, only the strongest survive.'

He watched helpless, as Pa grabbed a handful of writhing bodies, and shoved the kittens to the bottom of a sack that jumped of its own accord. The cast iron bucket stood waiting, filled to the brim, and Pa tried to hand him the bag.

'No,' he whimpered, hot tears spilling down his cheeks.

'For Christ's sake, boy, stop blubbering.' Pa pushed up his shirtsleeve with his free hand and plunged the bag into the water, sending up a shower of bubbles. 'It'll take three minutes,' he said, and looked at his wristwatch in the way he did timing the 100 yards sprint. Justin stood transfixed, desperate for the air bubbles to stop.

When the pulse of life was snuffed out, Pa let go off the bag. Small pale bodies floated to the surface. Justin saw Pa's face blotched with anger, and knew he was to blame. He ran out of the scullery, cradling the remaining kitten to his chest and waited for Ma to come home.

As soon as he heard footsteps on the gravel, he rushed out sobbing uncontrollably. Ma pressed his head against her bosom while Pa stood by, watering his pink geraniums.

The gutted fish and dead kittens had slyly superimposed themselves and brought back the shame at looking on helplessly, but this time he was the grownup and put a protective arm round Ma.

Kafka kindly framed another seminal moment, this one lodged in conscious memory. A holiday job at Pa's factory. The clerk put his wages in a proper pay packet, a brown paper envelope with a cellophane window. There were no notes in his, just a few bob pocket-money for sweeping and tidying round the men and their machines. A holiday job *in the real world*, Pa would say, always keen to remind him he'd have to step up to the plate one day.

On Thursdays Justin would mount the spiral steps and walk past the management offices to collect his wages. Pa's office was screened by panes of frosted glass. That day, someone must have opened a window to let in air.

Raised voices stopped him. It was Pa and Ken, the normally mild shop steward. Justin positioned himself in the shadows and tuned in to a stand-up row.

'If the men don't work overtime, we'll lose the contract,' Pa bellowed. 'Engineering outfits like ours are two a penny!'

'They'll need paying time and a half, in that case. It'll take a good two weeks to get the job out. The men won't do it for nowt.'

'Bugger that, Ken! The Christmas bonus covers overtime, that's the deal. We're all in this together, remember?'

'They've already worked their bonus, with them extra hours over Easter,' Ken answered back.

'Where's your loyalty, man? You can talk em round. You always do. I'll double your bonus, no questions asked.'

Justin gnawed his nails, waiting for Ken's reply.

'Not pigging likely! What d'you take me for?' There was a

crash, as though a chair had been knocked to the floor, followed by a slammed door and a clatter of boots down metal steps.

The following day, as Justin swept, the men bent their heads over lathes and milling machines, refusing to meet his eye. They see me as the enemy, he thought, as the thump and screech of metal jangled his nerves.

At tea-break, Ken came and patted him on the back. 'No need for us to fall out, Justin. You're a good lad.'

Tears sprang to his eyes. 'It's because of the Union, isn't it? Can anyone join?' He felt safe among these men who stood by each other and paid something called *subs*.

Ken's belly shook with laughter. 'Did you hear that, lads? Justin's going to join the Union! Well I never! Best not tell your old man.'

That evening, Pa exploded at the dinner-table. 'Lazy ungrateful so-and-sos,' (he never cursed in front of Ma and Molly). 'They're all commies, like my pathetic brother, Stan.'

He didn't yet know the meaning of *commie* except as a swear word, but had always liked Uncle Stan.

When the men walked out, Pa was stupefied. Forced to pay overtime, his revenge was to cancel the annual bonus. Soon after, Justin screwed up courage to announce that he had no intention of becoming an engineer or working in the factory. It was his first step towards breaking free of Pa's stranglehold.

With other people I felt guilty because of your attitude towards them—I felt implicated in this and had to atone for your words. And you always spoke badly of people that I had dealings with. In business and in the family you tried to instil a mistrust of people in my mind (when I admired someone, you buried him with criticism).

Justin didn't count himself a tortured soul like Franz, not at all, but the one-man show, performed from behind bars, had moved him deeply. When he'd told Molly about the dream, she said it was about guilt and shame, doubtless linked to Max.

'What d'you mean?'

'Work it out for yourself, Jus, it's something you have to deal with.'

The landscape flattened, the skies opened, and clouds billowed like giant sails. Crossing the spare and elegant Humber Bridge, he felt the sway, or imagined he did, exposed as it was to the wind. The route to the village veered left towards Grimsby, dwindling to country roads that erupted in potholes due to frost or farm traffic. Agricultural buildings clustered at intervals, dotted among fields along the way. The satnav insisted that he had to continue two miles past the village. She must live on an outlying farm, he thought, cut off from the world.

His faith in the satnav deserted him as it took him down an unmade road to a ploughed field. The undercarriage scraped the ground as he veered to avoid a large stone and rain splashed the windscreen in huge drops before slashing down in torrents. 'Jesus! I could have wrecked my car,' he said aloud.

At the end of the rutted path was a concealed right turn; a cottage emerged, screened by a copse of scrawny trees. If this wasn't her place he was going straight home.

The squall of rain stopped as quickly as it started and he pulled up outside the cottage next to an ancient jeep. *Earth to Earth* was painted on a sign above the door. There being no bell, he rapped the knocker and took a step back at the loudness of it. He waited, pulling up the collar of his parka, then gave a gentler more apologetic knock.

He heard a woman call, '*Il y a quelqu'un,*' and another more distant voice, 'Say I'm out.' The door creaked open as if not in regular use and a woman stood before him, looking for all the world like Sofia when she was young. Tall, with dark hair tied back, her expression combined suspicion and amusement. 'Nobody comes here except by appointment,' she embarked. 'Maybe you're lost?'

'I'm Justin, an old friend of your mother's. You must be Sofia's daughter. You're very alike.'

'Really? And I suppose you were just passing? You'd better come in.'

He ducked inside. 'I shouldn't have come unannounced, I'm sorry. I think she'll understand.'

Sofia's daughter, who hadn't introduced herself, threw him a look over her shoulder and said, 'Then you don't know my mother.' She led him into a low-ceilinged room smelling of wood-smoke that came from the stove under the chimney breast. Once his eyes adjusted, he saw shelves filled with plates, figurines and decorative pots, in varying greens, reds and rustic browns.

'Please sit down. I'm Rosalie, by the way. I'll see if I can persuade *Maman* to leave her workshop.'

He was left to choose between an upright leather chair and two settees draped in blankets in the same earthy tones as the pottery. He eased himself into a settee expecting to be there awhile. He didn't have long to wait. Sofia walked in and Justin leapt to his feet and they stood apart taking each other in. He'd forgotten how tall she was, her face was heavier and her hair a cloud of silver-grey. They jolted towards each other with open arms for a slightly awkward embrace.

Sofia said, 'Well, here's a turn up for the books,' and to Rosalie, 'Meet Justin, my old partner in crime. For a while I wasn't sure if he was your father.' She laughed, amber eyes glinting mischief.

Rosalie turned to Justin. 'Don't worry, I've heard that one before.'

'Look, I'm sorry, maybe this was a mistake,' he said, ready to run.

'Don't frighten him off, *Chérie*! We're only playing, Justin, we don't get much in the way of entertainment. Come now, sit down. I hope you haven't come to tell me you're dying,' said with a smile that didn't make it to her eyes.

'No, I'm not dying, Sofia, that would be too easy. It's about Max. He died last year, did you know?'

'Yes, I read an obituary by his wife. A touching piece, something about his charitable work with young people. Got an Open University degree in prison, I always knew he was bright. Did you keep in touch?'

'Not really, but I should've done, after, you know…' he trailed off.

'Rosalie knows everything,' Sofia interjected.

'Which doesn't mean I agree with your politics. As my mother will tell you, I've gone over to the dark side.'

Sofia shook an impatient hand. 'My daughter rejoices in the title, *human capital technology consultant*. Even Guy Debord couldn't have invented that. Rosalie is here to persuade me to move back to Paris. I won't of course. They'll find me stone cold on the workshop floor. I've made disposal arrangements.'

The daughter countered, 'There's always the kiln.' Justin was taken aback by their gallows humour.

'So, the past has finally got you by the scruff of the neck,' Sofia probed.

He looked at her from the settee as she sat magisterially in the upright leather chair, Rosalie at her feet. He rather hoped the daughter would go and fetch tea, even though he was uninvited.

'I'm trying to piece together who we were back then and you're the only person who can help. Don't get me wrong, this isn't some existential crisis. Max left a memoir and his son Stephen wants to make a documentary. I've agreed to be interviewed.'

'You agreed? But why? After lying low for so long?'

'I owe it to Stephen after what happened. It's what I'd expect if he were my son.'

Sofia snorted. 'You owe him nothing, comrade, and if you're getting involved it's for your own reasons. Sounds like you want to beat yourself up to expiate tedious middle-class guilt about having a soft life. Poor Max, who took a wrong turn and got chewed up by *The People's Militia*, is that it? I'd say he knew exactly what he was doing—he could have denounced us at any point. But he didn't. Respect him for that, but don't pity him. It's how free will works, we make choices for better or for worse.

'Still smoke?'

'Not officially.'

She lit a spill from the stove and he stood so they could both light up. He inhaled slowly and deliciously.

'For worse, in my case.' They both stayed near the stove. 'I need to fill in the past to come to grips with the present.'

'Ah, the old days! A shifting time zone that can't bear the weight of much reality, I fear. Let's just say, we were indefinable... an ideas cloud that absorbed the spirit of the moment, shapeshifters who melted away as quickly as we were formed.'

He'd forgotten her verbal flights. 'But what did we actually achieve, concretely? Did we change the balance of forces?' In his private mind, he asked, *did we do more harm than good?*

'That depends on your outlook. I imagine you've moved on, being a respectable academic, sorry, respected academic, I couldn't resist stalking you once the internet made it possible. Professor of Sociology no less. Where do you stand these days? Communism may be dead, but capitalism is looking pretty sick. What do you tell your students?'

Rosalie got up and said she could see where this was going, it was an excavation into the past and she had better things to do.

Sofia moved next to him on the settee and he relaxed. 'I'm not here to spar about politics, but I haven't changed that much.'

'I can see there's a lot at stake for you; your job, your reputation and your family. A wife who works for the CPS and you've become something of a public figure in your own way.' She brushed ash off her overalls.

'First, tell me what happened after you left. You left me for Gilles, didn't you?'

'I went to France for the revolution. But yes, I was living with Gilles.'

He swallowed hard. 'And then?'

'The police caught up with me in Paris after the Dublin bombing in '74. It was a 1st of May operation and I set it up. We attacked the Spanish Cultural Institute in retaliation for the execution of a Spanish anarchist. Rosalie was only a year old and I was threatened with extradition. My parents came over for a while. Gilles worked nights and my mother and I pushed the pram round the streets all day while he slept. I knew I'd have to send my child to my parents for safety if I continued to be active and I couldn't bear to part with her. In the event, the fascists were defeated the following year when Franco died and the case against me was dropped. No heroics on my part were needed. For the rest? I supported Gilles in his party and trade-union work until he died.'

'I'm sorry, I didn't know.'

'How would you? I cut myself off quite deliberately. I knew you had a better chance of making a life for yourself without me. In London I was always at risk of being arrested and I could pass unnoticed in Paris. And there was Gilles. It wouldn't have worked, you and me. I could see you were too attached to your roots.'

'I wish I'd known for sure about Gilles. It would have closed a chapter.' He blinked away tears from the cigarette smoke.

'I know. It was complicated. He was still married at the time. If I'd left you an address you'd have followed me, and I didn't want that. I was particularly sorry that I didn't ask after your mother. I presume she died soon afterwards.'

'She did. It was hard, losing both of you. I went a bit peculiar for a while and retreated into myself. It took a long time to get into a close relationship, but then I met Harpreet and count myself a lucky man. Since we're telling all, the weapons found at Rob's place, was that anything to do with you?'

She got up to attend to the stove, deftly using iron tongs to add a log of wood. 'That was also complicated... wheels within wheels involving the 1st of May Group.' Next to him again, she said, 'You mentioned a son?'

He'd never get a straight answer and decided to let it go. 'Yes, Sanjay. Girlfriend in Rojava and in danger of following her there,' he summarised.

'Really? You must be very proud. The revolution there has more chance of succeeding than it did in Spain.'

'I'm proud at one level, but shit scared he gets shot up in some ghastly war.' A silence followed and he felt the need to pace about to organise his thoughts. 'Going back to Max, should we have come clean? I mean me and Rob.'

'Absolutely not. We had a code of collective responsibility, remember? We'd have been blown wide open and all done for conspiracy. When they finally nailed Rob, Callum and Jess, that was the Prosecution's argument—that the three in the dock were involved in the same conspiracy. The verdict was a fudge—not guilty for Callum and Jess, set against clemency for Rob. Which the judge ignored.'

'Let's face it, for Max, it was a catastrophe. He spent all those years inside and nobody said, *Max didn't actually do it, even if he did know what was going on, and actually dozens of others were doing similar things up and down the country.* From Stephen's point of view, it's tragic.'

'As Max's son, obviously. But we weren't acting as individuals or on our own behalf. We were part of something bigger, a movement we believed in. It's society and the state that were to blame for Max's fate, not individuals in *The People's Militia*. We were caught up in a storm of rebellion—were we wrong to try? I don't think so. Should you apologise to his son? Go ahead, if you need to indulge your bourgeois conscience. But don't turn Max into a victim, he deserves better than that. He was a class-fighter, however old-fashioned that may sound.'

Justin stopped in his tracks. 'Yes, Max was what we all aspired to be, a fighter and survivor. I only wish I'd said so to his face.'

An electronic bleeper went off in one of her pockets. 'Drat, that's the kiln.' She went to the door and called out for her daughter to attend to it.

Facing him she said, 'You were such a beautiful man, Justin. Did I ever tell you?'

He looked away, embarrassed. Was she teasing him for old times' sake?

'We were young and hardly realised it at the time,' she continued. 'I never dreamt of turning seventy, did you? But, of course, you're younger than I am.'

'I'm history, old girl, a crumbling fossil in a brash and shiny Business School.'

'Well, that's hardly the end of the world, my dear. You've lived a full life and there are people who love you. What more can one ask? Except friendship, perhaps.'

By that time he knew they wouldn't see each other again. The present was hard at his heels.

Chapter 13

Pallid light seeped into the kitchen as he sat prepping onions, leeks, carrots, celery, parsnips and turnips for Harpreet's *pot-au-feu* and listening amiably to Vivaldi on the radio. If asked to describe his mood, it would be *allegro vivace* at the prospect of Sanjay coming home for a leisurely Sunday lunch. He filed for later any talk of driving a van of supplies to Syria.

This morning Harpreet had laughed at his joke about gardening leave and getting an allotment, and said it wasn't his style. A day without turmoil was rare and he was determined to make an oasis of this family meal. He had a good *Côtes-de-Beaune de Bourgogne* set aside and a fruit cup for his teetotal son. What could go wrong?

The lights went on and Harpreet said, 'What're you doing in the dark?' This was their regular dance; he switched off lights and turned down the heating and she turned everything on. He had a private theory that it was a male-female thing, based on vast empirical evidence and a sample of one.

'Getting your vegetables ready. Anything else I can do?' He looked up and saw she was wearing a glowing yellow shalwar kameez. 'You look nice—it's my favourite.'

She smiled, 'I'll take it from here, thanks. Sanjay promised to make an apple crumble. You could start peeling the Bramleys? He should be here soon.' She tied on an apron and took the meat from the fridge.

He set about the apples while she studied the recipe, involving beef shanks and marrow bones, from a serious looking cookbook. The air would soon be suffused with aromatic juices, redolent of family holidays in Provence. These moments were timeless, free floating above life's vicissitudes, when they were present to each other in amicable silence.

Harpreet broke in with, 'Molly called me yesterday.'

'Oh yeah?'

'I know, I couldn't believe it either.'

'What did she want? Not springing one of her surprise parties, I hope?'

'Nothing like that. She's worried about you, thinks you're going through some sort of crisis.' She looked up from her task of tying beef with string.

'It's been a tough time right enough, but we'll get through it.' "We" was him testing the water after her outburst a couple of weeks back—*I don't know if there is an "us" any more.*

'Yes, one way or another. There's so much in life that's beyond our control, don't you think?' He preferred her in angry mode rather than this tone of quiet resignation, which scared the hell out of him.

The front door clattered opened. 'That must be Sanjay,' she said, unnecessarily and wiped her hands on her apron.

'Hi!' Sanjay walked in beaming and gave his mother a hug. 'Hey, what's for lunch?' he asked, glancing at the cookbook.

'French hot-pot to you,' Justin said, as Sanjay clapped him on the shoulder.

'You won't be running off early, *meri jaan*, it takes hours to cook,' Harpreet said, laughing.

'No rush. I'll just get out of my cycling togs—I'm doing crumble, remember?' And he disappeared into the hallway leaving a vacuum. It was like this since he'd left home. As parents they hankered for when they were a family, and when he came home there was an adjustment for this grown-up son who loved them dearly but no longer needed them. He came back into the kitchen and settled onto the sofa. It was an unspoken rule that he helped himself to coffee or whatever he wanted as he was at home and not a guest.

Harpreet piled meat, marrow bones and vegetables into a cooking pot, added water and a bundle of herbs wrapped in cheesecloth and turned up the heat. 'That'll make a fine broth,' she said, and joined Sanjay on the sofa. 'Heard from Farida lately?' she asked. 'I read her blog.'

'Yes, she messages most days. Says it'll be months before she'll be on the front line, which is a relief, to be honest. She's with an all-women group and they're up at the crack of dawn for physical training. There are women from Europe and the Middle East apparently, and they speak a hotchpotch of languages but they're all learning Kurdish. It helps a lot that she speaks Arabic. The food is pretty rubbish and they're short of all sorts of basics because of the Turkish embargo. I know some guys who run supplies to the Jungle camp in Calais and there's a group of us planning to do the same for Kobani.'

'It's a bit different, isn't it? Calais and Kobani?' Justin said, objections lining up like dominoes that would be knocked down at the flick of a wrist.

Harpreet was subtler. 'I remember when we arrived from Uganda, people were so kind, they brought toys for us children and warm clothes for everyone. We'd no inkling of how cold it could be and it was only September.'

'You don't talk about it much, Mum. It must have been terrifying to leave your home almost overnight.'

'It was for your Dada and Nani who had to abandon everything and leave behind people they loved. I was only twelve and it was more like an adventure. I never imagined we'd be moving for good, that we'd never go back.' She tucked her legs under her and propped an elbow on the back of the sofa. 'There are Syrian refugees in Leeds, you know. Have you thought of doing something locally?'

Sanjay sprawled, hands clasped behind his head. 'I'm in touch with some of them and we're actually working on the convoy idea.'

'Convoy, is it now?' Justin interjected, still peeling and chopping.

'Look, it's got a way to go, but we're attracting a lot of

online support.'

'I've been thinking of a visit to Uganda,' Harpreet announced, to no one in particular. 'I'd take Dada and Nani on one last trip, a sojourn into the past, so to speak. They like the idea.'

'Really?' Justin dropped the knife, which clinked against the bowl. 'I think I need a drink,' and proceeded to open the *Bourgogne*.

'It'd be a break for me—I'm worn ragged at work and need time out.' She touched Sanjay's arm. 'You could come too, see where I was brought up.'

'What's wrong with you both?' Sanjay said, sitting upright. 'Haven't you talked about this?'

'Evidently not,' said Justin, angry and hurt she'd aired her plans without consulting him.

'Your father's over-reacting, I just need a bit of breathing space,' Harpreet said lightly. 'There are people in Kampala close to Dada and Nani who still keep in touch.'

'I remember seeing these amazing stamps as a kid. When they wouldn't answer my questions I understood it was painful,' Sanjay said, leaving her invitation hanging.

Justin drained his glass, before pouring Sanjay a fruit cup. He didn't want to drink alone.

'I'll make the crumble,' Sanjay said, getting to his feet. 'Thanks for doing the apples, Dad.' He gave Justin a comforting body nudge. Opening and closing cupboards, he assembled flour, porridge oats, flaked almonds and butter, for his signature dish.

'Look, I know this thing with Dad is affecting you both, and I think we should get it out in the open. I'm talking about Stephen and the film. What's going on with that?'

Justin nursed his third glass at the well-worn table. 'It's going okay,' he said, trying to sound low-key. Stephen had sent more extracts from Max's diary, filled with vivid descriptions of the daily indignities of prison life. 'He wants to know why Max and I didn't keep in touch after he left prison.'

'Why didn't you?'

'Oh, you know, work and family. And my own cowardice. Max wanted to make peace with Peter Haddon, the man who's house we bombed, me and Rob, that is. He emailed asking me to go with him to apologise.'

He could see it now, Max getting the train south and heading across to Parliament Square, on foot, most likely. He'd enjoy the novelty of being back in London a free man. There'd be the usual inspection of credentials at the gates, before being ushered in and met by Peter Haddon. He was in the House of Lords at this stage. They'd have walked along carpeted corridors filled with illustrious portraits and eventually descended to the basement to the Peers' Visitors Café. He'd been there, when called as an expert witness to a select committee on rough sleeping. Peter Haddon would have put Max at ease and the grandeur wouldn't have bothered him. He'd have said how sorry he was for the upset caused to the family and talked about his own son and stepdaughters. Haddon would have drawn him out on his work with a children's charity and congratulated him on his achievements. An intern would have done the homework, briefing him on his supposed attacker's career.

'My biggest regret is that I didn't have the decency to reply. He deserved better than that. That was the last time I heard from him.'

'That's harsh,' said Sanjay. Harpreet got up to stir her concoction. Justin swilled his wine round the glass until streaks ran down the sides. *Le vin pleur*, as Harpreet had said, presciently.

'D'you want to know what I think?' Sanjay said rhetorically. 'Forget all that shit from the past. This isn't about you any longer. Use Stephen's film to talk about today's struggles and the revolution in Rojava. What have you got to lose?'

'Seeing as I'm royally fucked, anyway?' he said, and realised the wine was talking.

'Give over,' Harpreet said sharply, and handed him a bowl of Bombay mix. She steered the conversation to safer ground and they talked about the bike cooperative and plans to expand the workshop at *Mellow Vélo*. Justin dipped in and out of the easy exchange between mother and son while his mind drifted to building site days.

A pall of depression weighed on his shoulders as he sat on the top deck. The bus filled with high-heeled secretaries gasping the first cigarette of the day before teetering downstairs to join the phalanx of bowler hats that advanced like ants on the city. It distracted him to observe through a sociologist's lens the changing layers of society as the bus progressed towards the East End of London. Men started to wear caps and women wore serviceable macs and headscarves against the rain.

Passing Whitechapel he looked out for Bloom's, the kosher restaurant where Sofia had introduced him to chopped liver, Gefilte fish and potato Latkes. It was over sweet-noodle Lokshen pudding she'd told him more about her mother whose parents were killed by the Nazis. From that day on her mother refused to speak German.

It was hard to live up to that degree of suffering as a child. I learned that the only way to survive was to take up the political struggle, knowing that nothing I did could redeem what my mother had endured.

To hear this was to see another side of Sofia. He'd seen the anarchist father in her, and now there was this other aspect. It helped explain her quick temper and impatience towards him when she guilt-tripped him about being middle-class.

The bus was nearing his stop and he saw light penetrate

the early morning drizzle. The building had grown to two storeys, so with luck he'd be working on the inside with Carlson. By now it had become evident there was no plan for a fire-escape, only internal stairs either side of the block. This added to the undertow of distrust among the men, who complained about the low quality building materials.

He set about cleaning mugs, scraping out thick black deposits with rough sand until they gleamed inside and out. He wiped the transparent polythene sheeting on the table covering pictures of the Derbyshire Peaks he'd placed underneath. At the centre was the summit of Kinder Scout surrounded by dark gritstone and purple slopes. Even Mervyn, with his fondness for pinups, gave it the thumbs-up.

Kelly, the Union man arrived before Jim the foreman, which was unusual. Kelly had taken a shine to Justin, one of the few labourers to join the new Union.

'Doing overtime, son?' he asked, as Justin set out a row of mugs.

'Unpaid as per usual. Fancy an early brew? I make one for Jim before the lads get in.'

'I'm alright, thanks.' He was holding a sheet of paper. 'You've got an education, Che. Would you read me this?' He handed a letter from the newly formed UCATT and Justin ran his eye over it. He understood the Union planned to negotiate a wage increase from £20 to £30 a week and a reduction in hours for members. 'That's great news. D'you think more men will join?'

Kelly fixed him with piercing blue eyes. 'Read it to me, son. Twice will do nicely, if you don't mind.'

Justin read the letter in full with its detailed proposals as Kelly listened and nodded, closing his eyes occasionally as if to seal in its contents. At the end of the second reading, his shoulders relaxed. 'Thank you, that's grand. I usually ask Jim, but I like to spread my favours,' he said mischievously.

Within ten minutes, the shed was crowded and noisy and Jim knocked on the table. 'Okay lads, Kelly's got something to say from the Union.'

Kelly took the floor to good-humoured groans, the letter dangling from one hand. He recited it from start to finish with no pretence at reading and Justin realised this feat of memory was taken for granted by the others. He continued to fill the men's mugs and listened as they debated the pros and cons of joining and turned the air blue with cigarette smoke. John thought the Union was a rip-off and there was no way he was paying subs. As a skilled man he was on a regular wage and that was good enough.

'If more of us joined we'd all get better conditions,' Justin argued. 'It's about time we stopped being paid on the lump and got holiday and sick pay.'

Bert, who was cracking eggs into a can of milk, said, 'I don't take holidays and I'm never sick.'

Carlson was all for a thirty-five-hour week. 'That's like being paid five hours to stay in bed,' he reasoned, followed by a slew of lewd suggestions from the others.

Justin was stirring cement on a plastic sheet while Carlson nailed together a wooden mould to receive it. Carlson was quieter than usual, and Justin sensed he was out of sorts.

'Something up?'

'Had a scrap with my dad about getting mixed up in things. He gets my goat sometimes.'

'Mixed up in what? I thought you kept your head down,' Justin said, surprised.

'I've been thinking back to the Mangrove demo, now the case has finally come to court. It sickens me, how people hate us because we're Black.'

'I see,' said Justin, out of his depth. It was the first time he'd heard Carlson speak so openly about racial prejudice. He'd once seen a door daubed, *Keep Britain White*, and felt ashamed.

'My dad's old-fashioned and still thinks he's lucky to be in England. I told him I'd heard Darcus Howe's speech and it made me proud. He talked of brutality in a different way. The brutality of the police, of housing, of education, in everyday life. Then it made sense why the police kept raiding the Mangrove. My dad blew up at me and said the likes of Darcus bring trouble to Britain and we don't need Black Power over here.'

'I'm sorry, mate,' Justin said, chopping cement with the blade of his spade. There'd been inflammatory headlines about immigrant mobs and attacks on police, but little about the demo itself. 'I saw a banner in the paper, saying, *Our Only Crime Was We Dared*. That really struck me.'

'Tell me about it. I ran away before I got beat up. There were literally hundreds of police as we marched and they must have radioed for more, because vanloads arrived and they blocked the road. Police with batons poured out, like an army, and the peaceful march blew up into a massive street fight. People were screaming and there were sirens and blood on the pavement. Somehow I managed to get out and legged it home. Dad said I was a fool, but he soon quieted down when he saw the news that evening.

'Last night, I told him I'm joining the Mangrove Nine defence campaign. That's what the row was about.' He started hammering nails into the wooden shuttering, leaving Justin to his thoughts.

Max's campaign was flagging and his lawyer had told him to plead guilty. There was talk of a grubby plea-bargain in return for a reduced sentence. The Mangrove Nine campaign seemed different and set to take on the courts. They had the backing of a growing Black Power movement, whereas Max was increasingly isolated since Rob, Callum and Jess had been kept in custody. It was time for a radical rethink.

'Ready, Che?' Carlson prompted. 'The mould is ready,

and when you've done, Jim wants us to unload the lorry.'

Justin shovelled in the cement and Carlson stood by, ready to smooth it off before it set. 'Thanks for telling me about the Mangrove and your dad,' Justin said, as they worked.

'My old man's okay, I suppose. He was brought up different, it's a generation thing.'

Job done, they clambered down the scaffolding to ground-level, and Justin geared up to shift bricks, the heaviest task of the day.

True, no one called him a shirker, but he was keenly aware that men twice his age could do double the work. He'd gained in muscle and body weight in the last year and could do most things required of him.

Sofia would pretend to complain that his hands were rough, while running hers across his expanding chest and taut leg muscles. The thought aroused him still.

RojavaSyria Blogspot 2

Let me take you to the heart of Kobani in the words of those who defended the city under brutal siege by ISIS. Thousands tried to flee. "They were mostly women, children, elderly people. People were crossing with giant bags of stuff, with cars and sheep. There was no water and food. The Turkish police opened fire with teargas."

By October 2014 It became clear that Kobani would fall. Turkey said it considered all Kurdish fighters (not just the PKK) to be terrorists, no better than ISIS. Meanwhile, shipments of weapons went to ISIS from Turkey and the gravely wounded were treated in Turkish hospitals, according to one ex-jihadi. In a diplomatic faux-pas, Joe Biden commented that Turkey was letting through a lot of foreign fighters to join ISIS.

At the eleventh hour the US announced that while it still considered the PKK a terrorist organisation, the PYD was not (the political arm of the YPG/YPJ), and it would therefore provide air support to Kobani.

The YPG/YPJ command told The Guardian, *"Air strikes alone are really not enough to defeat ISIS in Kobani... they are besieging the city on three sides, and fighter jets simply cannot hit each and every ISIS fighter on the ground."*

A YPJ woman commander interviewed for the New York Times, said, *"We will never give up. But we need more than merely rifles and grenades to carry out our responsibilities and aid the coalition in its war against the jihadist forces..."*

A YPG fighter described it thus: *"There were dozens of Alamos in that city no one will read about...hundreds of small little battles in small ugly broken houses no one will ever care about. It was like Stalingrad. At night it was haunting to see how much it looked like the moon."*

In January 2015 the YPG/YPJ replaced the ISIS flag with the Kurdish flag and celebrations broke out everywhere. More than 80% of the city was reduced to rubble and children were playing innocently alongside unexploded bombs. Today, the city remains a wreck and there has been an embargo on cement and building materials. Since the elections in Turkey this month, NGOs are prevented from entering and Doctors Without Borders have been turned away.

There is progress on the military front, however, spurred by the Kobani victory. There's a new military alliance of Kurds, Arabs, Syriacs and Yazidis under the banner of Syrian Democratic Forces (SDF).

On 15th October this year, US planes dropped 50,000 tons of ammunition. Sinjar in Iraq, has since been recaptured by the joint forces of the Iraqi Peshmerga, Syrian YPG/YPJ and Yazidi militias. The defence of the region will depend on continued international support to drive out fascist jihadis. The debate in the UK parliament next month will determine whether this is forthcoming from Britain.

The military principles of the revolution in Rojava were explained to me like this: *"Our theory is the theory of the rose, a flower that defends itself with thorns. Every being has to create methods of self-defence according to its own way of living, growing and connecting* with others. The aim is not to destroy an enemy but to force it to give up its intention to attack. It's a principle that works in other areas as well. National armies serve the state, but they leave the people without defence."

If you are a friend of the revolution in Rojava, shout out that Rojava is for a new democracy hand in hand with the freedom of women. As one woman fighter put it, "Armed women fighters break a taboo, since weapons are a symbol of male domination. They also signal a transcendence of gender differences, and insofar as they are perceived as a threat to men, they endanger male privilege. That's the philosophy of our movement. Men have been running things for five thousand years."

If your concern is primarily for national (your own) security, be afraid. There will be many more Bataclans until the scourge of jihadism and its causes are overcome.

Farida
25 November 2015
Kobani

Chapter 14

That night he'd felt Harpreet's comforting hand on the back of his neck, as if to soothe their present and coming losses. Their marriage would never be the same. The moment crystalised and he saw that he defined himself against the firm contours of her being. Harpreet grounded him in a way that Sofia never could.

In hindsight, it was clear why Gilles must have been irresistible. Sofia, evanescent and mercurial, Gilles, emanating an animal magnetism that attracted men and women alike. Gilles, next to Sofia and Rob, had made a great impression on him.

Rob was a different kettle of fish. Apparently cold and detached, he drew people in with an incisive intellect. Stephen had asked if they'd crossed swords, and he'd replied yes, over Max's campaign.

It was a lazy Saturday afternoon when a report of an explosion flashed across the TV screen. It was at the home of the Ford's boss and had blown out the French windows.

'Nice one,' said Rob. 'Looks like the Paris Commune bomb started a chain reaction. That'll be good for Max's campaign.' He'd looked at Justin.

'You know my views on that. Linking Max to a bombing campaign does him no good. If he stands trial, we want the Jury to think he was just a regular activist, not connected to any organised group.'

He remembered being riled by Rob's response. 'Thanks for your thoughts comrade, but you're wrong. Our politics is our only defence and we have nothing to hide. If we isolate Max from politics, there *is* no campaign. It will be us next.'

Sofia had talked about security, keeping campaign files off the premises because sooner or later there'd be a raid. Rob warned them to keep address-books safe as these had disappeared from squats and would be used by cops for cross-referencing. The net was closing.

'We should call a halt on all ops until Max is in the clear. Let others take the heat.'

Rob shook out a last cigarette and crumpled the battered packet. 'That's somewhat abstract, comrade, as we're out of supplies. I've got news on that front. Word has come from Paris and I'm going over to meet them.' He snapped a plastic lighter to the tip of his cigarette and drew on it heavily.

Typical of Rob, to sidestep the question. 'Is that the 1st of May Group?' Justin suspected they were a slicker and more experienced outfit.

Sofia cut in. 'Jus, the less you know the more useful you are, right?'

'No way! I've taken risks the same as you, or am I still on trial, for Chrissake? You can't keep me on the outside for ever.' He stormed round the room, anger bubbling.

'You're overreacting,' said Sofia, with maddening calm.

'So, just who *are* you meeting in Paris?'

Rob's tone changed. 'If you're admitted to the next level there is no going back. We need to know you're not here for the ride, on a break from real life. Ask yourself, are you ready to blow up your father's factory? Or your private school? Seems to me you've got more to lose than us. You have to expunge lingering attachments before becoming a true revolutionary.'

In a face-off with Rob he yelled, 'I'm not taking this mind-game shit any longer! Haven't I planted bombs? And I'm the one working my butt off on a building site!'

Rob gave a dry laugh and Justin saw a flicker in his eyes. 'I think it's time. This is what I've been waiting for, to see fire in your belly. Now I know you're ready. I'll introduce you to Gilles. He's our contact in Paris. He fought on the barricades in '68. And for the record, there'll be no mention of Max in the next press release.'

The raids came thick and fast as the Prosecution got their teeth into the case. The Notting Hill People's Association and the Agitprop Bookshop were turned over. Justin lived in fear that the cops would turn up something that linked Max to *The People's Militia*.

'They'll be going nuts searching for lists of members, looking and seeing nothing,' said Rob. 'There were over a hundred explosions last year and they've no idea who's behind them. The politicians will be pushing for charges, surely there's *something* they can use to incriminate a bunch of dope-smoking layabouts? They probably suspect the Russians! It must blow their tiny minds.'

Rob had loosened up since the row about Max's campaign. Justin learned that calls from Paris were relayed to designated public phone boxes and Gilles was the go-between. It was as if he'd stepped into the outer ring of a hidden constellation of revolutionaries that stretched across Europe and it was thrilling.

'Sorry about the other day,' Rob said, sensing a residual resentment. 'I had to put you to the test. The rest of us knew each other, but when you and Max came into the picture, it was different. You could have been anybody.'

'A spook or something?' Justin said, incredulous.

'You wouldn't be the first. Actually, I thought you might be collecting material for ethnographic research on the quiet.'

'Of course, a Masters in urban terrorism! I can think of better things to do.' He pointed at Rob's scribbled notes, written in an out-of-date desk diary. 'Could I help with your research? I'd like to get to grips with this housing stuff.' He knew Rob was investigating slum landlordism.

Rob stubbed out a fag-end. 'You're on, comrade, you can help write this pamphlet. Jess is going to add snarky cartoons. Can I give you a whistle-stop tour of the Housing Finance Bill?' He looked up from his desk with pale owl-eyes, vulnerable without his leather cap.

Rob launched in. 'Okay, so it's about ripping off for the poor. Nothing new there. Central government wants to shift housing subsidy to local government. Rents will shoot up and likely double to £4 a week on average. Got it so far?'

'Unpack the bit about rents, for me.' Rob had a habit of running ahead.

'Right you are. Let's go back a step. Instead of Local Authorities setting council house rents, this will be done centrally. The scheme imposes so-called fair rents on millions of Council tenants, which involve means tests and rebates. Read this. It's by the MP for Grimsby.' He handed Justin a typed sheet.

The only proper and sensible principle is to set rents at a level which most people can pay without a means test and without a rebate. That principle has been utterly discarded in the Bill and we shall have millions of tenants eligible for rebates. If we have a low take-up, which seems likely, we could have serious family hardship with rents at double their present level.

The motive behind the Bill has nothing to do with housing policy. It is concerned with Government financial and budgetary policy. The instructions were to lop off £200 to £300 million off the bill for housing subsidies, which the Chancellor of the Exchequer could then distribute in tax concessions to the better-off.

'I like him already.'

'Anthony Crosland. He's still part of the establishment,' Rob said tersely.

'What you're saying, is that Local Authorities will have to implement this, according to law.'

'Exactly. The Tories' line of argument is that better-off council tenants will subsidise the less well-off; it will all balance out. The reality is that by cutting subsidies and forcing up rents, people will be tipped into unregulated private housing. And here's the thing. The Bill allows landlords to make home-improvements under threat of a court order. Then they'll hike the rents.'

'And there'll be masses of people pushed out of their neighbourhoods?'

'Gentrification in a nutshell,' Rob affirmed. 'Property will be rented or bought by the middle-classes and the locals will be priced out of the market. It's already happening in Kensington. Swathes of the city will become no-go areas for the working poor.' Rob thumped the desk for emphasis.

'Bastards!' said Justin.

He'd quoted Rob many times since in lectures on, *The Systematic Pauperisation of the Working Class*, though he didn't relate the class-act that followed.

It was a perfect Situationist stunt. Reverse sociology, Rob called it. 'We'll beat the property dealers at their own game. It's like playing Monopoly.'

'You look the part,' said Justin, eyeing Rob in his shiny suit and polished brogues.

Vera was fussing over Rob's tie. 'I've never seen you so smart, *del*. You suit a tie.'

Sofia came downstairs carrying an armful of laundry and said, 'I wish I had a camera!' She returned from the kitchen and gave Justin an appraising look.

'Will I do?' he asked, shyly.

'Stand straight, so I can see properly. That's better, now give me a twirl.'

He obliged, shrugging his shoulders inside the second-hand leather jacket and feeling self-conscious. The last time he'd been this dressed up was for a student ball with a fey young woman who'd been desperate for a date. It seemed a lifetime ago.

The drift of her shoulders softened. 'You look fabulous darling, like a rock-star, with your builder's Club Med tan. I'd fall for you any day.'

'You're taking the piss, right?' This earned him a playful cuff on the chest. Last night she'd said, 'I love you, Jus, but don't let it go to your head.' It had gone straight to his heart.

Rob frowned. 'Where's your tie, mate?'

'I don't do ties. I'm going for the laid-back too-loaded-to-care look. Let's hope I can pull it off. God, if this was for real, my old man would die happy.' He looked at his watch. 'Hey, let's get moving. Got the catalogue?'

'Sure, it's in here,' Rob picked up a battered satchel.

'Don't be daft, you can't take that,' said Vera, and took out the property folder and put it firmly under his arm.

'Bye, girls,' said Rob, his feminist credentials slipping in the excitement.

Justin led the way down the street, doing a Monty Python Silly Walk. Rob followed suit. If they'd looked over their shoulders, they'd have seen the women laughing helplessly, leaning on each other for support.

The auction room premises were disappointingly anonymous, situated on the first floor of a modern office block. Justin expected more pomp for the exchange of such vast sums.

He walked abreast of Rob, who clutched the Kensington and Chelsea Council property catalogue. Their research had been thorough. They knew by heart the reserve and guide prices of the houses they would bid for and planned to exchange casual glances and the unstudied look of property tycoons.

They found seats with a clear view of the auctioneer, who stood at a tall desk. He was round and balding, in a tight grey suit that reminded Justin of a Latin master at school who made free with the cane. The room filled with people of all descriptions and no obvious dress code. Property developers clearly came in every guise.

'Gentlemen, please,' said the auctioneer, calling the room

to order. He ran through the nature of the sales, all Local Authority properties ripe for renovation.

'Gentrification,' Rob whispered in Justin's ear. When the bidding opened, Justin felt his chest tighten and saw beads of sweat gathering on Rob's forehead.

'Property number one in your catalogue, gentlemen. A beautiful Victorian home with five bedrooms and a large garden with planning permission. It has enormous potential. Starting at thirty thousand pounds, do I have an offer?

'Yes, the gentleman at the back at thirty thousand, can anyone offer me forty, forty thousand pounds, gentlemen, do we have an offer for forty thousand in the room, yes, we do, the gentleman here in blue at forty...'

Mesmerized by the rhythm of the bidding, Justin heard fifty, sixty, seventy thousand pounds, well over the guide price, and he raised a finger at the next hike.

'Yes, I have seventy five from the gentleman in the leather jacket, any advance on seventy five, I see eighty thousand, eighty thousand to the gentleman at the back...' His voice went up half an octave. 'Ninety five, yes, for property number one I have ninety five from the bidder on my right,' which was Justin, who winced as Rob stamped on his foot.

'The gentleman there at the back again, at a hundred thousand.' The auctioneer's face was pink from exertion. 'Property number one at one *hundred* thousand pounds, going, going, gone!' He cracked the gavel to break the spell and there was a collective exhalation of breath.

Justin's eyes darted to Rob, who raised a nonchalant eyebrow, then pretended to study the catalogue, which quivered in his hands. A rush of adrenalin masked his fear, like being at the races with Pa on a winning streak.

They didn't bid on the smaller properties but bid up as close to the limit as they dared on the larger ones and managed to duck out in the nick of time. By mid-morning they'd doubled the guide price of five properties to the tune of half a million.

The auctioneer cracked the gavel to make an announcement. 'Gentlemen, the auction is hereby suspended as I suspect foul play. Would the gentlemen on my right care to identify themselves?'

Justin jumped to his feet with raised fist, shouting, 'Down with capitalist exploitation of property!' They both headed through the door before security staff could stop them. Justin's heart raced as they hurtled downstairs and Rob still clung to the catalogue.

'Keep moving,' Justin said, as they hit the street, and they didn't break stride till they reached the Underground.

'Christ, I was having an effing heart attack there,' Justin said as they juddered to a halt on the platform. They watched the tail-lights of a train being sucked into the tunnel, followed by a draft of sooty air. Justin cleared his throat. 'Want a smoke?' Justin offered his cigarettes.

'American shite!' Rob said, seeing the packet of *Marlboroughs*.

'Better than French shite,' Justin responded, and they both guffawed.

'It's addictive, isn't it?' Justin said, meaning money and power.

Rob spoke over the sound of the approaching train. 'It comes to them naturally, owning capital and making it work for them.'

'And we made monkeys out of them!' Justin said, feeling invincible.

Stephen had chortled at his account of the foray into property dealing, and said it would play well in a piece framed by darkness and light.

He still wondered at his own motives at the time. Would he have been so gung-ho if Sofia hadn't recruited him? The phrase *horizontal recruitment* was uncomfortably apt. Her previous bloke had been ditched over political betrayal, there was no other kind, and he eventually became a Labour councillor. What if Sofia had been called to Paris sooner by 'her people' as she called them? Would he have stayed with *The People's Militia* in London, while she carried on the revolution there? Unlikely, he had to admit. His commitment had been contingent on his infatuation with Sofia, and once deserted, disillusion set in.

Sanjay was doing things differently. His love for Farida had let her fly free, so strong were their shared beliefs. What had he said? 'This isn't about you anymore, Dad,' and the germ of an idea came fully formed, though he didn't know where it would go.

Chapter 15

'It's me, Pa. You okay?'

'What's up? You never call in the morning.' Pa didn't like being taken off guard.

'I'm fine. Just thinking of Ma.' It was the anniversary of the day she died and for once, Justin had remembered.

'Good woman, your mother. The best. Can't believe I lost her so soon.'

Ma was sealed into the folds of their lives like an ammonite created from a collage of memories. It was striking how differently they remembered her.

'She was a great letter writer,' Justin offered. 'I was the envy of boys at school when I got five or six pages from home. Did you ever write to each other?'

'Never had occasion to,' Pa said, wistfully, and Justin recalled his painstaking penmanship in the factory ledgers. He and Pa had never written to each other and Ma would sign letters from them both.

What he remembered was Ma peeling and chopping potatoes while listening to the wireless and Molly chattering at her side, while he did his homework at the kitchen table. He conjured the sharp winter evenings when the stove blazed and sheets hung damply on the rack above and he breathed in the sweetness of fresh laundry.

'Molly coming over later?' he asked, knowing she would be.

'Yes, after work. You joining us?'

'Not this time, Pa.' It was a ritual he always avoided. 'I'll be working late at the office sorting out the merger with the Business School; I mentioned it, remember? Looks like I'll be out of a job by the end. Bit of a bumpy patch, to be honest.'

'I hope they're paying you redundancy. I had to work till I was seventy.'

'Unlikely. Let's say I'm leaving before I'm pushed.'

'Like that is it? I'm sorry to hear it, son.'

The expression of genuine concern left him winded. 'Thanks, Pa,' he managed.

It was what Ma would have wanted, for them to be reconciled. Or maybe the old fellow was going soft on the hormones he took for his prostate.

'I'll be seeing more of you, then?' Pa went on.

'Yes, we should do more together,' Justin said, with a pang of remorse for his churlishness. 'Make use of that National Trust Membership of yours, come spring.' Pa was a lifetime member—he did nothing by halves.

'I'll say hello to Molly. She'll be here by six.' Which meant, we'll be thinking of you and Ma, here in spirit.

'Thanks, Pa. I'll think of you too. Speak soon.'

He wouldn't be at the office today, as he'd woken with limbs like lead, a blinding headache and a throat rough as sandpaper. Harpreet had already left for an early meeting. He'd emailed to cancel a couple of supervision sessions, his only appointments, and planned a day at home.

The weather was foul, a ghastly storm raging, and he sat at the kitchen table in his dressing-gown with a freshly brewed pot of coffee to catch up on last weekend's papers.

MPs vote 397/223 to authorise UK airstrikes against IS in Syria

Debate in Parliament about letting Donald Trump enter the UK after his statement on barring Muslims from the US

Lately, he was seeing the world refracted through the war in Syria. He still couldn't endorse the bombing, despite his efforts. IS had to be pushed back, Sanjay would remind him, and Islamophobia was central to the playbook of the likes of Trump. In his most lurid imaginings, he could never have foreseen that the maverick politician would be invited as president, to be feted and dazzled by royal bling in the interests of the "special relationship".

He took a slug of black coffee, felt revived and repeated

the dose. Flicking to the centre pages he lighted on reports of flooding in Cumbria and evacuations: Storm Desmond had hit hard. Those poor people were still reeling from Storm Abigail—what was the world coming to? Appeasing the gods of nature by banning free plastic bags wouldn't cut it. He flicked on to read that combat roles were now open to women in the US army, and thought how this held a totally different social and political meaning to the participation of women soldiers in Rojava. He earmarked it as a promising topic for a future seminar.

Reaching for a jar of stubby pencils, he turned to the Sudoku at the back of the paper. Like physical jerks, it stretched his mind and provided an excuse to put things off, *things left undone*, as Ma would have said, pricking his conscience. He was able to ignore the battering wind until the squares of the puzzle were pleasingly filled with numbers. He shivered and went to switch on the All Day heating, and made a mental note to follow up on installing solar panels, however hideous.

Enough of malingering, it was time for the hot-shower treatment. He took the stairs two at a time in a surge of energy that blotted out the pile of marking and the plague of emails that awaited.

Rob and Gilles were easily spotted, sitting in a wood-panelled nook in the pub. As he neared them, Justin heard them speaking French. After introductions and handshakes, he asked if they could continue in the vernacular.

Gilles looked puzzled.

'Il ne parle pas français,' Rob explained, and Gilles said of course, my friend. His smile displayed crowded teeth and his face had a lived-in look, with laughter lines.

'Pints all round?' Justin offered.

'Thanks mate.' Rob answered for them both.

'After, I'll tell you what this meeting is about,' said Gilles.

Justin returned with a tray of frothy beers and set the glasses on the table. Gilles reached out, relaxed and unhurried. 'Tell me about yourself, Justin. What brings you to this point?' He paused and clarified, 'I mean, to the revolution. What is your journey until now?'

'Oh, you know, a northern middle-class boy escaping his origins. I studied Sociology and began to understand why I hated working in my father's factory.'

Gilles smiled encouragement. 'It interests me. Go on.'

'I explored various political groups and then met Sofia, Rob and the others and saw it was possible to build a completely new society. No point tinkering with a broken system.'

'This is true. Your Irish struggle still continues and we must act against this new law...'

'Internment, that's imprisonment without trial,' Rob supplied.

Justin nodded, recalling the "supplies" Rob had smuggled in his rucksack, along with a cargo of cheese, peaches and wine, in red and white *Monoprix* bags. When Justin had objected to the explosives, Rob said, cool it, I'm dropping them off at the locker.

Bert at work, had started a whip-round for the families driven out of their homes after a round-up of nationalists. Said his Da had had fought for independence after the Great War. He'd clammed up after, claiming that Irish meant terrorist over here.

Gilles talked about the barricades in '68 when folk came out to give food, and rags soaked in sugar-water which served as tear-gas masks. A workman had shown him how to use a pneumatic drill to dig up the cobblestones, used as ammunition. They'd battled nightly with the CRS, the riot police, who finally pulled back.

'We won concessions but not enough...' Gilles took a mouthful of beer and pulled a face. 'Your beer is like piss, *pardon, mais c'est vrai.'*

'You were saying,' Justin prompted.

'Strikes spread like lightning and soon there were ten million workers from factories, shipyards and hospitals out on strike or they'd taken control of their factories. Even farmers showed solidarity with tractors in the streets.'

'It was as if a dam had burst!' said Rob, pulling off his cap to give his scalp a vigorous scratch.

Gilles patted his pockets. '*T'as une clope?*' he asked Rob.

Rob fumbled for a packet of fags and offered them round. Gilles flicked a lighter between nicotine-stained fingers and they all lit up.

After a long inhalation, he sat back. '*C'était un festival, un raz-de-marée, la révolution en fait.'*

Rob took up the story. 'De Gaulle tried to quell it by appealing to *La Patrie*, but street fighting carried on. The crowd set fire to *La Bourse*, that's the Stock Exchange.'

'At Renault where I work,' said Gilles, 'they chanted for a People's Government. By then, we wanted more than better wages, we wanted to take control of our lives.'

A silence fell between them, as if imagining what might have been. It was only three years ago but far more remote. Justin knew the rest of the story as Rob told it. The French Communist Party and CGT Union worked with Prime Minister Pompidou to end the strike in return for miserly concessions. Slogans were daubed on walls: *Ce n'est pas fini.* There had to be hope.

'Tell him how close it came, when De Gaulle went to Germany,' Rob said.

Gilles inhaled until his eyes watered. 'De Gaulle went on a secret mission to rally support. The ruling class thought it really was the end for them. You won't read that in the capitalist press.'

'Why Germany?' Justin asked, mystified.

'To meet General Massau, the commander of the French

troops who was based there. And De Gaulle got what he wanted. Massau agreed to march on Paris, if necessary. He returned and warned the people of the danger of a communist dictatorship, and cried, *Sauvez La Patrie!* He called a general election, troops were mobilised and tanks appeared on the Paris ring-road. It was serious.'

'So, what went wrong?' Justin asked, frustrated.

'A problem of leadership, comrade. The Communist Party had no intention of seizing power and the revolutionary moment slipped away. The Communists sold us out. The Gaullists won the election. *La vieille France*, old France as they say, came to the rescue.'

'Otherwise De Gaulle would have presided over a military dictatorship?' Justin whistled in amazement.

'It's not so surprising. Collaborators from the Vichy regime are still in government. It isn't a big step.' Gilles shrugged, as only a Frenchman can. 'For us, the struggle continues. But you can help keep the flame alive, comrade. Are you with us?'

Justin felt a thrill, heady as falling in love. 'Yes, I'm with you, comrade.'

Rob gave a rare and lovely smile. Justin would take over from him as go-between, fielding calls from phone-boxes at pre-arranged times.

'Will I have to make collections from Paris?' he asked, hoping it wasn't so.

'No, I'll still do that,' Rob reassured. 'And don't tell the others. We have to keep operations in silos in case anyone is caught.'

'You already have a comrade in prison, so you know the risks,' Gilles reinforced.

Justin nodded, his brow creased. 'Will we meet again?'

Gilles fixed him with intense blue eyes. 'Perhaps, comrade, but it's not important.' This power-pack of a man stood up and gave him a manly hug, and said, *'Venceremos,* comrade, and welcome.'

PRESS RELEASE 4

Thousands made homeless, 24 dead, over 300 interned without trial in the six occupied counties of Ireland. This is the true face of British Imperialism. Don't be fooled by the army recruitment campaign. If you join, you'll be trained in Belfast, Derry and other working-class ghettoes to murder and brutalize ordinary people. Next, troops will be sent to Clydeside, Merseyside, Tyneside, Birmingham and London, and other working-class districts throughout Britain. Which way will you point your gun, when the officers order you to shoot against the people of your own town?

Don't join the gunmen in khaki. This war of terror is carried out by the boss class.

Not in our name.

The Angry Brigade Moonlighters' Cell

Justin's confidence in Rob's leadership was already wearing thin and the pub meeting was a tipping point. It wasn't just the business of Max's defence campaign, but Rob's stubbornness. He had an irritating habit of knocking twice on a surface before raising an objection. He did this when Justin proposed they should have cover-stories in the event of arrest.

Rob tap-tapped. 'No Comment is our position, or the bastards will tug at the corner of a web of deceit and unravel the lot.'

'It's harder to be criminalised if we present as regular activists,' Justin argued. 'The Feminist Collective is a cover for the women, I'm doing Trade Union work, and you're active in the Claimants' Union. Callum, well, he's a bit of an all-rounder. Better keep quiet about the bookstall.'

It was stalemate, Rob sidestepped the issue and said Justin was over-worrying. Everything changed after he met

Gilles, who gave shape to his revolutionary longings. He'd often wondered whether history would have been different had he got out in time.

The tape-machine clicked on. 'For the record, this is Detective Inspector Havering interviewing Justin Caffrey on 17th August 1971 at seven thirty a.m.'

Bleary-eyed, Justin looked up after a sleepless night in the cells. He felt for his watch, then remembered it had been confiscated.

'I'm expected home for breakfast; let's make this snappy,' Havering said.

Justin glanced round the interview room, no more than a cubicle, and ran his tongue over furred teeth. He'd been over to Rob's place after Vera had taken off for Wales. Just for a week, she'd said, for headspace.

When Rob didn't answer the street-level bell, he assumed it was broken and walked up the two steep flights to the bedsit. He should have smelled a rat when he saw the door wide open. A man was slumped asleep in a chair and he heard the electric crackles of what sounded like a badly tuned transistor radio. At the squat, the slumberer could have been a comrade passing through, overnighting before a demo or rally. But the clothes were wrong.

It happened in a split second. The man jerked awake and sprang to his feet, quick to recover himself. 'Who are you?' he rasped, and by now Justin had figured he was a cop.

'I've come to see a mate,' he replied, weighing up his chances of making it down the fire-escape. Too late for that.

'What is your name?' the cop enunciated, as if addressing an imbecile.

'Justin Caffrey. Like I said, I'm just visiting. What's up? Where's Rob?' He decided to play the innocent, heart racing.

'He's helping us with our enquiries,' the cop said with a sneer, 'and I reckon there's a thing or two you could tell us yourself.'

There was another crackle on the police radio and heavy footsteps mounting the stairs. Two uniformed men appeared in the doorway. One looked like a schoolboy.

'About bloody time,' said the one caught napping. 'Take him down to the station.'

That was yesterday. Now he was starving as well as pissed off.

'Now then, Justin, may I call you that? No need for introductions as we've already met. We've found a quantity of explosives, and it would help us greatly if you could identify them.' The D.I.'s gnarled fingers fumbled inside a grey folder, pulling out a large photograph he placed carefully between them. 'For the benefit of the tape, I'm presenting the suspect with item A.'

'Christ, what's that?' Justin said, shocked. He'd never seen so many sticks of gelignite.

'Don't feign surprise. I'm willing to bet you've seen something of the sort before. You told me yourself, you believed in violence to bring down the state.'

'I did not. Those were your words.' He knew this would be a cat and mouse game. 'I demand to see my solicitor, it's my right.'

'Of course, far be it from the police to deny you your rights, sonny Jim. This is just an informal chat.' He switched off the tape-machine. 'Is that better?'

It felt like a well-practised trick to lure him into letting down his guard. 'Does my girlfriend know I'm here?'

'She does.' The detective tapped the photo with a thick finger. 'This is what we found in a locker at Victoria Station. We know you recently met a Frenchman who calls himself Gilles. If I told you he was wanted for murder, would that surprise you?'

Justin's brain went into overdrive as he sifted fact from

fiction. Was there an undercover cop at the pub that night? They'd sat in a secluded corner, so there was no way they'd been overheard, unless there was a wiretap under the table. The cops knew about the locker, but there was nothing to connect either him or Rob to the drop-off arrangements made over the phone. The stash of explosives could be fake, to make him panic. The murder charge against Gilles pure fiction, unless he was mixed up with the German Red Army Faction.

Havering was trying to extract a confession based on tenuous leads, and most likely trumped-up evidence. The pile of gelignite was a lure and he wouldn't fall for it.

'I don't know anything about this,' he said, pushing back the photo. He wasn't even going to admit he knew what it was.

Havering sat back and softened his gaze. Justin was acutely aware that the man already knew too much about his personal life, making him vulnerable. The attack, when it came, hit him in a different spot. 'We have your comrades in custody, all of them, including your girlfriend. Some of them are being remarkably cooperative.'

Was this true, even Vera? He felt ice down his spine. 'As I said, I want a solicitor.'

Havering's head tilted, which in a different setting, could have passed for a look of paternal interest. 'How's your friend Max? I believe you've been to visit him six times since he's been in custody.' He leaned over and consulted a document from the open folder. 'And your friends have attended the court hearings in Barnet. Max has vociferous support.'

A reminder that they were being watched. Rob had predicted that Havering's team would be liaising closely with the Bomb Squad who'd have a Special Branch man on board, so information would easily change hands. The comrades had assumed that Max's visitors would be logged, and it was becoming clear a detailed dossier was being compiled on people's movements and affiliations.

'Yes, Max's friends know he's been framed, and we'll fight for justice.'

The sly smile on Havering's face made him instantly regret being drawn.

Havering switched the tape back on. 'For the record, I am showing the suspect item B.' He pulled out another photo from the grey folder, placing it next to the first. It showed a table laid out with a canvas bag, two automatic guns and a pistol. There were also three cartridges. He played with the biro behind his ear. 'Recognise these?'

Justin said, 'Fuck no.' Sweat ran down the side of his face.

'Just in case you didn't know,' Havering said with an edge of sarcasm, 'here we have two sub-machine guns—a Sten and a Beretta—and a Star automatic pistol. We know for a fact the Beretta was used in the attack on the American Embassy. Ballistics have confirmed a match. That puts your girlfriend in the frame, given her connections.'

The interview had switched to super-formal and if he put a foot wrong, they'd all be in the shit. The cops were within spitting distance of piecing together vital information. He breathed deeply to stop himself from passing out. 'I know nothing about these weapons. They are nothing to do with me.'

'You're looking peaky, Justin.' Havering got up and opened the door. He had a word with someone outside and two glasses of water appeared. Settled back in his chair, he said, 'I think you *do* know about the weapons, Justin. We found the arsenal at your friend's bedsit. Robert Rigby kept them under his bed and in the wardrobe. Almost unbelievable, isn't it? But true. And I accept you may not be fully conversant with the full picture, so to speak, you're a new boy after all, but you ought to know what you've got yourself into.' He pushed forward the photo. 'Whoever's charged is looking at a very long sentence once we've ironed out some minor details. Interpol is on the case, needless to say.

'Robert Rigby went to Paris recently, as we both know. I'm sure you're aware he brought back explosives, even if you won't admit it. Don't dig yourself any deeper, Justin. I suspect you're being used in a much bigger game and it's time to quit. Difficult, I know, with your girlfriend involved. You're a man of principle in your own way, very loyal, particularly to Max Scott. But you need to call time on this before it's too late. Your solicitor will advise you, I'm sure.' He gave a complicit smile.

Draining his glass, Justin said, 'You've got nothing on Max Scott, it's all hearsay…'

'That's where you're wrong,' Havering cut in. 'The trial date will be announced tomorrow. If you're so sure he's innocent, perhaps you could name the culprits? We know full well he didn't act alone.'

Justin felt the bile of anger rise in his throat. 'Let me be completely clear: I won't condemn the explosions that you've pinned on Max, and as far as I know, a man can't be jailed for his opinions.'

'Ah, as opposed to the dodgy regimes you support, where people are locked up for their political views? In England there's no such thing as the thought police, or political crime for that matter. Rest assured, we *will* find out who carried out these crimes, and in the meantime Max Scott is likely to go down for a string of them.'

Justin grappled with the improbable notion of a weapons arsenal in Rob's wardrobe. It was ridiculous. Of course, Rob wouldn't be so stupid, the police must have found a way of planting the stuff when the flat was empty, and the scale of weaponry was far beyond anything they'd handled. Unless this was linked to a deal with the 1st of May Group. It was possible they required weapons to be stored and distributed in exchange for gelignite, and Rob had agreed to it.

'Thank you, Justin,' Havering said, standing and tucking the folder under his arm. 'You've been a great help. It's often the case that what a person doesn't say gives away more than what he says. You're free to go, lad, I won't detain you longer.' He looked at his watch. 'The time is eight twenty-two a.m. and this interview is terminated,' and clicked off the recorder.

Justin watched as Havering lumbered unsteadily out of the room with the sway of a man whose hips are awry.

He blinked in the early morning light and put his wristwatch back on. His first port of call would be the Law Centre, to move heaven and earth to get the others released.

Chapter 16

Today was the second meeting at HMP Brixton to prepare the defence for Rob, Callum and Jess. The comrades on the outside would act as *McKenzie Friends*, an informal legal back-up team. The charges were grave: possession of weapons and conspiracy to cause explosions.

Vera hadn't been detained, as D.I. Havering claimed, but returned from Wales a woman reborn, fired up by the campaign. The three women huddled on one side of the Formica-topped table and the men sat opposite. A male and a female officer perched on stools in a corner of the windowless room.

Justin took the lead. In fact since Rob's arrest, he'd been finding his feet. He was at pains to observe a formality, partly due to the presence of the screws, and because there was a lot to be covered in the brief time allowed. 'We need to lay the ground-rules for our defence, assuming this goes to the Old Bailey.' He had their attention. 'First, we'll challenge the Jury and demand to be judged by our peers. It worked for the *Mangrove Nine* and we can learn from them. We need to draw up a list of questions with yes or no answers to minimise the risk of a hostile jury. Okay, go ahead, Jess,' he said, as she raised a finger to speak.

'How about, *Are you a member of the Conservative Party?*'

'Yup,' Justin said, noting it down.

'*Do you have relatives in the Army in Northern Ireland?*' Callum offered.

'Brilliant, Cal,' said Rob. 'Add to that, *Are you associated in any way with the Police?*'

'Now we're cooking with gas,' Justin said, scribbling. 'Anything that covers the economic side of things?'

'*Have you ever lived on Social Security?*' Sofia offered.

'Also, *Do you consider yourself working-class?*' Justin said, still taking notes. He looked up at Vera.

'How about, *Are you against anarchism?* It would be an opening to demystify the term.'

'Nice one, sister.' Justin glanced at his watch. 'Anything else before I run through the guidelines?'

Jess spoke up. 'There's been some vicious coverage in the Press, like, *drop-outs with brains try to launch bloody revolution*, which would prejudice any jury. I propose we apply for the whole thing to be postponed and get bailed in the meantime.'

Callum looked amused. 'Cool idea, babe, but zero chance the judge will agree to it.'

'It's a neat idea and puts us in the driving seat,' Sofia countered, leaning in. 'We should also complain that we've been refused access to key documents on the grounds of so-called public interest, which means the interests of the prosecution, in this case. And while you guys are on remand, it's hard for us to get our act together. It's against natural justice.'

'That's right,' Jess agreed. 'And if the judge refuses to postpone, the jury will see him as unreasonable. They probably won't want to be there anyway.'

Justin felt the three women eyeballing him across the table. 'Okay, we'll apply for a postponement and also take on board Sofia's point.

'Moving on, we must see the court as a place like any other, where we act collectively. They'll use the law to intimidate, to try and isolate us from each other. We're pleading Not Guilty, not begging for forgiveness. The central plank of our defence is to challenge the prosecution's attempt to put us on trial for our beliefs. We'll paint a picture of our everyday lives and values in a way the jury can relate to; helping claimants, standing up for women who suffer domestic violence, fighting landlordism, and remember, the jury will be mostly council or private tenants, they'll get it…'

His flow was interrupted by the distant jangling of keys, a

warning that the meeting was about to be cut short. Rob and Vera leapt up spontaneously and fell into each other's arms and Jess and Callum were kissing like crazy. The screws yelled, 'Cut it out!' before the door burst open and more screws filled the cramped space.

The couples released each other and laughed and laughed, turning to wave as they were led away. Rob and Callum would be taken to the wing and Jess escorted to Holloway; Justin's heart clenched with sadness to see them go.

He sat back in the chair in front of what had once been Rob's desk. Research for the trial and attending court had taken over his life and building-site days were a distant horizon. He bumped into Carlson on the Portobello Road occasionally, who said the men often talked about him and followed the case in the Evening Standard. The flats had now reached fifth floor level and there was overtime to be had at weekends. Somehow, the easy rapport they'd had at work didn't translate to home-turf and neither of them suggested meeting for a drink. They bumped fists on parting and Justin hoped Carlson would give him a favourable report in the hut over the early-morning brew.

Sofia had landed a well-paid job, so money wasn't an issue. She was giving evening classes at a Spanish investment bank in anticipation of Britain joining Europe. They both enjoyed the irony of bankers being taught by a libertarian socialist and Justin was happy she no longer stripped for life-drawing classes.

The trial at the Old Bailey started the year following their arrest, after months of legal wrangling. *The Notting Hill Three* were a *cause célèbre*, not least because it had become the longest running trial. They'd got to know the Jury, endlessly second-guessing their reactions. It was a solid bench after dispensing with a stream of candidates, including the man holding a bowler hat and carrying the *Financial Times* under one arm. There were seven men and five women and an age-span from mid-twenties to early sixties and two of the jurors were Black. They'd weeded out a policeman's wife, an ex-squaddie, and accepted three people who'd been on Benefits even though they didn't agree with anarchism or communism. You couldn't have everything.

Rob was a star, running rings round the Prosecution by discrediting the evidence on the arsenal found in his bedsit. He'd cross-examined police-witnesses to show they'd had opportunity to plant the weapons in the time he'd spent in the toilet before being taken down to the police-car. There were also no fingerprints on the guns or explosives. He'd said privately to Justin that the place was used as a temporary cache by a group under Gilles' command. As Justin had suspected, when Rob had made the deal with Gilles on supplying explosives it came with the territory. Gilles hadn't been charged with murder, but it was a relief to know the links with him were finally severed.

For months, Justin's job had been to source documents, find witnesses, and keep up morale. He acted as Rob's McKenzie friend, while Sofia and Vera supported Callum and Jess respectively. Vera had turned up trumps on the investigation. A key piece of evidence against Jess was a pair of gloves with traces of gelignite, found in her jeans pockets. Jess had never carried explosives, so this was definitely a plant. Vera's persistence gained her access to the jeans in question and when examined it turned out that they *had* no pockets, so the evidence was blown sky-high. It made the police look inept if not downright dishonest.

In the quiet of the afternoon, Justin leafed through his folder to capture the sweep of events that otherwise felt random and disordered. He stopped at an article torn out from *Time Out* magazine, held in place with a paperclip.

…long-haired men and women in jeans bring a freshness into the

stuffy court. Quite a contrast with the cut-glass lawyers and shifty Special Branch types, hanging about in the lobby. It is clear from the word go that this trial will break with convention. Potential jurors are quizzed for their social and political affiliations until "The Notting Hill Three" get the Jury they want.

Against a backdrop of charges of conspiracy to cause explosions and possession of weapons, the defendants argue they are on trial for their beliefs and that there is a conspiracy by the state to convict by any means necessary. On the walls of the Old Bailey itself, Whose Conspiracy? has been daubed in white paint. In a supercharged atmosphere in the highest court of the land, this trial promises high drama and surprise twists and turns. A Comedy of Errors *or* Much Ado About Nothing? *Watch this space.*

It cheered him to read an up-beat perspective and helped calm his fears as the day approached when the comrades would make their final speeches in court.

They'd refuted the evidence dragged up from articles comrades wrote in the underground press on the Industrial Relations Act, the Fair Rents Act, the *Miss World Contest,* the law on Internment, and associated political targets.

They'd dealt head-on with the charges of twenty-five bombings between 1968 and 1971, which had been claimed by groups as diverse as the 1st of May group, the *People's Militia, The Wild Bunch* and *Butch Cassidy and the Sundance Kid.* Okay, some groups had taken the piss, but that was the point.

After six months in court it was time to make an honest assessment of the likely outcome. What were their chances? Justin took comfort in the fact that the *Mangrove Nine* were eventually cleared of the most serious charge of incitement to riot. He'd learned since, that the police had considered deportation as an alternative under the new immigration law. The *Nine* had faced down the establishment and their strategy paid off. He wasn't convinced that the *Notting Hill*

Three would fare as well. They may have won the political battle, but waging war on the state wouldn't go unpunished.

He flipped to the start of the folder, where he'd kept a record of the Judge's opening address:

Now, members of the Jury, it is my task to tell you what this case is about. The allegation is that these three defendants, calling themselves revolutionaries and anarchists, under various names, sought to disrupt and attack the democratic society of this country with whose structure and politics they apparently disagree. To disrupt it by a wave of violent attacks over quite a lengthy period; that is, by causing explosions aimed at the property of those whom they considered to be their political or social opponents. They have all entered Not Guilty pleas and it is your task to determine the truth.

The transcripts of the speeches and statements he'd obtained during the course of the trial had proved invaluable as the weeks turned into months, recording the unfolding story in a dystopian reality.

Sofia popped her head round the door. 'Leave it Jus. You've done all you can.'

He couldn't help feeling he should have done more, including for Max, whose appeal depended on the verdict. Max had been in touch with news about Daisy and their growing relationship and Justin had promised to visit him in Full Sutton once the case was over.

He hadn't been home last Christmas as he'd half-promised, but phoned Ma occasionally to show he was still alive. She hadn't been herself, and it wasn't her nerves this time. Molly had dropped him a line to say Ma was sicker than she let on and he'd better visit soon. That was almost a year since.

Sofia crossed the room and ruffled his hair, and he looked up in surprise. There'd been a cooling-off between them and he'd supposed it was stress, until he found she'd been in touch with Gilles. It's political, she'd said, brushing it off. Why didn't you tell me? he'd asked, not unreasonably. You know the rules, she'd said, Intel is on a need to know basis. And you've taken against Gilles after what Rob said about the explosives found in his bedsit. Too right, he'd retorted, I'm amazed you want anything to do with him.

They'd left it at that, there was so much else going on, but now he knew the question of Gilles had to be dealt with.

'I can guess what you're thinking,' she said. 'Let's talk about what we both want after the trial.' She'd insinuated herself into his lap. 'How long can we carry on like this?'

This was typical. She'd ask a question to leave him guessing, and get annoyed if he guessed wrong. The worst thing to ask was, What d'you mean? He opted for saying how he felt.

'What do I want? I'd like a break, to be frank. A holiday. Time to absorb what we've been through these past couple of years.' She wanted to hear that he was battle-ready, he knew that. Anything less, and there'd be no room for him in her life. He felt her body stiffen.

'Sounds like you've got doubts,' she said, her hair coppery in a stripe of slanting sunlight.

'Not really,' he said, equivocating. She'd once accused him of wearing his principles lightly, and it had hurt. 'I'll find a job, maybe teach. Get some money together and we could go abroad for a bit?' It was his way of asking if they had a future.

'Maybe. I've had enough of teaching city-types and I'd like to go to Paris.'

'Has this got anything to do with Gilles, by any chance? And I don't mean politics.'

She got up from his lap and walked to the window. 'You know the two are one and the same for me. I can't be involved with anyone who isn't a hundred percent for the revolution. I'm fond of you, Justin, but I'm not sure you've got the stamina.'

'*Fond* of me? Jeez, Sof, is that the best you can do? Is this you letting me down gently?' His heart burst out of his chest.

She wouldn't answer. 'If the comrades go down, it's just a setback, Justin. The road to revolution isn't straight and its rules aren't written on tablets of stone. Once this is over, we take stock and plan the next stage in the struggle.'

His stomach hollowed as she spoke. He saw she'd already steeled herself against the worst and wore the revolution like a shield to protect herself against her own vulnerability. He'd seen this brittleness before and been able to reach past it, but now he wasn't sure.

When they had sex that night it was fierce and desperate as if they both knew something was irredeemably broken. The next morning he woke with a tingling anxiety that reached to the ends of his fingertips. He would have to dig deep to rally the comrades in these final days in court before attending to his own wounds.

Chapter 17

'What's up, son?' Sanjay looked as though he'd been punched in the vitals.

'I dunno. Guess I'm worried about Farida.' Justin watched his son flick on the kettle and crack open a bag of coffee, releasing a cloud of caffeine. His gestures were slow and deliberate.

'The risks seemed abstract at first, but she's been telling me stuff that scares the shit out of me.'

Justin thought of Sofia and the appalling risks she took for the 1st of May group, fearless and reckless. What Sofia and Farida had in common was total commitment to a cause. He recognised in Sanjay the dawning realisation that he'd always play second fiddle to Farida's passionate engagement, and he was hurting.

'Don't underestimate what your love means to her, even more so from afar. Remember she'll be surrounded by people with several years of combat under their belt who'll look out for her,' he tried to reassure.

'If she's killed, I'll be destroyed.' Sanjay's face crumpled as he poured hot water onto the coffee.

Justin went to his side. 'I didn't exactly raise the flag when you told me about Farida going to Syria,' he said, an arm round Sanjay's shoulder. 'You've convinced me otherwise. Mum and I think she's a fine young woman and we'll do anything we can to help,' he said, unsure of what that meant.

'Thanks, Dad.' Sanjay brushed tears away with a sleeve. They headed to the kitchen table with mugs and coffee pot, where time was marked by decades of family meals. The thought put him in mind of a lifestyle guru who asked an audience how many weeks they estimated remained to them on earth. He did his own rapid calculation; if he lived to his mid-eighties it was just over a thousand, which brought him up short. He'd noticed that young people doubted they'd survive their natural lifespan if economic collapse and climate disaster prevailed. There was an urgency to their concerns which he'd once felt, without today's generation's fear of extinction. Among his students there were women who declared they'd never bring children into this world, and others who became frenetic activists as though their days were numbered, which was the guru's point.

'What's this she's been telling you, then?' he asked, and waited for an unburdening.

'There's an association in Kobani that supports families bereaved by war. Farida spent a day with them, visiting homes and talking about their loved ones. What got to her was seeing the family of a YPJ fighter who's end was beyond shocking. ISIS took her body and publicly beheaded her, making a video as a warning to female fighters. Farida said she sat holding the hands of family members and looked at photographs while the family talked about her. "She's even more precious to us now than she was before," a friend and comrade said, who came to mourn. The saddest sight was a little girl sitting stone-faced in a corner, so traumatised by what she'd seen she'd become mute. These aren't things you'll read in her blog, but she has to share the horrors with someone.'

'And that someone is you,' said Justin, meeting Sanjay's eye.

Sanjay nodded. 'All I can do is listen and it leaves me feeling heavy and sad.'

Justin stared into space in the silence that followed; coils of memory unfurled, bringing back the old fear that Sofia wouldn't return, the not knowing.

'War is like that,' he said eventually. 'The big beasts of the world broker the lives of the little people, and just sometimes the little people fight back. That's what's impressive about the SDF, the Syrian Democratic Forces.'

'You know about them?'

'I've been doing my homework.'

'They only formed a couple of months back. It was a re-branding exercise to placate the Turkish government and allowed the US to become involved. It's actually led by Kurdish militias though Arab groups are involved. That's what I was telling you about the YPG, they're tactical in their alliances.'

'And they're deeply embedded in their communities. In my day, we convinced ourselves we were in the vanguard, which we definitely weren't.'

'Did you doubt yourself ? Were you ever scared?' Sanjay asked, brown eyes glistening.

'I was scared I'd blow myself up, I was that cack-handed,' Justin said, in self-mockery. 'And yes, I had moments of doubt. When I argued for my beliefs with my builder workmates, it was clear our group was isolated and hid behind imagined certainties. We believed a wave of strikes and social unrest would shake down the establishment and our actions would help tip things over the edge. When the revolution is a living reality as in northern Syria, theory informs practice and vice versa. I don't think any of us truly believed we were about to overthrow capitalism. I guess Max was the only one with his feet firmly on the ground in all that turmoil.'

Sanjay looked quizzical. 'You haven't spoken about him much.'

'I've read his memoirs, at least excerpts Stephen sent me. He realised too late we were a bunch of amateurs, though he's remarkably forgiving on that score. I'm shocked at the violence he describes in prison, the bullying and punishments meted out by fellow inmates. He kept his head down in Brixton, but in Full Sutton it was another story. His saving grace was studying for an Open University degree and working in the library. The villains still got to him and threatened Daisy and her children if he didn't play their game. He refused and they broke his jaw.'

'For what?'

'They wanted Daisy to bring in drugs and he wouldn't hear of it. He was above suspicion, you see, so it would have been easy. He told Daisy to stop coming until things settled and anyway, he didn't want her to see him in that state. Max was the most principled man I ever knew.'

Sanjay frowned and scratched his three-day stubble, which Justin had noticed earlier. 'You going for the rugged look?' he asked, amused.

'Don't tell Mum or she'll take the piss,' he said with a lopsided smile.

Justin grinned. 'It suits you! By the way, how's it going with Stephen? Is he still up for doing a film about Rojava?'

'Yes, he's read Farida's blog and says it'll be his next project.' Sanjay glowed with his usual warmth and geniality and Justin basked in the energy of his beautiful son and wondered what he'd done to deserve him.

Soon after Sanjay left the spell was broken. His phone pinged with a link from Molly:

#70sbombprofexposed

Professor Justin Caffrey lied to avoid justice sending Max Scott to jail after 70s bombing of Minister's home. Max's son Stephen seeks to clear father's name in no-holds-barred documentary.

Followed by: DON'T IGNORE THIS JUS. IT'S NOT GOING AWAY. CALL ME.

RojavaSyria Blogspot 3

Rojava (Autonomous Administration of Northern Syria), comprises three cantons and a swathe of territory along the border with Turkey. The battle for Kobani this year secured the integrity of the region, linking the daisy chain. The SDF coalition led by Kurdish forces make daily progress across the desert, liberating villages from ISIS as they go. US support from the skies has helped make this possible.

My job is to learn about the revolution before undertaking military training. It will be months before I'm ready for active service and Commander Hanife tells volunteers not to be in too much of a hurry. After my visit to the Women's Recuperation House I understood why. Everyone was under thirty, some in their late teens. Call me naïve, but I was ill-prepared for the scourge of young flesh leaving deep holes penetrated by bullets. Two women had lost a hand, another a foot, and one had half a leg blown off. This was during the siege of Kobani, which will one day be recorded as one of the worst massacres by ISIS.

'They disguised themselves as Kurdish security forces and crept in at night, shooting civilians with assault rifles and rocket propelled grenades,' one woman told me. 'They also used car bombs and suicide bombers to terrorise the people. There were many losses.'

By the end of June ISIS were driven out, and six months later the wounds of war, both internal and external, are clear to see. The Recuperation House was one of the first new buildings, rising above the surrounding rubble.

What struck me on my visit was the warmth and camaraderie between the women, and how young they are. They make light of their disabilities, determined to take up roles where they can still be of use. Later, I listened to Hanife (a nom de guerre) challenge young recruits to consider what kind of women they wanted to be. Not chained to childbearing, but embracing the freedom to create a world where women are equal with men. 'We show our love for our land through suffering,' she said. 'If we are attacked we must defend what is dear to us. ISIS are animals, they enjoy killing and beheading and leave civilians dead in the streets. They want women to be slaves. We fight against everything they stand for.'

Women preparing for a mission roll up sleeping mats and pack cooking utensils, ready to make camp. The atmosphere is gay, festive even, as the women pile into the battered grey trucks carrying

AK-47s. They wear olive-green fatigues and camouflage jackets, but nobody wears body armour or a helmet. Their confidence is infectious as they laugh and joke, belying the danger that lies ahead.

Many have faced down patriarchal pressure and taken their futures into their own hands, defying clan tradition. They are led by veteran women with an authority that is beyond question. I saw this in action when we went to a village that had recently come under attack by ISIS. Hanife approached an elderly man dressed from head to toe in white, every inch the head of the village. She spoke to him calmly and firmly and said they would secure the surrounding area. Women and children were directed to a safe house, the women first frisked for weapons. There was no question of who was in charge, Hanife's manner was completely compelling. She squatted to the level of a sobbing child and flicking back her braid, told him he mustn't be afraid.

Good news spreads fast, such as when a group of Yazidi girls held as sexual slaves by ISIS were rescued and taken to Kobani to recuperate, before being returned to their families in the Sinjar mountains.

One evening, we volunteers sat round with the women who were prepared to share their stories. Arabic was spoken for our benefit and my ear tuned in to the language. We sat cross-legged on mats and chewed sunflower seeds while sipping hot sweet tea. The young woman, who I will not name, had escaped her ISIS husband in Raqqa and got away to her mother's house. When her husband found out, she was sent to jail, which she described as a rape camp. A group of women staged an escape, preferring to risk being killed in a minefield than a living death. She'd heard about the women's militias and wanted to join them. And here she was, a year later.

The quality of listening was profound, as the room heard this woman's affliction. We bore witness to a degree of suffering that turns a human being into a thing, a level of distress and degradation that destroys the soul. 'My body was a corpse still breathing,' she said, 'it was worse than being dead.'

The yellow-bordered green shield of the YPJ came alive for me, shown alongside images of women who died in battle. The women who fight on, speak for themselves and won't be told what's good for them, they want freedom right away.

I admit I was sceptical about the omnipresence of PKK leader Abdullah Ocalan, locked up in a Turkish one-man prison for the past fifteen years. When I raise this, I'm told that the autonomous region has made his ideas its own. They are fighting for a region that goes beyond a Kurdish enclave, to include Arabs, Christians and Kurds and where Kurdish, Arabic and Syriac will be the official languages. In its constitution, women and men will have full rights before the law and women guaranteed 40% representation on all governing bodies. Much of this is already in place. I overlook the photo of a youthful moustachioed Ocalan displayed in every official space and focus on the ideas that he represents. 'A country can't be free unless the women are free,' is his central tenet. The women who teach me have taken this to their hearts.

Farida
15 December 2015
Kobani

Chapter 18

December 1972

The court smelled of beeswax and ancient dust with a fruity finish of old socks. Justin waited dry-mouthed for the comrades to be produced from the cells. Next to him were Sofia and Vera conferring in low voices.

The level of hubbub rose half an octave when the wigs and robes swept in, followed by a flock of court officials. Next came the three comrades, huddled in the dock looking more like amigos than defendants on conspiracy charges. There followed the Judge, whose person and character were indecipherable behind heavy jowls and thick spectacles. The court got to its collective feet like reluctant church goers, then sank back down once the Judge had lowered himself into his seat. The daily ritual had the effect of lulling everyone into their allotted roles. Like a medieval pageant, Justin thought, or a pantomime without the jokes.

Justin's stomach felt like the contents of a porringer. Yesterday, Callum had made his final appeal to the Jury and today it was Rob and Jess's turn.

Rob stood without notes, his face pale above his black polo-neck sweater. He turned to the Jury. 'The charges against us relate to many more incidents than those claimed by *The People's Militia*, whoever they may be. The state accuses us of bombings and shootings undertaken by groups with very different political agendas over the past three years. The Prosecution claims that it is all the work of a small and isolated gang of madmen, and women for that matter.

'Let me tell you who we really are. We are part of the revolutionary movement resisting oppression wherever it exists. We are part of a social force growing in power, energy and coherence. I spoke about the women in Kirkby defying the so-called Fair Rents Act. They are part of that movement. The marchers and strikers who resist the attacks on workers' rights, are also part of the movement. The twenty-eight protesters shot down by British soldiers for demanding an end to internment in Derry are at the heart of the revolutionary movement. We salute and honour them.

'The ruling class relies on the myth that subversive groups and troublemakers are at the root of political action and must be weeded out. During the miners' strike, Peter Haddon claimed that, *there are small but virulent minorities in our midst.* In fact there were no violent infiltrators, just the solidarity of miners fighting against dangerous conditions and miserly wages.'

Rob's passion radiated across the court room, a *tour de force* from someone with a normally muted emotional palette. Justin held his breath, riveted.

'We have described how we lived in North Kensington in the shadow of the very rich. We acted in solidarity with fellow Benefits claimants, defying attempts to humiliate us; we walked shoulder to shoulder with women, Black people and gay people who faced oppression. In this very court, you saw allies from the Gay Liberation Front belittled.

'Our work has been to shine a light on the workings of class society: to track down those who profit from slum conditions; to flush out those who use political influence in the service of corporate greed, like Freshwater, London's largest private landlord.' He pointed a warning finger at the imaginary culprits.

'The arrest and imprisonment of our comrade Max Scott is a part of a general campaign of legal repression. Every revolutionary worthy of the name must take the blame for his fate. We are not co-conspirators, but part of one and the same struggle.

'For the state, making an example of people fighting for justice matters more than smashing the so-called *People's*

Militia. The authorities must still be worried about the continued bombings, as they've assembled a large Bomb Squad. Believe me, putting us behind bars is not going to stop the wave of rebellions.

'It is for you to decide and not for anyone else. You are twelve independent people who live in the real world and you are the people with the power. I have been working together with those in the dock for a happier and more peaceful world. That is who we are. It is your decision.' Rob made his way from the stand back to his place next to Justin.

'Brilliant, mate, the Jury loved you,' Justin said, with an elbow nudge. Yesterday, Callum had also spoken well, but the Jury seemed restless. No doubt they were impatient to get back to their families after this marathon of attack and counterattack, witnessed in silence. Justin couldn't imagine what they made of it, sifting truth from lies, weighing character and motive.

Next up was Jess, looking neat and tidy in a navy trouser suit. She took the stand with a sheaf of notes and laid these out in front of her, appearing calm and collected.

'It seems to me that a whole lot of people are angry. Groups up and down the country are protesting, and we've heard D.I. Havering say that *The People's Militia* is one of these organisations. Well, not an organisation as such, but an idea or philosophy anyone can join, according to him. Which means anyone he counts as an anarchist can be lumped under the same heading and counted as a conspirator. However, since no such group or organisation has been identified in the six months we've been here, there is no basis for charging any of us for conspiring to cause explosions in its name.' She flicked back her shoulder-length hair, now unadorned with beads.

'Let me be clear. I believe politics can be pursued by argument and persuasion, and by living and working alongside people whose lives are blighted by the power structures we live under. I consider the attacks flashpoints, advance warnings of what is to come, when groups of the oppressed join to get a fair share of the cake.

'I was personally involved in disrupting the *Miss World* contest, to protest the way women are used as sex objects for the enrichment of the Mecca Leisure Group. Why does this matter to me? Because women's liberation is about claiming our rights as full human beings. Workers' rights are women's rights! We stand shoulder to shoulder.

'You've already heard about our research into the upper echelons of society. What's that all about? It's a bottom up approach, where we expose the hidden networks between banks, business and politics operating outside democratic controls. These networks have tentacles that reach downwards, in the form of Social Security files, personal debt records, lists of workers seen as troublemakers, keeping us in our place. We call it *reverse sociology*.

'We are not saboteurs of society, quite the opposite. We've been called communist, anarchist, revolutionary, all meant to discredit us. If you convict us, we are not going to change. We will still be who we are and what we believe, and I trust you to see the truth.'

She picked up her papers, which she'd hardly glanced at, and walked with dignity to sit next to Vera. Justin felt proud and humbled and shot a smile in her direction.

Before the Jury withdrew to consider their verdict, the Judge had the last word. It was to clarify what was meant by conspiracy. 'The Crown does not have to prove that any of the three actually caused any of the explosions, simply that they agreed to it. As long as you know what the agreement is, then you are a conspirator. You needn't necessarily know your fellow conspirators, nor need you be always active in the conspiracy. It can be effected by a wink or a nod, without a word being exchanged. It need have no particular time limit, no particular form, no boundaries.'

This totally played in their favour, Justin thought, the Judge had finally come out with it. All three were deemed capable of conspiracy over the three-year period, covering the set of twenty-five bombs. Surely the Jury would see the injustice of defining conspiracy so broadly.

'This is not a political trial. Political trials are trials of people for their political beliefs which happen to be contrary to those in government...we do not have them in this country.'

The Jury were whisked away to a secret location and the Judge said he'd be available to them and expected a verdict by Monday morning. The comrades exchanged power salutes before parting company, high on the speeches, which distilled everything they'd been arguing for months.

The twitter storm took him by surprise and shot him back to those crazy days.

This time he'd turned to Harpreet for advice. She'd softened now all the hurtful things had been aired and they'd reached an unspoken truce. He knew well she might walk out of the marriage altogether or else settle for living in its shell, and he didn't know which was worse. In little ways he showed how he loved her, beyond cooking her favourite meals. For years, she'd asked him to clear out the spare room, a dumping ground for old books, and he'd never got round to it. Something clicked one day and he got rid of the lot, filling dozens of bags which he took to a charity shop.

The woman looked askance at the out-of-date academic archive and suggested they go for pulp. 'Pulp fiction?' he'd quipped, but the joke was lost. It had made Harpreet laugh after she'd opened her eyes to the room made unfamiliar by spartan shelves and a rearrangement of furniture. 'We could turn it into your office, pet, I could put a desk under the window and you'd see the cherry blossom in spring.'

She turned and stroked his cheek. 'When I think of you,

Justin, I think of home. That will never change.'

They sat a little apart on the narrow spare bed which was covered by a faded candlewick bedspread. He didn't dare reach for her hand.

'I honestly don't know how I'll feel after taking Mum and Dad away, that's the truth. The visit has brought up a lot of stuff from the past,' she said, hugging her knees.

'If I hadn't barrelled into your life, you could have married someone more suitable, closer to you in age.'

She turned to him, amused. 'A nice Indian boy, d'you mean? I don't think so. I was attracted to your easy confidence and calm. You've never cared much about what others think, and I like that about you. You're a curious blend of maverick and English, with a disregard for respectability for its own sake. You're still part of the establishment, whatever you may think. You have the luxury of criticizing your origins without fear of the consequences. I felt you belonged and that made me feel safe.' She patted his hand. 'Now I have to find my own equilibrium; going back to Uganda is part of that. I need to disentangle family stories from faded memories and find out who that little twelve year old girl was.'

He scratched his beard. 'How come we've never talked about this before? It's obvious, now you bring it up, and I wish I'd asked more about what happened. I've taken a lot for granted, haven't I?'

She shook her head. 'I wouldn't have known where to begin. It's only recently things have started to surface. Leaving your life isn't something easy to articulate and I think we just got on with it. I reinvented myself, acquiring a Yorkshire accent. There were a couple of others of us in the class. We soon learned you don't stand up when the teacher speaks to you, like at home. What the school hadn't realised was that we came with a solid education from an English medium school, so we romped ahead. I was determined to be the clever and successful girl my parents wanted me to be, and I somehow was cast as the teacher's pet. I was chuffed to bits to get a detention for hiding in the cloakrooms with a bunch of other girls, skiving off netball.'

'Sounds like a horrendous balancing act,' Justin said, quietly.

'I guess so. It was okay by the sixth form, when most of us wanted to go to University. For me, studying law was the epitome of fitting in. But who was I supposed to marry? Then you came along, gentle, allowing time for our relationship. You were always clear that if I said "no", that would be alright too. That's why I fell in love with you, Jus, you saw me for who I was. After all the interviews with Mum and Dad for your doctorate, I felt as though you knew us better than we knew ourselves.'

He nodded, feeling tears prick his eyes.

Justin remembered how their lives were blitzed overnight by Idi Amin, when they had to flee their sprawling bungalow and comfortable life in a suburb of Kampala. Harpreet's dad had gone from managing a soft drinks factory to setting up a chain of clothing stores in Leeds and Bradford. In between, they'd shared a house till they got back onto their feet and her dad had packed shoes in a factory. He remembered odd details from their testimony; how Harpreet's mum had never before worn a cardigan, and how they bought full sets of winter clothes at C&A with vouchers issued to refugees.

'I remember you saying that you had to smuggle in packed lunches at school because you couldn't eat the food.'

'Goodness, I'd forgotten that. Food was a nightmare, because we were vegetarian. Faced with spam and fish fingers what else could we do? They relaxed the rules over pack-ups in the end. How we missed the abundance of fruit, not just bananas as people imagine. We had papaya, guava, jackfruit and mangoes, which you couldn't find here until everything was globalised.'

This time he took her hand. 'It's a shame it's taken so long for us to talk like this. I hope it's not too late.'

'Let's see how things go, Jus,' she said, but didn't pull away. 'About that twitter business, I agree it's unlikely to be Stephen who started the media leak; it would be stupid of him to alienate you. However, I do think you need to decide what to say publicly. Molly is right, this isn't going away.' She was back in trouble-shooting mode and he felt he'd lost her. How tenuous the threads that bind us, he thought, as we try to make sense of who we are. Sanjay was the unbreakable bond that defined them, whatever the future might hold.

Chapter 19

He'd taken a late train north on the evening of the summing up, after receiving a telegram saying that Ma was in the final stages of her illness. Inoperable cancer. She'd refused treatment for the sake of a few extra months and would soon be flying into the arms of Jesus, as she put it.

Waking in his old room, he looked at the built-in wardrobe painted with a red fire-engine, a silver aeroplane and a blue racing car, all zipping across a cloudless sky. He remembered the moment when the mural was revealed. It was breath taking, as if the world outside had burst into his bedroom.

Two years later he was at boarding school and had never properly inhabited the room since. There were school holidays, but these were tainted with sadness from the outset. The time for repacking the trunk approached at the speed of a runaway train, signalled by Ma stitching nametapes into his new clothes. She would iron and fold each item she placed carefully in the trunk as neatly as could be.

When the boys arrived at school the trunks were ready and waiting in the dormitories. Ma's way of packing was special, he could see that by looking at other boys' trunks. It hurt him dreadfully to undo her loving care as he unfolded each garment and caught a faint whiff of her perfume.

Birthdays were the worst. Happy the boys who had theirs in the holidays. The unfortunates with term-time birthdays were bounced in a sheet and flung to the ceiling by older boys, and always landed badly. After the first time it happened to him, he'd begged Ma and Pa not to send cards and to make sure nobody else did either.

If nothing else, school gave him an insight into military discipline: the housemaster was the officer in charge, the prefects his sergeants and the boys were the men. Stretching under the covers of his childhood bed, he remembered *Jankers*, an idiotic punishment meted out by prefects. Christ, he hadn't thought about that in years. It meant having your clothes messed up and shoes muddied several times a day and being made to clean up until the prefects got bored of forcing you to do it.

Pa had laughed. 'Jankers! They still do that? It's an old army trick to keep men on their toes. Won't do you any harm, lad.'

He would show no sign of weakness after that.

Across the landing he could hear the comings and goings of Molly and the nurse as they made Ma comfortable; low voices, the occasional clink of china, water running through the pipes from the corner hand-basin.

She spoke openly of dying, impatient with any pussyfooting around the truth. Yesterday, this had taken a particular turn.

'When I'm gone, make it up with your father.' Each sentence was an effort of will as she lay propped on pillows.

'After all that's happened? He's never forgiven me for not taking over the business.'

'You've never forgiven him either. I fear we lost you after you went away to school.'

'Sent away,' he corrected, and regretted it. Shifting awkwardly in the wicker chair, he looked past her to the steel stand where the oxygen mask hung.

'Don't blame him for everything,' she said, a film of sweat breaking out on her brow. 'There's something I want you to know.'

He handed her a glass and she took a sip. Her skin was translucent and he longed to transfuse her with his own vitality.

'There was someone else before I met your father. A Polish pilot.'

He watched as she caught her breath and was struck by how he took the simplicity of breathing for granted.

'I was sixteen. His name was Gabriel. We were secretly engaged.' Her eyes brimmed with tears.

He leaned over and took her hand. 'What happened, Ma?' He already knew the answer.

'He was killed on a mission.' She pulled a handkerchief from her bed-jacket sleeve and dabbed her eyes. 'Afterwards I wasn't myself for a while. Nearly everyone had lost someone, so I didn't make a fuss.'

He'd once found a photo of Ma in the bottom of her sewing-basket while rootling for a cadet uniform button. It was dated on the back in pencil. *Summer 1944.* A girl with a halo of braids was laughing at the person behind the camera. Ma had caught him and snatched the photo.

'I met your father after he was demobbed. He was very kind to me and said getting married could mend a broken heart. He'd had a tough time of it in Burma and we helped each other. He's a good man, Justin. You should know that.'

Justin nodded and tried to marshal his emotions. 'We're very different, Ma. He wanted me to be something I wasn't. He thought school would sort me out and it just made me miserable. Did you know that I slipped pathetic SOS notes into letters home? I wondered if you ever found them.'

'There you go again, blaming anybody but yourself.' A spot of colour came into her cheeks. 'Some'd say private school was a privilege not a penance. I know he went too far after...'

'...don't worry, Ma, I'll try and make it right with him, I promise. Rest now.'

'You mean save my breath?' she smiled wanly. 'The only point in knowing you're dying is to make sure those you love look after each other.'

She coughed, and he saw it was one of those fits that left her heaving and gasping for air. The nurse, who'd waited discretely outside, came in and together they propped her up and the nurse placed the oxygen mask gently over her nose and mouth. Ma's eyes followed him, fluttering like moths as her breathing came under control.

'I'll be back,' he said, and squeezed her hand before leaving. The sadness he'd felt when he first knew Ma was dying had deserted him and he felt distant and drained.

'She said what?' said Molly.

They sat either side of the hearth in front of a blazing log fire.

'That she was still in love with a dead Polish pilot when she married Pa. And Pa said he'd help her get over it. Did you know that?'

'Yes, more or less. Was there anything else?'

'She wants me to kiss and make up with Pa. Even though he was a brute.'

'Come on, Jus, don't exaggerate. Did he ever raise a finger to you?'

'He didn't have to. Remember those ghastly Sunday lunches when he'd launch into some topic, capital punishment or whatever, and make me argue against him. He'd set out to flatten me, then swap sides. What was that in aid of?'

'Men's stuff, I suppose, toughening you up. It was all wrong, but given his past, it's not surprising.'

'You mean the war? Ma said something about that. Whatever happened?'

'I doubt even Ma knows. It must have been pretty ghastly.'

'As a kid, if I asked him about it, he'd reel off lists of foreign sounding places and names of campaign commanders. The only detail I gleaned was that they lived in tents and malaria was rife; and he was in the Royal Engineers. Mending bridges didn't sound that dangerous.'

'We've no idea really, have we? Our generation.'

'I once asked if he had any snaps of the war. He said, *Snaps? What d'you think it was, a fricking holiday camp? There was nothing you'd want to see in an album, take my word for it.*'

'Maybe now's the time to share your feelings? It could do you both good.'

Molly had become sure of herself since she'd started social work training and talked about *Gestalt* theory; it was something along the lines of integrating past and present. Dealing with the present was a full-time job, as far as he was concerned.

'How would that go? *Pa, my mates are on trial for blowing things up, but it was all in a good cause.* That should knock his socks off,' he said crossly.

He watched as she took off her specs and rubbed her eyes before refocusing. 'That's typical, hiding behind sarcasm. You think you're on the frontline, but you just can't hack it, can you? You have to deal with your relationship with Pa, now Ma can no longer act as a buffer between you. She'll be gone soon, that's the reality. You can't spend the rest of your life blaming the parents.' She gave him an unpitying look.

He considered whether there was a chance of making a truce with Pa. The alternative would be easier. To cut ties after Ma died. He couldn't do that to Molly. 'I'll give it a go, Sis. I'll talk to Pa.'

She got up to feed the fire and they sat staring until the log took flame and the silence between them stretched companionably.

Justin noted the fault lines creasing Pa's forehead, like the folds in an old map.

'Grand girl, your sister,' he said, settling to the boiled eggs Molly had cooked for breakfast, before leaving to sit with Ma.

The newspaper on the chair between them was a lure and temptation from the conversation Molly had engineered. Justin took the plunge. 'I'm sorry about Ma. I didn't know she was so sick.'

Pa looked up from under dark eyebrows. 'Life won't be the same without her,' he managed, before turning to his egg.

Justin ate his toast in silence and waited for the right words to come. Now they'd spoken of Ma, neither could retreat behind the paper. 'We haven't always got on, you and me. We've never really talked, have we?' Justin said.

'That's your mother speaking, I presume.'

'What if it is? She's giving us a chance to, I dunno, to be a normal father and son, whatever that means.'

Pa wiped his lips with the linen napkin. 'You want my opinion, son? You're wasting your life, working on a building site.'

This was classic Pa, throwing an opening punch. It was going to be hard to meet him half-way.

'If that's all you can say, this isn't a conversation, is it Pa? I'd hoped we could get beyond that. You have to accept I'm living my life and that means making my own mistakes if necessary. I know things were different in your day.'

Buttering his toast, Pa said, 'At your age I'd been three years in the war, and I'd seen and done things that I wouldn't wish on anyone. Youngsters today have everything dished up on a plate. A dose of National Service would do you a power of good.'

Justin despaired of making headway and tried to recall the last time they'd connected, certainly not on family holidays. Erecting a tent was for men, and Justin became cack-handed. He would misjudge the distance of guy-ropes, and when the *choc choc* of wood on wood sank a tent peg awry, a volley of invective followed, leaving him cowed and shamed. Now, for Ma's sake, he was scratching for the man beneath the bluff exterior.

'I'm trying to see things from your point of view, Pa. Let's start with when I went away to school. You showered me with advantages you never had, and I've thrown it all back in your face. I can see that now.' He saw Pa's face redden.

'When I was expelled, it was the breaking point for both of us. It was the moment we stopped talking in any meaningful way.'

'You didn't exactly cover yourself in glory, did you?' Pa said, unable to contain himself. 'Getting on your high-horse over a couple of boys found in bed together, when it had bugger all to do with you.'

'The younger boy was raped, Pa. I knew him, he was in my dorm. I got up a petition because *he* was expelled instead of the boy who molested him.' He watched as Pa took his time chewing toast, thickly spread with Ma's homemade marmalade.

'The lad came back in the end,' Pa said smugly.

'How d'you know? Why didn't you tell me?'

'I heard it at a Rotary Club dinner. Some talk about a boy whose father had paid the fees of another over a regrettable incident. I knew straight away who it was. I kept quiet about your disgrace.'

Justin was struck dumb. He felt the shame of the boy who'd been allowed back, who'd curled up foetus-like on his bed leaving blood-stained sheets. 'Let me explain why I do what I do,' he said, mustering the last ounce of patience. He could have told him about Carlson and Kelly and Polish John and the cheaply built flats a bus-ride from the Stock Exchange where traders juggled short and long for shareholders' profits. The builders and traders were all part of an invisible machine that reinvented itself and played fast and loose with human fortunes. He decided on a different tack. 'I've met so many families on the edge and the only thing that stands between them and destitution is help from neighbours. People on our street could be made homeless overnight if rents went up in a system rigged against them. The marches and campaigns I'm involved in aim to change all that.'

Pa weighed in. 'They've got it a lot better than when I was

a lad and there was no such thing as the dole. It's being out of work that strips a man of dignity. I saw the Jarrow hunger marchers. They'd been on the road weeks by the time they arrived in Sheffield. Whistling and playing their mouth-organs, they were.' He cleared his throat as if affected by the memory.

'What was it like, Pa?' Justin urged.

'The crowds came out for the spectacle and the cause pricked church-going consciences, but it didn't result in work. The war took care of that, when steel was needed for ships and armaments. The world turns on a bigger axis than you or I can alter, son. But I see you're bent on learning the hard way. I know about the case you're meddling with.' He pointed at the unopened paper for emphasis. 'I trust you've got the wit to turn over a new leaf afterwards, because whatever the verdict the authorities will have you under suspicion. Clear out of London and make a fresh start. It's what your mother would say, and you listen to her.'

'Right Pa, I'll think on it. I have to get back tomorrow when the Jury announces its decision. You'll read about it soon enough, no doubt. And I'll come straight home when Ma's time comes.'

The McKenzie friends arrived at court in good time and raised victory fists to supporters holding banners on the pavement outside, before going into the lobby to wait. It was to be a long morning and Justin was grateful to Sofia and Vera for bringing a flask of coffee. They watched as Special Branch men, whom they recognised now, chatted to reporters in the fizzing atmosphere.

At midday something was clearly afoot, and they later learned that the jurors had sent a list of questions to the Judge. It was five o'clock before the Jury returned.

It was strange, following events from the gallery and

seeing Rob, Callum and Jess alone in the dock.

An exhausted looking Jury foreman stood before them in shirtsleeves. Justin's head thumped as the verdict was read out.

The foreman announced that Callum and Vera were acquitted of all charges, it was unanimous. The three clung to each other in the dock before Callum and Vera were led away. There was a long pause and Justin chewed his nails, already bitten to the quick.

The Jury found Rob guilty on the main count of conspiracy to cause explosions and also guilty of possession of weapons, by ten votes to two. When he'd finished, the foreman turned to the Judge and said, 'Us members of the Jury would like to ask Your Lordship for—I believe the word is leniency or clemency—but that is what us members of the Jury would like to ask.'

There wasn't a flicker on Rob's face, and Justin could have wept at his courage. The sentence was yet to come and Max's fifteen years rang in his ears.

In his preamble, the Judge said, 'For the purpose of the sentence, I propose to disregard any of the incidents which occurred before responsibility is claimed by *The People's Militia* press releases. That shortens the period and reduces the number of explosions.

'The means that you adopted could have been even more lethal than they were, but I am satisfied on the evidence that the devices you used were not deliberately designed to cause death or serious injury, but rather to damage property. Nevertheless, in every one of these cases, there was that risk. It is fortunate that no one was killed.

'Your participation arose because you objected to the orderly way of society. I am not going to lecture you. I am sorry to see such an educated person in your situation. Undoubtedly a warped understanding of sociology has brought you to the state in which you find yourself.

'I treat you as a person of good character. You have sought in many ways to do good and I count that in your favour. But when all is said and done, the public is entitled to protection. Everyone must know that anyone who seeks to behave in this manner, holding explosives and weapons, must expect severe punishment.'

Out of the corner of his eye, Justin saw Sofia and Vera hold hands, while he held his arms tight across his chest. The sentence came like a hammer-blow: seven years for conspiracy with six years concurrent for possession.

Justin looked across to check he'd heard right and saw Vera's head buried in Sofia's shoulder. It was far worse than anything they'd imagined, even though conspiracy carried a maximum of Life.

He heard Rob say, 'I would like to thank the two members of the Jury who had faith in me,' as he was led away, showing no anger or defiance at the verdict.

Justin looked on, horror-struck. It was a tragedy, a farce. Possibly both. His own life would never be the same again.

He tasted something warm and metallic and touched his lips. His hand was covered in blood. A massive nosebleed was flowing copiously down his freshly pressed T-shirt and his head pounded, fit to explode. Sofia and Vera guided him out of the court room as he cupped his hands to catch the worst, leaving a scarlet trail in his wake.

Chapter 20

The *bombprof* twitter storm wasn't all bad. Tweets plopped in from unexpected quarters: freshwater fishermen and the hunting and shooting brigade, who decried state interference in their chosen past-times claimed him a visionary. At the other end of the spectrum were the anarchist Black Cross and various anti-capitalist groupuscules who took him to their breast. In the midst of this, came a defamatory piece in the student newspaper, *Shout!* When the Politics Society invited him to speak in a debate on *What is Terrorism?* he was dubious.

'You should do it,' said Harpreet. 'It will help diffuse the hype.'

'Going public is a hard ask right now. I need to get my story straight.'

'That's the point, Jus. You need to have a convincing narrative. Preferably one you believe in yourself.'

She had a point. There were so many facets to the truth, he didn't know where to begin. Harpreet said he should brace himself for a backlash from the University.

'Kyle won't love the idea, but so what? He's got it in for me anyway.'

It was clear what he must do. He needed Daisy's blessing before going public. Stephen would put them in touch. His stomach churned at the thought so he knew he was on the right track. The only time they'd ever met was in a prison waiting room and she'd been hostile.

'Sure,' said Stephen, 'good idea to break the ice.'

She called a few days later while he was drafting notes for the debate. 'Justin, it's Daisy. This a good moment?' She sounded warm and friendly, as if they'd spoken only yesterday.

'Thanks for calling, Daisy. How are you and the girls? Both married, Stephen tells me.'

'Yes, I'm a proud grandma now.' He pictured her surrounded by a parade of silver-framed family photos displayed on gleaming furniture, a gallery of two generations in defiance of their orphaned childhoods. His image of Daisy, long out of date, was of a young woman with a round face and bubbly blonde hair. What did she make of him, with his posh voice and a slightly inflected Yorkshire accent? She'd remember him from the waiting room, the awkward moment both their names were called. There'd been a mix-up over the visitors' passes and they ended up visiting on the same day. She'd lashed out at him with such bitterness he'd put up his hands in self-defence and backed away.

'Stephen's told me all about the film he's making about Max and you're giving a talk about him.'

'That's right, Daisy, and I'd like very much for you to come, if you're able. I wanted to speak to you first. I'm sorry I haven't been in touch sooner.' It had been a long journey from Stephen's first email; back then the idea would have filled him with dread.

'What d'you want people to know about him?' he asked.

'I've been thinking about that a lot, and most of all, I want people to know about the person he was after those difficult early years. He was his own man and I don't want him coming over as a victim, d'you know what I'm getting at?'

He hunched forwards. 'I imagine he thought we were all idiots, the rest of us in the squat, I mean.'

There was an audible intake of breath. 'Bunch of middle-class wankers, pardon my French, except for Vera. She made something of herself as a Welsh MP and he liked that. He blamed Rob for dragging everyone along. Max said that a lorry driver's son who got into Oxford should have known better.'

'And Callum?'

'He said he was a freeloader who sponged off Jess. Loveless Jess, he called her, who lived on guilt money from her divorced parents. As for Sofia, she was off-the-scale crazy and dangerous to know. Sorry, I know you two were together, but you must have realised she was nuts.'

Justin laughed, 'You don't mince words, Daisy! And what was the verdict on me, dare I ask? Don't hold back,' he said, half joking.

'Max thought you were naïve and a bit messed up, but your heart was in the right place. You didn't mind getting your hands dirty, and he respected you for that. If you want my opinion about the envelope signing business, I always said he should have dobbed you in to get himself a lighter sentence. Max wasn't like that.'

'Listen, Daisy, I'm deeply ashamed of my part in what happened. I absolutely should have handed myself in, it's blindingly obvious. I'm so sorry.'

There was a tense pause. 'Well, that's not enough, Justin. *Someone* has to be accountable! What I want is for Max's name cleared, not in a legal sense, it's too late for that. People tell me to move on, but I can't. I want to tell the world he was a wonderful husband and dad, who was cheated of ten years of his life. That's what makes me so angry.'

'I get it, I really do.'

'Do you? Really? How will this talk change anything?'

'It's a debate on *What is Terrorism?*'

'So, you'll be saying that Max was a terrorist?'

'No, no, not at all. My view is that he was framed and harshly punished as a warning to others. I'll say that he was let down by his comrades, me included, as we hid behind political rhetoric.'

In the silence that followed he heard her sniffing. 'He was a good man, Justin, and I miss him terribly. We'd known each other since we were kids and there were no secrets between us.' He could hear her blowing her nose. 'Sorry about that. We both had our ups and downs, depression and that, but we coped. We had a good life together and we were happy. You can't ask for more than that, can you?'

'Ah, a good life, that's quite something.' Could he say the same of himself?

They talked about Sanjay and Stephen and how the two might work together on a film about Syria. 'Stephen says his film about Max is up for an award, and he'll get the rest of the money through crowdfunding.'

'That would be grand,' said Justin, sealing his intention to take part in the debate.

If the sky fell in he'd pick up the pieces later. He switched off the phone strangely elated.

January 2016

The lecture theatre was a windowless cube with zigzag patterns along the walls, which made Justin feel as if he were falling, as he sat on stage looking at the gathering crowd. Sanjay was there; Vanessa of course, and Kyle, and he spotted Stephen and Daisy on aisle seats.

Harpreet had already gone to Uganda and he felt her absence cruelly, like the ache of a missing limb.

He sat between two speakers, one from *ConSoc*, the Conservative Society, and the other from the student rag, *Shout!* Justin was clearly the main attraction, which made him go hot under his lilac collar.

After introductions by the President of the Students' Union, the *Shout!* speaker spoke about 'no-platforming' terrorists, lost her thread and became confused. The *ConSoc* speaker was more sophisticated in her arguments and spoke passionately against domestic terrorism and its effects on minorities, like herself.

It was Justin's turn next. He picked up the mic and stood to one side of the podium, weighing the mood of the audience. He pictured the cherry tree from the window in Harpreet's study, showering snow like white confetti in a quiver of wind. His spirits rose.

'Okay, let me get one thing straight. The reason I've been invited to speak, is because when I was about your age, I joined a left-wing urban guerrilla group called *The People's Militia*. We ran a bombing campaign and I blew off the back door of a government minister's home, while someone else blew off the front door.' A ripple of reaction ran like a Mexican wave along the rows in front of him.

'Was this an act of terrorism or an act of political protest? I'll leave you to think about that as the story unfolds. The bombings led to two high-profile trials, and although I was questioned, I wasn't charged. At the time, it seemed like an immense stroke of luck. Or *was* it? It's something I've had decades to consider. Max Scott served the longest sentence of the two comrades who went to prison. We'll return to him later.

'The world I grew up in was marked by major political upheavals, both here and abroad. We marched, we stood on picket lines, but it soon became clear that the conventional levers of democracy wouldn't allow for fundamental change. So we harnessed the power of disruption to release energy, to make space for new social forms to emerge. The process was unpredictable, but there were signs of hope: worldwide street protests against the Vietnam War, a militant women's movement, and in 1968 a near-revolution in France. That was two lifetimes ago, but in many ways it's recent history.

'Today's generation, young people like you, face the twin crises of poverty and climate disaster in the wake of the financial crash. On a personal level, many of you face a lifetime of debt and precarious work in the so-called gig economy. You'll struggle to afford a decent place to live unless your parents are able to help. We now live in a debt creation economy, which is a form of social control.

'Despite that, unemployment is at its lowest in forty years. How is this possible? By driving down wages through privatisation, coupled with the atomisation of work while the global elite has hugely increased its wealth. Wealth that moves seamlessly around the globe. The leaked Panama Papers exposed a money Laundromat which goes unchecked. It's a form of legalised dispossession, or to put it bluntly, robbery. Your future has been sold down the river.'

'*Fuck capitalism,*' came a cry from the back of the hall.

'Thank you, my friend,' Justin replied. 'Let me be clear: planting bombs wasn't the answer then, and it certainly isn't now. What I learned from my actions concerns my friend Max, who changed my life.

'When we met, he was a man who'd survived life in an orphanage, worked on the railways, and had recently fallen on hard times. Some would say he was typical of the flotsam and jetsam of society. In reality, he had a deep understanding of the kind of solidarity essential to survival.

'Max moved into our squat, which was a household of young intellectuals full of revolutionary ideals, and a seriously inflated view of our own importance. Max was definitely the adult in the room.

'He was tried separately and was the first to go to prison in 1971. He knew of our plans but didn't plant any bombs or handle explosives. He was charged with conspiring to bomb the Employment Secretary's home. The attack was in protest against the Industrial Relations Bill, which curbed the right to strike and empowered courts to arbitrate on industrial action. The proposed legislation was bitterly opposed by the Unions.

'To paraphrase our message to the Press, we said: *British democracy is based on blood, terror and exploitation. It has a brutal police force whose crimes against people the media refuse to report. The government has declared vicious class war with Peter Haddon's Industrial Relations Bill. We're fighting back and the war will be won with bombs.*

'It was meant to be hard hitting, but the bit about the working-class using bombs was pure fantasy. The police got lucky and found evidence that Max had addressed a couple of press releases. He was charged, not with the actual bombing, but with conspiring *with persons unknown* to commit the crime. The judge sent him down for fifteen years. This was later reduced, but that's beside the point. To our minds, the sentence stood as a declaration of war by the establishment.' His eyes narrowed as he stepped forward to make the next point.

'Now comes the tricky part: Why did the rest of us stay silent? Because, we argued, we were part of a mass insurgency. There'd been a wave of bombings across the country and breaking cover would have crossed class lines and endangered others. The second trial was of three comrades, the supposed *persons unknown*, who used the stand to appeal to the largely working-class jury and to some effect. Two of the three were acquitted.

'And what of Max? I visited when I could and continued to see him after he was moved to a prison in Hull. For political reasons he was considered a security risk and held in a high-security jail for seven years. There, he studied and got a first-class degree. He also fell in love with a childhood companion and eventually married and had a family. I regret to say that we lost touch—I lost touch, and he died last year.

'His son, Stephen, wrote to me recently, calling me to account. He wanted to know why his father served time while I went free.

'The answer is simple: we betrayed him. Working class solidarity, which he understood better than any of us, should have trumped all other considerations. We should have admitted our part in the bombings and taken the consequences.

'It's the take-home message for today, my friends, and it's

taken me a lifetime to get it. For this, I'll always be indebted to Max.' He swallowed hard to harness his emotions.

'Why should you care about any of this? Today, terrorism is not an abstract question, as countless innocent people are killed or maimed in terrorist attacks. Let's zoom in closer. We know citizens of this country have been radicalised and joined the jihadists as foreign fighters in Syria. What would you say to those who want to come back, having experienced the brutal reality of ISIS? Not just the insurgents, but the women who signed up as jihadi brides. The gut reaction of many would be: too bad, you betrayed your country. Don't come back.

'Citizenship, we're told, is a privilege not a right, and so, the argument goes, traitors should be stripped of citizenship. If we follow it through the implications are sinister. The rights of thousands of citizens could be in jeopardy.

'I have in mind those who came decades ago to work in the so called Mother Country, and more recently those fleeing war and persecution, who risk deportation. Some have already been shipped out. We live under a regime of internal policing and racial profiling, where universities, hospitals and landlords are required to check on identity, on a person's right to be here. It amounts to an internal border control that should concern us all. And the definition of who does and doesn't belong keeps changing. If you don't look right or sound right you will be checked, or simply stopped by police on suspicion. Your landlord will check your Right to Rent with draconian powers to evict. It's all part of the deliberately hostile environment this government has created in the name of national security,' he said, oozing contempt.

'Let's return to the example of a woman seeking asylum from ISIS. Should she be allowed to come back to her family? My reply is a resounding *yes*, because if we collectively turn our backs, if we strip her of citizenship, we collude with the state in its war against its own citizens. It's a form of modern exile.

'Not that the public is duped. Confidence in democracy is dwindling and the far-right fills the void. People know the system is rigged, aware of the growing disconnect between themselves and the decision-making processes.

'Who will save us? Not the socially minded plutocrats who gather to put the world to rights. Like the fictional aristocrat in Lampedusa's *The Leopard*, the elite knows this all too well: *if we want things to stay as they are, things will have to change*. The rich have their own vested interests. You get the point.

'Wars continue to rage, the planet is imploding and millions flee for survival. Walls, borders and demagogues will not save us. Fixing capitalism isn't an option. We know that boom and bust economics burns itself out, and that bailouts won't keep the financial bubble afloat indefinitely. We have living examples of alternatives, however short-lived, such as the revolution in Spain in 1936 when people organised along libertarian socialist principles. In everyday life communities have always been capable of organising and providing for each other in times of struggle or disaster. Today there's an autonomous region in northern Syria, where democratic forces are pushing back ISIS, led by militias of young men and women. The constitution gives women 40% representation on all governing bodies, in a regional revolution that includes Kurds, Arabs and Christians. There is reason for hope.' He was on the home straight and modulated into an optimistic key.

'Many of you are fighting back, building campaigns and networks with a flexibility undreamt of in my day. The campaign against climate change, the fight for gender, race and class equality, the anti-war protests, all these join and intersect to create alternative models inside capitalism's decaying shell. It's not an exaggeration to say that the struggles of today are laying the foundations for the future of humanity.

'In conclusion, I'd like to dedicate these thoughts to my friend Max Scott, who gave the best years of his life to the cause. He is my inspiration. Rest in in peace, Max.'

Justin returned to his seat as the hall sat in silence for what felt like an eternity. That's when it started. People were on their feet clapping and whooping, and he wondered if some other speaker had taken the stage. It seemed not, as the Union President went to the podium, thanked the speakers and invited questions.

A forest of arms shot up and volunteers in turquoise t-shirts ran around with mics. *What would happen now that he'd owned up to the bombings? Was he an anarchist? Was he soft on terrorists? Hadn't politics moved on from the left-right divide now that global warming threatened extinction?* He fielded these as honestly as he could, acutely aware of Daisy and Stephen in the audience, who'd set him on this dizzying course.

Chapter 21

Those were the days my friend, we thought they'd never end, played in an endless loop in his head as he drove to work for the last time, recalling his former purity of purpose. There had been no room for equivocation, no blurry edges under the lightning rod of action. Since then time had tempered him and in the slipstream of life he faced the harder task of living with the consequences of his actions.

He parked in front of the sixties' prefabs that had been 'home' for decades and unloaded flat-pack boxes for the final stage of clearing his office, walking upstairs instead of his usual two-at-a-time fitness routine.

It took an hour or so to pack up the remaining books, clear his desk and stow the outdated photo of Harpreet and Sanjay. He prepared himself for one last visit to Vanessa. She swung round on her chair in a swirl of brilliantly coloured kaftan. 'Hey comrade, come in,' she greeted, less exuberant than usual, for they both knew this easy relationship would alter once he'd gone. 'Final trip?'

'I reckon. The library only wants a fraction of the books. So much is online these days.'

She nodded in sympathy. 'I'm sorry about the debacle with Kyle. He's been a total arse.'

After the student debate, Kyle had summoned him. This was to be no cosy roundtable chat. In his opening gambit, he'd offered to stay on till Easter to set up the Centre for Sociology, then retire.

'That train's long gone,' Kyle had gloated. 'The department is merging post-haste with the Business School.'

'There's something I should have told you earlier,' Vanessa said now. 'Kyle has asked me to manage the merger.'

'Really? I thought management wasn't your thing. What's the catch?'

'No catch, but there's a sweetener. He's thrown in a research assistant.' Her dark lashes fluttered floorward.

'Sure, I get it. Watch he doesn't dump a load of other stuff onto you,' he said, unable to hide his dismay.

'Not a chance,' she said with mock bravado. 'There's something else, and I don't want you making a fuss. There's a surprise send-off at *The Feathers* tomorrow evening. I didn't tell you earlier because I knew you'd duck out.'

'You're joking!' He made as if to check his phone. 'Drat, I'm meant to be visiting my old man in Sheffield then.'

'You'll have to try harder than that, fella! Seven-thirty prompt, smart casual. I'll give you a hand downstairs with the boxes, so you can't cry off with a bad back.'

'You know me too well, Vanessa.' He couldn't quite bring himself to say, *comrade*.

Since Harpreet had left for Uganda, he'd forced himself into a strict routine: shower, breakfast, and an early morning cycle come rain or shine.

He was downing a bowl of shredded wheat when his phone buzzed and he saw it was Harpreet calling.

'It's you, pet! How are you?'

'I'm, fine, just wanted to let you know we've settled in and everyone's incredibly kind, it's overwhelming, actually. Mum and Dad are in their element. I've met all sorts of distant cousins I never knew. How are you?'

'I miss you, that's all. I've been helping Sanjay decorate his flat and…'

'Justin, I need to warn you. The CPS called me…' The line crackled and he couldn't make her out.

'*The CPS?* What did you say?'

'Yes, the CPS! Look, I'll text you, I'm sorry Jus, I didn't think…' and the connection died and when he tried to redial the line was engaged. He could see she was texting when the doorbell rang.

Hurrying barefoot to the front door he heard a great commotion and wondered what was going on outside. When he opened it, he was dazzled by a blaze of flashbulbs. Shading his eyes, he saw people wielding cameras and microphones and a small crowd gathering at the gate. Photoflashes popped right and left and a young woman thrust a mic under his nose.

'Professor Caffrey, were you a member of *The People's Militia?*'

'What d'you say to bombing charges?'

A hush followed, peppered by camera clicks, and later he would see himself splashed across the local rag in a black Lycra onesie.

'Is this about Max Scott?' he said, with a hammering heart. 'I made my views clear at the Student Union.' He supposed the mention of charges was a shot in the dark.

'What d'you have to say to Lord Haddon's family, Professor Caffrey?'

'Why did you bomb his house?'

'Where's your wife, Professor Caffrey? Will she stand by you?'

He clung onto the door feeling faint under the assault, then a postwoman stormed through the press pack, shouting, 'Move! Get out of my road!' She strode up the front steps, letter in hand. 'Get back inside, mate, they're just hyenas,' and she thrust the letter into his hand and pulled the door closed, leaving him alone and shaking.

Sweat dripped from his forehead as he staggered into the kitchen and slumped at the table. He grabbed the water bottle readied for the ride in what seemed like another life.

His mobile buzzed and he looked around helplessly until he saw it abandoned on the dresser. He picked up and heard a woman's voice. 'Professor Caffrey, this is Detective Sergeant Kowalski. Is this convenient?'

'Oh God, what's happened?' His first thought was for

Sanjay.

'Sir, I'm sorry to take you by surprise. I'd hoped you'd be expecting my call as I've already spoken to your wife out of professional courtesy. We're reopening a file on bombings in London in 1970 and 1971. We need you to assist with our enquiries. I'd be glad if you'd come to Leeds Central Police Station at 2pm. Ask for me, D. S. Kowalski. It shouldn't take long, an hour at most.'

'I'll be there,' he replied, flatly. He scrolled down and saw Harpreet's message, too late. The envelope lay next to him addressed in Molly's rounded hand, posted from Nepal, bright with foreign stamps.

The Detective wore a thick polo-neck sweater and a wide smile and straightaway put him at his ease. He readily admitted to his part in the BBC van bombing and to blowing up the back door of Peter Haddon's home. When he talked about Max and a miscarriage of justice she held up a warning hand. 'In the event that charges are laid, you should consult a lawyer.'

'That won't be necessary. I'll plead guilty and present my own case.'

'I was afraid you might. Let's cross that bridge if we come to it.' She stood to escort him out and chatted about her PhD in Criminology, all the way to the front desk. He left light-headed and wondered what had just happened. Was the CPS going through the motions for appearances? He knew a number of historic cases on both sides of the Northern Irish divide had surfaced recently, which the establishment preferred to bury. Worst case, he'd be looking at a fistful of years in jail. He wouldn't come out of it well.

The bike ride home pumped him up and he swung into the driveway, now free of blood-sucking journos. How they'd latched onto him he could only guess, a leaky toad at the CPS perhaps. He wanted to tell Harpreet what he'd been through, but was stopped in his tracks by a message from Sanjay:

Farida badly hurt. Worried sick. You around?

He typed back: *I'll drive over.*

He jumped into the car and a message pinged back: *Thanks.*

Questions crowded: Farida hurt, but how? She wasn't a combatant. It must be serious if they'd contacted Sanjay. Would he try to go to her? What if she died? His pulse raced ahead of the unthinkable, the far from improbable, and the car screeched to a halt at a red light as traffic roared in front of him at a busy junction. He sat, fingers thrumming on the steering wheel. If only Harpreet were here.

Sanjay lived in a downtown flat above a newsagent and Farida had moved in a couple of months before going to Syria. Justin ran up the stairs and knocked. There wasn't a bell.

'Thanks for coming over, Dad. I don't know what's going on, it's very confusing.' He sounded oddly calm. Justin laid a hand on his shoulder. They sat in the freshly painted living space, warmed by a gorgeous floral rug Farida had brought with her.

'They texted that she'd been involved in a vehicle incident and she's in hospital. Nothing more. They said to wait for further information, it wouldn't help to call.'

Neither voiced the fear that she could have been hit by a car bomb.

'The last I heard, she was going to visit an eco-fertilizer project for household waste to reduce the use of imported chemicals. It's all part of cleaning up the environment and becoming more independent. They're planting trees between farmlands, it's like a massive ecological upgrade...' His voice cracked and he held his head in his hands, shoulders heaving. Justin stroked his hair until Sanjay looked up, fiercely brushing away tears.

'Here, use this,' Justin said, handing him a handkerchief.

He swallowed hard, sitting out the storm of grief.

'Sorry,' Sanjay said, blowing his nose, and turned to him with reddened eyes. 'They're crowd-funding for the fertilizer plant and I promised to get sponsored for the *Tour de Yorkshire…*'

'Re-cycling for Rojava?' Justin said, trying to lighten the mood and was rewarded by a watery smile.

'What would I do if anything really bad happened?' Sanjay said, tearfully.

'Let's hold our nerve,' he said, over-heartily. 'You know I'm here for you, whatever happens.'

'Thanks, Dad. I know it's not easy for you, with Mum away and everything.' This sideways reference to his parents' contretemps was the closest he got to talking about it.

Justin let it go. 'About the ride, I'm in a bit of a fix, but I can get you sponsors, no problem.'

Sanjay's brow furrowed. 'Is it your dodgy heart, Dad?'

'Nothing like that, no. I'll explain later. Let's eat. Where's good round here?'

They sat on orange plastic seats in a restaurant run by a middle-aged Kurdish couple. When Sanjay introduced him, they gave him a warm welcome. 'We love your son, like our own family,' they said.

The table filled up with mezzes: humous, fetta, aubergine and peppers, fresh figs, tomato and cucumber and more, before they'd even seen the menu. 'You are our guests,' their hosts explained.

Sanjay tucked in. 'What's going on, Dad? The thing you were you saying earlier.'

'Nothing to worry about. Just a nudge from a nice lady detective who asked ever so politely whether I'd planted any actual bombs—the bombs I'd laid claim to at the student meeting—or was that just for dramatic effect. I told her it was all true.' She'd raised an eyebrow and her shoulders slumped. It wasn't what she'd wanted to hear.

Sanjay looked up. 'Was this on tape?'

'No, off the record.'

'Why now, Dad? I don't get it.'

'I want to do right by Max. I'm hardly a risk to society.'

'You could have spoken up when Max was still around. Why didn't you go with him to apologise to Peter Haddon, when he asked you to?'

'That's easy. If they'd come after me then, I'd have risked losing you and Mum, my job, everything. I couldn't do that. If that makes me a coward, so be it.'

'Sounds like you were a temporary terrorist. Seriously though, d'you think you were one? A terrorist?'

'Good question. If terrorism is the use of violence in the pursuit of political aims, then yes, I was. At the time, I considered myself an enemy of the state. That was before the war on terror was invented.' He heard how pompous he sounded and could have kicked himself.

Sanjay shook his head. 'Let's hope come May, we'll both be cycling our butts off for Rojava and you won't be doing porridge.'

'And that Farida is safe and well,' Justin said quietly.

Sanjay nodded vigorously, staving off tears.

Justin met his eye. 'It's going to be alright, son, I feel it in my bones.' He looked down at his phone blinking on the table. 'Christ, it's Vanessa, I clean forgot. I'm supposed to be at *The Feathers* for my leaving do.'

Sanjay threw back his head, laughing. 'You know what Mum would say? You'll be late for your own funeral!'

'I will that. I'll keep the buggers waiting if it's the last thing I do.'

Chapter 22

By the time Justin stood before the Magistrate, Farida was dead.

An improvised explosive device had cost the lives of three YPJ fighters as well as Farida. The bomb had been planted under their lorry and was missed by the bomb detector sweep, used religiously before any journey. Sanjay first knew of this on WhatsApp, as shocking as any World War telegram bringing death to the door. Justin contacted the Foreign Office in case there'd been a mistake and it was confirmed a British National had been killed in the region, but they wouldn't provide names.

Those injured, Sanjay would learn later, had been taken to hospital, but none survived. Farida had suffered, that was certain, but he'd never know how or for what duration. Burials were swift in the manner of the Middle East and he only knew of it after her body was sealed in the earth.

Sanjay was unreachable and walked in the shadowlands of disbelief, his normally warm complexion grey and his eyes like stones. Justin did what he knew best and cooked. Veggie curries, moussakas, Jerusalem artichoke pie, delivered to the flat each day. Sanjay wasn't ready to talk, but took the offerings gratefully. He emerged from the first crisis of grief, something Justin dimly remembered after Ma died. Raw reality forced his son back to work and Justin would pop into *Mellow Vélo* for a coffee. The white walls and bright lights created an anonymous space, which gave Sanjay permission to talk about his guilt and how he wished he'd gone with her.

Her comrades had carefully collected her belongings, including three sealed envelopes. One each for her parents and one for Sanjay. It was the first Justin knew that her mother had been bitterly opposed to Farida going to Syria and blamed her father for his radical influence.

'I'm going out there, Dad, I have to. I need to be near the people who cared about her. It's what she would have wanted. Stephen's all set to start the film project about the YPJ and he'll follow on.'

Stephen's film about Max had met with some success in small circles and there'd been talk of a second wave of the *Free Cinema* movement. Most of the interview footage with Justin had been cut, to his relief, as the film's themes became broader.

'I get it son, I just don't want you to come to any harm,' and he wondered what Harpreet would have to say. Her only son risking his life in a war zone? He could hear her now. 'Have you been in touch with Mum?'

'Don't play the mum card, it's too late for that. She can't really object, can she, after flying off to Uganda?'

'I'm pretty sure she can,' Justin cut back, and they both laughed complicitly. They cared about her deeply, but had struck a new chord together in her absence.

'Mr Caffrey,' said the Magistrate, looking up from behind her glasses.

Justin stood in the dock, though you wouldn't know it from the court layout that was designed to eliminate hierarchy. Or at least its physical manifestation. So his mind mused, reflecting on his attendances at various courts, none of them appearances. The outcome of Max's Committal hearing had ricocheted down the decades to the charges he faced today, for which he too would likely be sent up to Crown Court. Max, his onetime friend who'd made him bite on the pith of reality. In the days of milkmen, when columns of frozen milk rose up and pierced silver bottle tops, in the days of the dustmen's strike and rat-infested bins, in the days of joining picket lines like joining a queue, Max had looked at him with a question flickering across his face.

'What is it?' Justin asked.

'You had it all, man. Why are you here? Picketing?'

'When everything comes easily, nothing is real,' he'd replied.

A scattering of uncertainty crossed Max's brow and settled into a frown.

'I guess that sounds like I'm on my own trip,' he'd continued, as icy rain trickled down the back of his neck. 'Standing here makes more sense than all the talk about class and revolution. I feel it in my gut.' He remembered punching himself in the midriff to make the point.

Max had stamped on the smouldering stub of his rollup and spat out a stray strand of tobacco. Whether or not from disgust wasn't clear.

'Are you with me, Mr Caffrey, or a little hard of hearing? You appear distracted.'

The rebuke brought him sharply back. 'Forgive me, Ma'm, I can hear perfectly.'

She cut an unprepossessing figure in the Magistrate's black leather swivel chair, similar to the one in his study. He stood hands behind his back, ready to take what was due to him. He listened as she listed the offences, namely conspiring with others to use explosives; possession and use of same, on two occasions in 1970 and 1971. There was no mention of the political context, just the bald charges brought against him by the CPS.

'Do you plead guilty or not guilty?'

'Guilty, ma'am,' he heard himself say.

'I have no choice but to send you to Crown Court, Mr Caffrey, given the seriousness of the offences. I see there is no defence lawyer present to request bail on your behalf.' She glanced over at the prosecutor who looked haggard and bored, clutching a sad sack of a briefcase. He didn't look inclined to object.

'In which case, I grant bail on condition you appear whenever you are called.'

The Court Clerk sprang to life. 'The accused is free on bail.'

Justin gripped the side of the dock shaking his head, overcome by a dizzying wave of pent up emotion. 'I'm sorry, I'm sorry, I'm sorry,' was what came out and his eyes ballooned with tears.

'You may go, Mr Caffrey,' said the Magistrate, gathering up her papers.

He stumbled from the dock and into brilliant sunshine outside. Seeing a bench, he kicked aside empty cans and slumped down, head in hands. Was this the bargain? A spell in jail in exchange for clearing Max's name? Or more exactly, for clearing his conscience, he could hear Harpreet say. Her voice was always there. She'd told him she couldn't love him until she knew who he was. That could take a while, he'd replied, until he'd fathomed it for himself.

A squirrel scratched in the dirt under a tree and traffic rumbled by. The build-up of tension since Stephen's first email was physical, and as it drained away he was left limp, the stuffing kicked out of him. A brindled pattern of sunlight shifted on the pavement as a light breeze rustled the leaves overhead. His ramshackle thoughts settled on a municipal display of pink geraniums that brought Pa to mind.

He'd noted a softening in him since Magda had moved in and was grateful he had a live-in carer. Or so he'd thought, until Pa said, 'We're living together proper, like. I don't want you thinking she's a gold-digger, son. She's a great comfort to me and I'm fond of the lass. The best thing that's happened to me since your Ma died.'

Molly had guessed at the fondness between them from video chats, when she saw Magda tenderly stroking Pa's hand as she held the iPad.

Justin had tried to hide his discomfort with, 'There's life in the old dog yet,' while his more generous sister suggested they send the couple flowers and a card.

The month was June and the evening thick with the day's heat as young people flowed in, filling low seats bordering the room. On the walls were photographs of YPJ and YPG fighters lost in battle, hung with green and yellow pennants each pierced with a red star.

Justin had arrived without fanfare bringing a handsome donation for the eco-processing plant, raised at the *Tour de Yorkshire*. Farida's family and the Kurdish couple who'd taken Sanjay to their hearts, had used their networks to sponsor him for generous amounts, despite the fact that he'd had to abandon the ride half way, hit by exhaustion.

Going to court was a turning point, followed by a week's hard walking in the Yorkshire Wolds. It could be as long as two years before his trial and meanwhile he determined to make himself useful.

After landing in Erbil, the journey to Syria was coordinated by the Iraqi Peshmerga, on a tried and tested route. He still had the retinal imprint of huge billboards that greeted him on arrival in Kobani, showing joyous young women in uniform, smiling and waving YPJ flags to celebrate a victory over ISIS. Here, there was no space for complacency or self-absorption and he felt a lightness of being, buoyed by the occasion.

Tonight, the event was to honour Farida as well as welcome him. Sanjay and Stephen were in deep conversation with the young militants, some in uniform, others off duty in jeans and t-shirts. He had to remind himself it was highly unusual to see women and men working as equals in any culture and relished the energy. Heval Yezda stood and a hush descended. A woman in her late twenties, he guessed, and was later to learn she was one of their top commanders.

She laughed. 'I'm sorry to break things up, I know many of you haven't seen each other since fighting shoulder to shoulder, which makes this a happy reunion.' She looked up at the photographs. 'It is also a celebration of our comrades who died alongside us and who live with us still. Many of you have met Sanjay and Stephen, here from the UK to make a movie about our lives. Farida, who was tragically killed, was Sanjay's life companion, and his father, Justin, is with us today. Be welcome.'

There was a round of applause and Justin felt the warmth of shining faces. 'They are here to become our ambassadors, or influencers, I think you say, to sow the seeds of understanding of our mission to create a secular, democratic and federal Syria. Along this road we must eliminate *Daesh* to free our peoples, whether Kurdish, Arab or Syriac, indeed all ethnic groups, so that we may live together in peace.'

Her narration unfolded like a precious cloth glowing in the act of creation. 'Let me take you back to the beginning, to the revolution in Kobani in July 2012. Did we fight the regime? No, we took control of the roads into the town and we sent a delegation to the army. We said, if you give up your weapons, your security will be guaranteed. Almost all agreed. We talked to them and called their families to pick them up. Those who wanted to leave, we let them go to Turkey, but we didn't let them take their weapons. We didn't turn over a single soldier to the regime. When people woke and saw our flag flying over the rooftops, they were stunned.'

A young woman said, 'They were crying and threw rice with joy, people had no more fear.' She flashed a startling white smile under a bright headscarf over dark blond hair.

'Yes comrade, the liberation spread like fire across the region. In Derik we tried to hold back the people, but they pushed ahead and said give us weapons, and we distributed them.

'And so it went, until at the opposite end of Rojava, Afrin was liberated. We didn't want any fighting. In town after town, the people surrounded military bases and the troops withdrew.'

A young man with eyes like saucers, said for the visitors'

benefit, 'We weren't trying to grab some weapons and point them at the regime. We wanted to achieve a democratic Syria by peaceful means.'

'That's right,' a comrade said at his elbow, 'we're a defence force. We wanted to solve things by talking to people.'

'Many who had emigrated to other parts of Syria, returned to Rojava and the people celebrated, including Arabs,' said another.

Regime buildings were turned into cultural centres and schools, and in Derik, the police station was stripped of its insignia and people saw the basement torture chamber. 'The building is now the headquarters of the women's freedom movement,' said Heval Yezda, raising a victory fist to cheering.

Meanwhile, Justin heard American fighter planes humming in the distance, in the battle to destroy ISIS. He acknowledged the U turn he'd taken and saw that airpower was essential at this stage of the Rojava project. Why didn't they blame the West for destroying Iraq and creating the conditions for ISIS? Earlier, he'd put the question to a young man by the name of Destan.

'We understand imperialism very well,' he'd replied. 'It won't advance our cause to pick that fight now.' They'd gone on to discuss how Al Qaeda had spawned ISIS and Justin asked if they were really the same.

'Yes and no. For Al Qaeda, the US is enemy number one, but ISIS hates all the regimes in the Arab world who don't follow their crazy idea of true Islam and want to build a Caliphate today, not in some distant future.'

Justin said that one could draw a direct line from the destruction of Iraq to mass death and destruction of the twin towers, to the train bombings in Madrid, the Manchester Arena bombings, the Berlin and Vienna Christmas markets attacks, and last year's massacre at the Bataclan concert hall. He asked Declan if he believed waging war on terror would make the world a safer place.

Declan's eyes sparkled and a seraphic smile spread across his face. 'Forgive me comrade, but the war on terror was invented by the imperialists. This is the way they control their own citizens and limit their rights. They make normal the hatred of Muslims. I know this from my cousin who is a refugee. They say immigrants are terrorists and closing borders is the only solution. In Rojava we have a different vision and for this we must also get rid of ISIS. We want all to be equal, starting with women. I see this in my own mother, a member of the women's council. When my sister wanted to join the YPJ, my mother told my father, yes, our daughter is right, if her brother can go, so can she. This is a big change in our community.'

'Aren't you afraid of what will happen in the future? If it doesn't work out?'

'Liberation is like a new born child, comrade, we don't know how it will grow up.'

Justin heard his name called and got to his feet to accept thanks for raising funds and for returning to spread the word about the revolution.

Later that evening, he stood alone under the velvet black sky pricked with stars brighter than any he'd seen. He felt his smallness in the sweep of events that brought him here, a world in the process of creation. He'd add his grain of sand and speak with passion about all he'd witnessed, for you never knew whose heart you touched.

'They call it *Kobanigrad*,' said Destan, taking Justin on a tour of the broken city. In January last year they'd recaptured the hill where ISIS had planted their flag three months previously, and now rebuilding was well underway, Destan explained. It would take years, Justin thought.

'Turkey's embargo on materials and cement make the task doubly difficult, but for now, we recover what we can from demolished buildings.'

They passed the shell of a house and a line of washing hung along a perilous ledge of a collapsed upper floor. They crossed a street made impassable by waist-high rubble where shop signs clung to masonry and a rolled up awning in candy stripes lay askew a doorframe.

'How do people survive?' Justin asked.

'There are standpipes and generators,' Destan said, as they walked along a bustling street of makeshift stalls selling bric-a-brac and pots and pans, and an assortment of children's plastic shoes.

To his shocked silence, Destan said, 'The people here are lucky. There are thousands whose homes were destroyed and who live in refugee camps. We will visit before you leave.'

He'd have to strap on his courage first.

Sanjay took him to see Farida's grave in The Martyrs' Cemetery on the outskirts of town. Hundreds of identical marble graves lay in rows, filled with flowers and photos of the loved-ones. The earth was newly turned at Farida's spot and her beautiful young face smiled up at them. Justin felt his chest heave with sobs and clapped his hand over his mouth.

'It's alright Dad,' Sanjay said, 'I know she's safe here, among others who gave their lives.' In her final letter, Farida had told him not to martyr himself, but to continue the work in other ways. 'She said, *let your tears fall like sweet rain on the green shoots of revolution*. I'll always love her, Dad, till the day I die.'

Justin took his son in his arms and they stood like this for a long moment under a relentless sun, until Sanjay pulled away. 'Let's go. We shouldn't keep the driver waiting.'

Justin cast a last look at the monuments in the eye-throbbing glare and it came to him that his lifespan was equal to three of those young lives. The least he could do was to make the best of the time that remained.

He landed at Heathrow at 5am and found himself on the

wrong side of an interview desk. They'd picked him up on a spot check and found a stash of flags, pins and other paraphernalia that would come in handy at meetings.

'How do you explain this, sir?' asked the customs official.

'It's to help support the People's Protection Units in Rojava, Syria,' he said, evenly. He felt both weary and calm. Whatever awaited him was as nothing alongside the dangers faced by the young men and women he'd just been with.

He was escorted behind a panel along corridors to a cell-like room, offered tea and made to wait. 'Am I being detained?' he asked.

'No, sir. We've sent for a colleague to ask you a few questions.' Special Branch, he presumed. He decided not to make a fuss and to sit it out.

A woman with deep shadows under her eyes appeared, and settled opposite. 'Why did you go to Syria, Mr Caffrey?' she asked, unsmiling. It was an early shift.

'I'd raised money for an eco-processing plant and went to meet the people it was for,' he replied.

'Which organisation would that be?' she asked, head to one side.

'The PYD,' he replied, without elaboration.

'You mean, the YPG and YPJ who are under the direction of the PKK, a terrorist outfit,' she said, wearily.

'The people I support are fighting the Islamic State, backed by the US military who are providing airpower. I don't think that makes them terrorists.'

'The PKK is deemed a proscribed organisation by Turkey, the US and the EU, just for starters,' she said, more animated now.

'Since this country has just voted to leave the EU, that's okay then,' he hit back.

She ignored this and continued, 'Under the Terrorism Act 2000, it is illegal to support such an organisation, including the provision of money. It is also illegal to meet representatives of a proscribed organisation, and it appears you have broken the law on both counts. Penalties are up to ten years in prison, and or a fine.' She sat back with folded arms.

He said nothing.

'In case you're wondering, this also applies overseas. Extra territorial jurisdiction was introduced in 2006.'

By now he was hungry and irritable. There was no way these wankers were going to bang him up, they were just toying. He should demand access to a phone and call Harpreet. 'I want to call my lawyer. Now.'

The woman sighed and shook her head as if to say, fat difference that will make. He was escorted to another cubicle with a phone fixed to the wall. He punched in Harpreet's number, grateful he knew it by heart. They'd relieved him of his mobile.

'Justin, you're back! Thank God!' A pause. 'It's six in the morning. You okay, dear?'

'I'm at Heathrow—they picked me up on a random check on the way out. Sorry to do this, I know you warned me.'

'You're being held? What the hell?'

'For dealing with a proscribed organisation, apparently. They're incapable of distinguishing between the YPG and the PKK. Some guff about extra territorial jurisdiction. By now they probably know about my record, which won't help.'

'The law's still being tested—nobody really knows if it applies to the PKK. You've fallen unlucky, but it worries me about Sanjay getting back.'

'I didn't mention him, obviously.'

'I'll speak to someone—hang in there love. Tell them you need breakfast. We'll play for time.'

His heart swooped at her calling him love. He just wanted to go home. They were living apart but together, which was a step closer than together but apart. She needed space and he respected that. He hoped to woo her back along the secret paths of their walks in the dales and on the windswept moors, however wending that might be.

Six hours later they let him go, unceremoniously. He walked into the June day, light as a bird and as happy as he'd ever been. If this was it and he was granted a dying wish, it would be that Sanjay and Stephen get back in one piece. He asked nothing more of the universe.

A number of books and websites have provided invaluable background reading in writing this novel. In particular:

Gordon Carr. *The Angry Brigade, A history of Britain's first urban guerrilla group*. PM Press. 2010.

Guy Debord. *The Society of the Spectacle*. 1967. https://www.marxists.org/reference/archive/debord/society.htm

Franz Kafka. *Letter to his father*. Schocken Books. New York. 1966.

Richard Vinen. *The Long '68, Radical Protest and Its Enemies*. Penguin Books. 2019.

Alwyn W. Turner. *Crisis? What Crisis? Britain in the 1970s*. Aurum Press Ltd. 2013.

David Edgar. *Maydays*. Nick Herne Books. 2018 version of the play.

Michael Knapp, Anja Flach, Ercan Ayboga. *Revolution in Rojava, Democratic Autonomy and Women's Liberation in Syrian Kurdistan*. Pluto Press. 2016.

Gayle Tzemach Lemmon. *The Daughters of Kobani, The Women Who Took on the Islamic State*. Swift Press. 2021.

Guy Debord. *The Society of the Spectacle*, translated by Donald Nicholson-Smith (New York: Zone Books,1994) (quotation used with kind permission).